If Aurora Mattia is a switchboard operator, then **Unsex Me Here** *is her call log. Please hold. There's someone on the other line. A spider, a sibyl, an angel, a mermaid, a goddess, or an ex-girlfriend.*

Unsex Me Here is a prayer book tied together by the strings of a corset. Glamorous ramblers, haunted by the sense of another world drawing near, wander in and out of its inexplicable twilight. From a West Texas town with a supernatural past to a stalactite cavern in the birthplace of Aphrodite, from hotel rooms to gardens to the far horizon of a thought, they seek the source of the disturbance in their minds. Heartbreak is not so far from rapture; holy babble is another kind of gossip. Every pilgrimage is as dense with symbolism as it is refined by desire.

PRAISE FOR *UNSEX ME HERE*

"A fairy tale, in the classic, sparkling, and powerful ways."

—Michelle Tea, author of *Black Wave*

"Aurora Mattia writes from the point where passion, pleasure, and fury are transmuted into ecstatic vision. She intervenes into the perennial concerns of trans writing—how to confess without betraying, and how to resist the temptation to simplify experience to something coherent and false. These stories are ruptures in the taut skin of reality, but listen closely and you can hear the implacable, promiscuous mind of a trans woman of our era, trying again and again to break through to the real truth."

—Emily Zhou, author of *Girlfriends*

"With a favorite writer, there is a before and an after. Now I have read Aurora Mattia. These stories are so tender and cutting, almost mystical."

—Amina Cain, author of *Indelicacy*

PRAISE FOR *THE FIFTH WOUND*

"Aurora Mattia's *The Fifth Wound* is a strange book in all the best ways. Baroque and mythical, interdimensional and grounded, this novel is an exploration of passion, beauty, violence and loss. Chocked full of winding, brilliant sentences sure to turn readers' minds inside out, this is a tale of trans love and fantasy that engages with the full scope of the good, the frightening, and the profound."

—Isle McElroy, *Vulture*

"In her new novel, Mattia reinvents the roman à clef with a magical realist memoir that puts the dusty genre of autofiction to shame. Sifting from multiple narratives—and dimensions—*The Fifth Wound* is a romance, a meditation on transphobic violence, and a speculative tale of time travel, ecstatic visionaries, and mystical union."

—Ed Simon, *The Millions*

"I have never read anything like Aurora's writing. I would say less that I have read her work and say more that I have felt it, deep inside my body. It makes my heart ache. It also makes me long for a hard cock down my throat. Her work is a true spiritual experience, in that it causes me lust, grief, anger and ecstasy, sometimes one after the other and sometimes all at once."

—Carta Monir, author of *Napkin*

"*The Fifth Wound* contains some of the most deliriously, convulsively, terrifyingly beautiful writing I've ever seen. In the delicate, fleshy membrane of her prose, Mattia holds shards of pain, defiance, erudition, and above all passion—with all the biblical resonances of that word. The book is an astonishment."

—Barbara Browning, author of *The Gift*

"If Gertrude Stein had a child with Virginia Woolf, they would produce an exquisite comma/semi-colon named Aurora Mattia. In Mattia's highly magnetic & hyperconscious world of say boudoir shadows, sugarglass, operating tables, transsexuality, auroral wounds, strident malefic forces, a sentence, a paragraph, an entire chapter does bleed; and, it bleeds hyperchromatically, hyperphilosophically, hyperinventively, and hyper-nonbinarily from *The Fifth Wound*'s 'mouth, genitals, genitals, pores, eyes, ass, and nose' into her body's impeccable sheath."

—Vi Khi Nao, author of *Fish in Exile*

"This is a densely embroidered autofictional mythography, a surreal book of hours complete with self-flagellation, a Homeric urban odyssey, ecstatic and violent, tender, devastating, and triumphant, and a hallucinogenic yet visceral medical memoir. Mattia peels layer upon layer, cuts again and again, deep into the wound to spill the life inside."

—Sarah Gerard, author of *True Love*

"To say that Aurora Mattia's *The Fifth Wound* is not easily accessible to readers is to do it an injustice—the prose is winding, curving, explosive, and at times, completely unreadable. But that's the beauty of reading this book: getting lost in its delicious sentences as they turn and burn, coming to surprising and wonderful conclusions. . . . Mattia has a rhythmic, almost holy way of speaking at times, as if some greater power is speaking through her. "

—Joanna Acevedo, *The Washington Square Review*

UNSEX ME HERE

ALSO BY AURORA MATTIA

The Fifth Wound

UNSEX ME HERE

AURORA MATTIA

NIGHTBOAT BOOKS

NEW YORK

2025

Printed in the United States of America

ISBN: 978-1-64362-270-5

Cover design by Tree Abraham
Book design by Abbie Phelps
Text set in Adobe Garamond Pro

PERMISSIONS

An early version of "Ezekiel in the Snow" appeared in *Prairie Schooner.*
"Valentine's Day" previously appeared in *Joyland.*
"Via Crucis" previously appeared in *Zoetrope: All-Story.*
"Wild and Blue" previously appeared in *BOMB.*
"Il Santuario Madonna della Nulla" is forthcoming in *SPASM.*
"The Revelation of the Seed" previously appeared in *Yale Literary Magazine.*

The drawings on XVIII, 82, 129, and 162 are original works by CJ Mattia, created to accompany this publication, and are reproduced here with the permission of the artist. © 2025 CJ Mattia.

Man and I. V., 1994, is from the collection of the Metropolitan Museum of Art, New York, courtesy Alexander Gray Associates, New York. © 2024 Estate of Hugh Steers / Artists Rights Society (ARS), New York.

Original cover art for "Ezekiel in the Snow" © 2021 Hannah Marshall.

Artwork for "https://waterfall not found" © Angel Marie Light.

Cataloging-in-publication data is available from the Library of Congress

Nightboat Books
New York
www.nightboat.org

Pursuing you in your transitions,
In other Motes –
Of other Myths
Your requisition be.
The Prism never held the Hues,
It only heard them play –

—EMILY DICKINSON, J1602

In the middle of the 14th century there were at the Camaldolese monastery at Florence, two celebrated illuminators, Don Jacopo Fiorentino, and Don Silvestro. This Don Jacopo, according to Vasari, was the best large letter writer in the 14th century. He wrote for his monastery twenty folio choral books, the miniature illuminations of which were painted by his brother, Don Silvestro. Their right hands were preserved after their death as honoured relics.

—MRS. CHARLES B. COOPER, MSFA,
PLAIN WORDS ON THE ART OF ILLUMINATING

AUTHOR'S NOTE

So. I am sitting at a café on South Lamar, across from my best friend, Noel, who has flown down from New York to visit me. My great-aunt who, my mother tells me, was institutionalized in a Kerrville psych ward for her entire adult life, is buried in a cemetery just across the river; twice since moving back to Texas I've visited her grave. I wonder if the ward, which still exists, has any record of her—wonder what trace she left, if any, in the paper trail of Empire. Tomorrow I will be thirty.

The first two stories in this book I wrote when I was nineteen, when I thought womanhood was something I could only approach by a painful and asymptotic pilgrimage through phrases.

"Valentine's Day" is an attempt to express how much can happen when nothing is happening, or an attempt to fathom the height and depth of an instant.

"Via Crucis" I wrote in a rush of fantasia when I was twenty, left in a drawer for five years, then rewrote and rewrote again when I was twenty-five, with a new clarity of vision, because in the intervening years I had finally allowed myself to say *I will learn the name of the woman I wasn't, the woman who was buried in a pine box in the backyard of my childhood.*

"Wild and Blue" was the first story I wrote on commission. The assignment was open-ended; the deadline was not. The funnel of time forced me not to imagine but to see: not to tesselate a horror—to interrupt it with shimmer—but instead and simply to describe its inevitability.

"Ezekiel in the Snow" I began when I missed my ex-boyfriend but wanted a break from missing him myself, so I tried to imagine his sister missing him. Three years later I became interested in writing a story that claimed none of its realities as final, where reality was not the constant but the variable, so I rewrote that story about a sister and her sibling, and then I asked my other ex to typeset and design a digital edition—under the banner of our shared 'publisher,' Fascinum Press, which was me and Noel and Loretta in the living room, Noel's archival and aesthetic genius and my little scribbles—for which my ex-boyfriend, the same one I'd been missing, wrote the only blurb: 'Reading this story is like peering into a mutating queer crystal that rotates your heart through its shifting centers. Here, the "I" & its perpetually unsettled eyes provide a series of lavish apertures into dimensions both earthy & gaudy, musical & jolting, coded & vulnerable.'

But "Celebrity Skin," my first new piece of writing since *The Fifth Wound,* I wrote like a Stations of the Heart, a passion to which I submitted without faith, in the blank months of my life, the months when I hardly existed, when I was nothing more than a knot of muscles, alone in my room. Writing was no pleasure; it was a way of staying sane. But if I did not have faith, my fingers did. I clawed this story out of an absolute zero. The writing of it, with the blood-ink spikes of the Holy Nails, was like not believing in paradise, but with such fury and tenderness that I decided to create paradise myself.

"https://waterfall not found"—rewritten, reorganized and handled with sweet grief like shards of glass or broken-winged butterflies—began as the final monologue of my first novel, never to be published, called *Cradle Me, Lucifer.*

As for "Il Santuario Madonna della Nulla," I wrote that story to say goodbye to what Alan Jackson calls 'livin' on love.'

And "Cradle Me, Lucifer"—I wrote that essay because my python demanded it.

I signed the contract for *Unsex Me Here* in the nightmare psych ward at Bellevue in Manhattan; I finished the manuscript at a vital rehab in Los Angeles. Sometimes the course of life has a certain charm.

The Fifth Wound was autobiography as vision; *Unsex Me Here* is an autobiography of vision. If that book was about the development of my mind in the world, this one is about the development of my mind in the dream: it begins where I began, and ends at the present moment. So *Unsex Me Here* is not a sequel to *The Fifth Wound*, but a sequence of detours; a secret door, hidden within a dive bar Wurlitzer, to a garden of allotropes—or something like the 'dissolvent scenes' once projected by Monsieur Henry's magic lanterns. My obsessions at nineteen were not so different from my obsessions at twenty-nine. These are stories about attempting to outrun time; about trying to remember transfemme pasts; about magic touching everything except the possibility of lasting love. They are stories about attempting, by means of profusion and multiplicity, to evade the Imperial obsession with naming and classification, personified by the historical figure Isidore of Seville, who wrote the *Etymologies,* an encyclopedia of the unreal, that is, of all the realities that Christianity—in its capacity as the mystical arm of Empire—sought to enumerate, to absorb, in order to simplify them into nonexistence. I was trying to find a way to live in the world by imagining other worlds—I was trying, in one story after another, to make a paradise. But the desire to make a paradise bears the memory of might-have-been, irresolvable and unforgettable, which constrains me to insert, beneath each fern frond and within every ripening fruit, atoms of rot that threaten to corrupt and decompose the dream before I can speak the last word, as final and uncertain as the first.

[LOS ANGELES, CALIFORNIA, SEPTEMBER 29, 2022
AUSTIN, TEXAS, NOVEMBER 7, 2023]

POSTSCRIPT

This book was originally acquired by Coffee House Press. I terminated my contract five months before publication because, following their review of a petition signed by nearly seventy Coffee House authors, the board and leadership of the Press refused to sign onto PACBI, or to release a statement in support of Palestinian liberation, or even to acknowledge the State of "Israel"'s ongoing and escalating genocide against the Palestinian people, in Gaza and beyond—much less our manifold complicity in it, and our manifold responsibility to help ensure its end, which requires, too, the end of this Empire. The end of this Empire and the beginning of every way it could be otherwise. From the Jordan River to the Rio Grande, from the Gulf of Mexico to the Mediterranean Sea, 'Abolition,' writes Ruth Wilson Gilmore, 'is not *absence*, it is *presence*. What the world will become already exists in fragments and pieces, experiments and possibilities.'

[MY BEDROOM, JULY 25, 2024]

TABLE OF CONTENTS

APPENDIX

UNSEX ME HERE

INFRAPINK

LET THEM GALLOP. I want to unleash them from the night in which they cannot be free, the horses, because they are born just as the day is born, with the fragrance of flowers, with quiet sexuality, with the unfolding of wings, but I do not know how to let them out of me, they who I feel inside me at such a great distance, at such a depth, inside a night from which the morning must pour out, from which they must escape in order to be born, to raise themselves up on steady legs, to gallop, knowing they have no destination, but galloping anyway, because like a melody when the day arises, so do the horses, the flowers and the birds, together they are the song that I want to sing, but I am afraid, so I go on writing, creating my endless morning, but unable to let it be born, because I cannot bear it alone, can't bear the birth, which is an offering of myself, and if no one receives me I will be born alone, like a cathedral in a town of unbelievers, ungainly among the houses, too tall, beautiful and useless and foreboding, so I go on writing, I gallop for you, I am beautiful for you, I perfume myself, undress myself, a bird without wings, a useless bird, and I go to you, and I sleep with you, my body is young, I let you touch it, I let you kiss it, and for a moment I pretend that you are in love with me, and in that moment I feel the horses approaching, lithe and free, strong and unencumbered, and I feel my body, almost like a woman's, I can almost feel that I am a woman, that I could give you children, and how I want to give you that, but I am the boy who loves you, and inside of me horses are galloping, stuck inside an endless night.

[BEIJING, 2013]

RE: INFRAPINK

The cathedral is twenty stories tall. That is, according to my encyclopedia, 'above-average height' compared with other cathedrals in the world. The cathedral is also mentioned on pages 36, 59, 61, 278, and 340 under 'crucifixes per square meter' (ten one-hundredths), 'fires due to world events' (two), 'fires due to descent of the holy spirit' (three), and 'fires of disputed origin' (five). The last listing is for 'religious miracles' (one). Father Alessandro Ricci of Avellino wrote in 1609 that 'this cathedral is unique in the history of the Church for its unprecedented quantity of bells, which consume a full 80 percent of its architecture.' After consulting the prayer journals of clergy in fourteen disparate hamlets, located between twenty and two hundred miles from the cathedral, one modern scholar concluded, 'The bells were audible at a remarkable distance.' According to medical records of the time, residents of the cathedral parish experienced a high incidence of headaches, but also of spiritual revelation. And like an empty cathedral I write to you. I am a cathedral in search of a congregation—because the song which I feel inside my body, I cannot hear myself. I need you to hear it for me.

In return, I will tell you about a miracle: One morning I heard a flower blooming in the garden. And the song of a blooming flower—inside the song of a blooming flower were the bells of a cathedral that no longer exists.

[SPICEWOOD, TEXAS, 2013]

VALENTINE'S DAY

The individual is the seat of a constant process of decantation, decantation from the vessel containing the fluid of future time, sluggish, pale and monochrome, to the vessel containing the fluid of past time, agitated and multicolored by the phenomena of its hours.

—SAMUEL BECKETT, *PROUST*

Raphael rose from his sheets, shaking those copper curls which his paramours—curling a lock around their fingers in the prologue to a tryst—always seemed so pleased to describe as *cherubic.* He was tired of that epithet. A residue of cum lingered on his tongue. He sipped from a cup of cold rosehip tea left untasted the night before, but the tea was bitter—the tea was acrid. His throat clenched, his stomach spasmed coldly. He spat back into the cup.

The walls of the dorm room were wide and blank and tall. One window opened onto a silent green courtyard where sometimes a butterfly would streak yellow across the air before vanishing into the boughs of green trees. Heat and light conspired with Raphael's eyes to coat the courtyard in a breathless glaze: the leaves on the trees were as still and vivid as lost time. He felt suffocated with hunger, a hunger never satisfied because he never came any closer to the trees than looking: what a mouth wanted could be kissed or tasted, but what the eyes wanted, what else could the eyes do but see? The trees were green, they were bright. The walls of his bedroom met in high corners; the corners reverberated coldly along their edges. Everything profoundly revealed its own surface.

And there were no new notifications on his phone, either. He tossed it onto his pillow. The screen's dim glass reflected the green courtyard; the silent leaves; another fluttering daub of yellow.

Raphael was ashamed. After so many years of pretending not to want, he had said, at last: I want. But after he spoke, he heard nothing except the echo of his own voice. Day after day he waited. He had spent so many hours waiting, waiting—waiting for some other bespectacled sylvan fairy to see him standing in the hazy blue beam of a strobe and lift a delicate finger, beckoning him to a distant bed. But instead he had left Emily Dickinson half-read beside his pillow; had forgotten his cup of tea and danced half-heartedly at Melusina's Bath with some friends who he didn't much care for and who didn't much care for him, then absconded to a dim beer-encrusted bathroom and followed a succession of messages on Grindr to the bed of, for god's sake, an economics major. He had sucked cum from the man's cock like venom from a wound. He had swallowed it all, but returning along the quiet dewy streets of Asphodel in the early morning, opening the wrought-iron gate of the college and climbing a winding stone staircase, hadn't brushed his teeth, and fell asleep, in a fit of dizziness, atop his bedquilt. *To fill a Gap, Insert the Thing that caused it*

It was already past twelve. Morning had come and gone. Every time he woke late—every time he woke to a slant of light so firm and dead and alluring; a scene so established and impenetrable—he remembered that his seeing was not an essential function of the world. The early afternoon had already completed itself and in fact resisted his late arrival. He fell back onto his pillow, attempting to recall other mornings, untouched by memory because they had caused nothing, had been caused by nothing, were nothing more and nothing less than instants, full of the hot, mesquite-scented breeze, the clandestine tinkling of wind chimes, and somewhere in the strawberry bushes, a mourning dove whose spherical cooing broke upon his ears in sedimented rings of sound. Such mornings were his hoard of riches. But now, past twelve on a Friday in Asphodel, they failed to sweeten his mind; now, even though he closed his eyes, Raphael felt reverberating the dull intransigence of his dorm room—the walls, the corners, the rectangle of lurid immobile trees. He was alone. His tongue was sour with the tang of last night's cum.

♥

An hour later he woke again. A yellow rayon robe hung beside his bed. Eyes closed, he fumbled carelessly for the fringe, which slipped between his fingers, soft, cool, unworldly, so that suddenly, halfway inside a memory, Raphael was stroking the surface of a pond, and now at last he was sheltered, insulated by leaves and branches, folded into a beatific gloom: and this enfolding was composed neither solely of recollected senses, nor of nostalgia, but something more diffuse, more auroral—the haunting of his mind by an earlier version of itself. And though a perfect irrevocable Friday proceeded unaltered on the other side of his eyes, Raphael had proven, for now, that he did not need its nourishment.

He grasped a corner of fabric, pulling until the robe began to spill swiftly, silkily off its hook; then, with a flick of his wrist, whipped it toward the bed, where it fell and settled—in glossy folds and flat yellow lengths—on his chest. The room was offended at this sudden flash of extravagance. The walls loomed; the corners sharpened. But Raphael laughed. Raphael laughed and the room—the room which was only as powerful as his silence—winced, retreated, shrank back to its own proportions. He slipped the robe over his shoulders and slid off his bed, tying it loosely around his waist.

As he sauntered out into the empty living room, he wondered briefly and not without pleasure whether any of his roommates would open their doors at that moment, and the fantasy followed him into the hall; a still image of Valentine appeared in his mind; Valentine, partial to guitar riffs, mathematical riddles, and states of drunkenness so extreme they delivered him into a sort of glossolalic rapture, under whose influence he declaimed a homily on the nature of prisms which Raphael had now heard on three separate occasions, before three separate audiences; Valentine blushing behind his stubble in a pair of threadbare blue boxers, which so daintily draped his cock (the same cock which Valentine had once sheepishly described as *bent,* but Raphael had not so much as glimpsed save through light-limned cotton) that they inevitably formed a crumpled scrim upon which the silhouette of fact was decorated by the livid detail of Raphael's fantasies; and the irresistible intimation that the fragile blue fabric which clung so loosely to Valentine's hips was on the verge of floating away—like Aphrodite's ellipsis of sea foam—further vivified the vision, so that (thought Raphael wordlessly as he opened the bathroom door, recalling at the same time some memory of kitchen curtains lifted lightly by a breeze, inviting him to a grassy yard) 'my skin never fails to prickle whenever he glances my way . . .'

This image was followed by another—lips rouged, eyelashes long and languorous—of Raphael himself (like Marilyn in the wind), one leg bent coquettishly in front of the other, grasping his robe with an air of scandalized dishabille. But the bathroom door closing behind him, he immediately felt a hot gust rush from his head to his heart; because what if Valentine did not feel the same? What if this fantasy was less the elaboration of a fact than the inflammation of a delusion? But there had been details, so many details, foremost among them the intense awkwardness which—despite twelve months of gossip, vodka and autumn leaves; twelve months of condoms, snowstorms and shared silences; twelve months of ecstatic overwrought conversations whirling with forgotten and oft-repeated revelations and punctuated only by the burning orbs of cigarettes and joints which by dawn would disperse at last into slow eddies of incense while outside the windows water slipped from leaf to leaf and flowers yawned pinkly in sweet half-slumbering breaths—the intense awkwardness which hovered and haunted any room in which he and Valentine were left alone, sober: because they had cried drunkenly into one another's arms and yet? Yet lounging on couches in the vast thin silence before the bells began to chime for five o'clock, that silence as thin and flavorless as a final steep of tea, something more than late-afternoon lassitude hung pungently between them, rendering their glances half-covert, almost shy. At these times Raphael (who was now turning the shower knobs, testing the heat, stepping onto the cold brown tiles) sensed a fear emanating from Valentine, which sometimes exacerbated his shyness into a cagey, hesitant sulk, because the terms between the two of them, the terms of the intimacy from which speaking would or would not be possible, those terms were unsettled by Raphael's hope for romance with a willowy bookish boy, by which epithet Valentine could be described; but (thought Raphael, muttering, veiled in droplets of water) was that all? Was that really all? Because Valentine's fear (the ghosts of his eyes roving, seeking) seemed to be addressed to something inside himself (seeking, roving through the perpetual dusk of the mind), something of which Raphael's presence—and those rustling insubstantial wings rising from Raphael's shoulders which were his desire taking form, overhanging them both, enfolding them both in a canopy of blue etherealized feathers—had made him faintly aware, in the living room late in the afternoon. And this awareness, faint as it was, was extraordinarily unsettling: Valentine (conjectured Raphael soaping his skin) felt that if he were not careful, if he did not foreshorten his phrases, his glances, then something might happen (because there was a topaz pulsing, burning in some far crevice of Valentine's mind which his roving ghost-eyes forbore from revealing to him, a frozen topaz waiting to melt into a confession) which could not, most certainly could not happen because he loved women, and Raphael (thought Raphael, adorning himself briefly with Valentine's eyes) was not a woman. But what was he, really? Raphael (insulated from a flawless green Friday by the hot howling shroud of water pouring over his head in this stall whose narrowness offered him a brief privacy reminiscent of what he imagined nuns felt kneeling, praying in the cells of their convents as tongues of fire gilded their supplicating bodies), Raphael did not float through rooms with dainty butterfly-parabolic steps or execute those prototypical fey angularities of a flicked wrist and was too broad shouldered to even be considered epicene, except for the apparently cherubic glow of his cheeks; but within the domed desert of his skull, swarms of pearl-eyed rattlesnakes at all hours slithered and hissed on the scent of those rare iridescent eggs (those eggs—hidden and rehidden in an endless Easter panic—which Raphael called his 'pieces of mind') nestled in the crooks of prickly pears or cratered in drifts of sand, with whose silver yolks the snakes hungered to lacquer their lips, erasing meanwhile with innumerable slither-scribbles any brief attempt at language inscribed into the red dust by a wispy turquoisedissolving hologram of Raphael himself, hunched, shuffling slowly backward while composing stanzas with a branch of twisted mesquite and an irrepressible devotion to delicacy materialized in thoughts (too awestruck to be spoken, too involuted to be remembered, lost as soon as he thought to write them, in waking life, on a slip of paper) which rivaled the moon in their coldly amorous ventriloquism of a distant light—but the light of what?

"Morning," shouted Valentine as he blew through the bathroom to take a piss.

Suddenly everything became literal. Raphael was reduced to the proportions of his body. Or now at last, even if the vision couldn't nourish him—now at last he was a butterfly? Because he was pinned by tiny needles (the hands of the clock) to a frame (bathroom, September 15th) and there was no more fluttering of wings, no more colorful dust: no more loop-de-loop among the ribs of Proteus' glitching carcass. His visions were anesthetized.

Raphael turned the knobs; the water ceased. Now he was wet, pink, shriveled. Lost in the aftermath of a rebirth. The walls of the stall refused to acknowledge him; they stood expressionless and eternal, pretending to be a mausoleum for the embalmed corpse of a dead king. Living matter offended them. Raphael was an error. Something pierced him—and he opened the door, tumbling out unwillingly like the translucent flesh of a lobster. Onto the unblemished plate of a Friday afternoon.

"Morning," he said, shivering. Without a form to take. Valentine still stood unseen astride a toilet as Raphael—nauseatingly enthralled by the glittering plash of piss—dried off, wrapped the towel around his waist and once more donned the yellow robe, water dripping from his lashes. The cool contact of the fabric reminded him of some television rerun he fell asleep watching as a child (Dallas, winter, 1996) wherein a woman, seated above an array of creams, pigments and powders as mysterious as a painter's palette, prepares for an evening with a man, her lips parted, her eyes wide as she leans toward a mirror making quick black flicks along her lashes and slow red irrevocable strokes around her lips, then dreamy, coquettishly demure as she lifts a bouquet of roses from the vanity stool beside her, buries her face in them, inhales deeply as if absorbing their extremely mortal sensuality, then rises, ripples down the hallway in a shimmering robe, searching breezily for a vase—and remembering what he had imagined to be her pleasure in imagining the man imagining her rippling down the hall, half-dressed, flowers in hand, Raphael was able to absorb, in turn, the affect of a woman who has just smelled her lover's roses.♥

His faith was blithe; his cheeks were flushed. He reached for his toothbrush.

Meanwhile Valentine gave his cock a few final shakes, releasing one after another arpeggio of aural glitter, which Raphael's inner mind—longing for a past that never was—processed romantically, extrapolating a Roman fountain, green summer shadows, and honeysuckle tumbling from a ruined arch:

'Let me stroll your ancient streets . . .'

Because it was not Raphael himself who felt that longing, who

♥ This affect belonged not only to the 'woman,' but also the actress, who had perhaps imitated, in the conscious gestures of her performance, an old Hollywood black-and-white film she first saw as an adolescent, in which a woman receives roses from her lover—and certainly she had herself received roses from a lover at some point and at that point had imitated, less consciously, the same gestures, and was now, that is, in the moment of her performance, investing this third bouquet with the accumulated dream of the roses she had received and the roses, the silver roses, that she had imagined receiving when she first watched a starlet sigh on screen, so that by the time Raphael, preparing to brush his teeth, had unwittingly inherited it more than half a century later, the 'ritual of roses' had achieved the fortitude, not only of an affect, but of an artifact.

spoke those words, but the nameless woman behind whom Raphael—having steeped those roses, those lipsticks, that slow cascade of covert smiles, cigarette-swaying fingers and rustling fabrics for so many years in the liquoring swamp of his subconscious—had projected an extravagant past, longing, speaking wistfully through him as he lifted the toothbrush and pressed paste onto its bristles, while his sleeves slipped and collected in deep golden folds at his elbows with such an air of sensuous ease that he could not help but imagine her into more than his mannerisms, more than his expressions, but by breathless induction mistake her for himself until, lifting the toothbrush to his lips, he was not merely haunted, but possessed. *When we sit together, close, we melt into each other with phrases*

Valentine slouched out of the toilet stall and, insulating himself from the immediate coincidence of their gazes, rubbed his face vigorously.

'Am I Medusa, that you refuse to meet my eyes . . .' whispered the rustling woman.

But Raphael only said: "Have you had lunch yet?"

[BROOKLYN, NEW YORK, FALL 2019]

VIA CRUCIS

Then came the most exquisite moment of her whole life . . .

—VIRGINIA WOOLF, *MRS. DALLOWAY*

It's still happening.

—MICHAEL CUNNINGHAM, *THE HOURS*

. . . you just get stopped with whatever it was that ruined you and you make it happen over and over again and your life has—ceased, really . . .

—JAMES BALDWIN, *ANOTHER COUNTRY*

Aye, grief goes, fades, we know that—but ask the tear ducts if they have forgotten how to weep.

—WILLIAM FAULKNER, *ABSALOM, ABSALOM!*

I.

When I was what you might call a young man, I lived in a small West Texas town, on whose outskirts stood a rundown manor surrounded by high adobe walls. Behind these walls, so I was told, lived the descendants of the family for whom the town was named, drifty Deutschtexaners with cousins in Fredericksburg. But I never saw any of them with my own eyes—any of them, that is, except one.

One night in May a mule-drawn carriage approached the compound bearing baskets of fresh plums swathed in gauze. This was not, in itself, cause for surprise: the plums were delivered, the carriage departed. But distracted by the setting sun (forgive us, for dusk in West Texas is a premonition of paradise), the merchant, who had been entrusted with a set of silver keys, left the compound's front gate unlatched. Nobody noticed. Early the next morning one sylphlike insomniac scion of that fabled family, pacing in feverish loop-de-loops beneath his ancestral almond trees, discovered this error and fled into the desert.

II.

But I did not know that yet. I was alone in my parents' cottage. My father was long dead. My mother was traveling to a cathedral three towns away in order to consult a bishop about the matter of the demons in her garden. I was alone, listening to the breeze rattle the shutters, listening to myself deliver lines of dialogue to a firefly, which every few seconds exerted and exhausted its own splendor in some new corner of the room. I was alone, and in this sense that morning was like any other, because once I had been a 'sensitive boy' who wanted to wear perfume to church like his mother, but whose mother had smelled it and sent him to the bath, where she scrubbed his skin with such violence that he fainted, and they were both late for the service, which of course was his fault.

Put another way, I was a 'sensitive boy' weeping in a lilac briar after his classmates Brie and Albert told him boys could not have babies. Because earlier that day the teacher had asked her students to write stories about what they wanted to be when they grew up, and he believed that words made all kinds of wishes come true. After all, someone had written a book and then god came true. So he wrote: 'Once upon a time there was a boy who had a lot of nightmares and woke up at dawn which everyone knows is when miracles happen. One morning when his family was asleep, an angel walked out of his closet door and told him that god was going to give him a baby. God made an exception for you said the angel because you like to grow lavender in the garden and because at the proper angle you look like a little girl anyway.' That was his first story, and he showed it to Brie and Albert to see if he had spelled all the words right, because he thought it was a pioneering document and should look professional, like a priest wrote it. But Brie and Albert laughed and said he would get in trouble if he told the teacher a lie. "Boys can't have babies," they said. He thought they probably wouldn't write very good stories with that attitude. "What about seahorses," he said, like a hallelujah. But Brie and Albert only laughed again and went back to playing pat-a-cake, so he ripped up the story and ran into the lilac briar, whence he did not emerge until dusk. He prayed to god. He asked god to prove his classmates wrong. But god said nothing—so he decided god was silence. Which meant the devil was words, which meant he started praying to the devil instead. He figured god probably expelled the devil from Heaven because he talked too much. But maybe god was silent too much, and if Heaven was so silent, it was worse than a schoolroom.

So as that 'sensitive boy' aged into a 'taciturn young man,' he retreated more and more into what appeared to be narcissism or shyness, but was in fact a shame as unanimous as sunlight. Under the glare of that shame, he became: I.

I found shade only intermittently, beneath the brief ramshackle constructions of twig and gauze that are called dreams. I dreamed of love, of course; and between dreams (and sometimes below them, my hands moving in some distant world), I cared for the peacocks that roamed the scorched scrub wastes beyond my backyard. I fed them handfuls of sunflower seeds and maintained their roosts in the low branches of mesquite trees. I gave them names: Ellipsis, Semicolon, Comma, Etcetera, and in this way months passed, and years, and I finished my schooling, and remained in the attic of my mother's cottage, waiting for a sign.

Then came the day when I woke to the sound of bells ringing from the chapel. The bells always rang for births, deaths, and marriages, or to announce an event such as an oncoming storm or the arrival of a person of note; they rang when a man or woman was missing, when a new vicar was ordained, and when a miracle was officially recorded in the chapel ledger. But on this morning they rang because peacock feathers were blowing through the square.

III.

That sudden iridescent death—without a drop of blood spilled—would later be called the peacock blight. Because the birds had been no one's property, and especially because their nighttime shrieks had long disrupted the sleep of all and sundry, no one cared much to investigate the cause. But in a matter of days the feathers vanished—from gutters and creosote bushes, from the spokes of cart wheels—only to reappear not a month later in the market, and soon after in the bands of hats and the tresses of coiffures.

For the town, the blight marked the end of a fanciful epoch. For me, it marked the end of the town. At the same time (and my grief is herein encrypted), it marked the end of my asceticism. I refused any longer to store possible and impossible pleasures inside the cramped timeless bric-a-brac shrines I had built behind my eyes. There was an imbalance in my mental ledger. Reality had too little; fantasy, too much. A spiritual osmosis was required.

By and by I spoke my red secrets. I spoke them in a cottage in a small West Texas town. I became part of time.

So there I was, months later, watching a firefly flash and vanish. My mother was off consulting the bishop. (At three o'clock the previous afternoon her tomatoes had exploded in unison. Then her blueberries burst into flame. I watched from the porch as she whacked the burning fruits with a broom; when only ashen puree remained, she turned to me, tilted her chin upward, and gravely declared: "The devil is in the details." By evening she was gone.) And someone was fleeing a rundown manor on the edge of town; someone was walking with purpose toward my cottage, because someone was looking, though I did not know it, for me. I heard a tapping at the front door, faint but insistent, and peeked through the slats of the attic shutters to see a febrile fairy with languorously sloping lashes and eyes as impersonal as clouds babbling ravenously as though his skull were so full of phrases and so clotted with commas and semicolons that he had no choice but to expel them all at once, less as a form of communication than a form of exorcism.

"Please slow down," I yelled.

But he did not seem to see me, much less see what I saw. An unsaddled horse galloped down the dusty avenue; a mourning dove smacked into the side of a barn. Dawn broke open, as cool as the flesh of a papaya. And as the air ripened, his cheeks paled, but words still burst from his mouth like a swarm of butterflies. I could hardly breathe; fluttering wings were pressing into my throat, my lungs—an unbearable delicacy. And my hands were empty, I had no words of my own. But my terror was so sweet that I rushed down the stairs, opened the door, and took his hands in mine.

At last the present had arrived.

His eyes were the eyes of a young man.

He smiled.

He spoke my name.

He vomited blood at my feet, and fainted.

I gathered him in my arms and, halting every other step to catch my breath, carried him up the narrow stairs to the attic, where I nursed him for three days.

On the first day I brought him hot milk with creosote. When he swooned with fever, I fanned him with palm leaves and fed him chips of ice. In the afternoon he opened his eyes. His lips trembled as he attempted to shape a phrase. He gestured wanly, his wrists limp.

"Do you need another blanket?" I asked. "Another pillow?"

He said nothing. But he raised a hand to my cheek.

When he fell back to sleep, I stole down to my mother's bedroom, where I discovered beneath her bed a chest of sunken treasure: honeysuckle perfume, mother-of-pearl hair clips shaped like cactus needles, and a tube of coral lipstick unused since her wedding night. With all these artifacts I adorned myself before returning to the attic. From my own closet, I removed a nightgown: makeshift, ill fitting, and liable to tear at the slightest misstep, but which I had sewn myself from the windblown feathers I collected, covertly, in the panic of the peacock blight.

It was evening; his body was slick with sweat. I knelt beside him, writing in my diary with the tube of lipstick. He woke with a start, half-rising from the damp sheets, glancing back and forth. I snapped the book shut. A ringlet swung down from my messy coiffure. I blushed. At once his eyes shifted: their dull murk glazed, hardened to a bright blaze of marigold. Slowly, in the ray of his gaze, I rose from the floor. Light was glimmering into my mind.

you

One by one I removed his bloodstained blouse, his soiled underclothes, his trousers. Then his nakedness became my secret. I lifted a soapy cloth to his plum-wine nipples and the black brambles of curls under his arms, then—glancing up at his face, where his lashes fluttered like words—down and further down, while all across his skin my covetous strokes were reborn as bubbles that slipped along the curve of his collarbone and popped in the grooves of his hips. A mouth speaks, tastes, breathes; I knew that much. But until that fairy lay on my cot, I thought eyes knew only how to see. The blue breeze of my gaze hovered over him, banishing the bubbles—and gently but decisively he grasped my hair, lowering me onto that warm pink place from which I would draw out, like venom, his thick bitter milk.

Soon he kissed the lipstick (or its enduring red silhouette) from my lips; soon I rustled and deplumed my peacockfeathered skin; soon I recited to him pages and pages of crude baroque verses that I had written in hope of the audience he now formed for me and which would never again be recited for any other because I buried them two days later in an unmarked grave beneath a mesquite that grew in the wastes beyond my yard.

(A pearl is the silent howl of an oyster. In the beauty of my phrases seek their inverse.)

On the second day I made him oatmeal and asked how he knew my name. His smile faded. Suddenly he looked extraordinarily tired and took a long, slow breath:

"In the old days," he said, "the days of my great-grandparents, my family celebrated each Spring equinox by hosting a weeklong festival of drink and dancing, after which the whole town showed up disheveled and dissolute to Easter mass: and as young ladies and their mothers swished up the aisles in soiled dresses, the vicar would sigh and mutter under his breath that paradise was coming and he would be rid of us soon enough. In the midst of one such festival—unseen by some, unnoticed by others—an elderly stranger, dressed in silver robes and leaning on an aspen cane, appeared before my great-grandfather and offered to grant him a single wish. Convinced he was being tested in the manner of Solomon, my great-grandfather did not ask for riches or for immortality, at least not directly. He asked instead for what he called *hereditary vision,* by which he meant an agglutinating inheritance bequeathed to his children and their children and so on, composed not of gilded furnishings and bolts of silk and vellum-bound libraries and lemon groves and manor houses, but of the constellating speckles and filaments of experience, so that each successive generation would bear from birth the imprint of manifold memories, an absolute record of all that is trapped forever in a man's skull and rots when he rots: the nature of Saturn's rings, the sweetness of a wedding cake, the fragrances of the flowers and how to dance the Zwiefacher, and the freeze of 1933, the icicles long as the nights, and the woman on the train platform staring at you. Or drafting with the T-patchers, stumbling across the beaches of Salerno in the dreamlike green gloom—the unreal shrieking of shells, the unreal screaming of men, the strange fact of Roman temples in the distance, like islands of silence . . . or your lover lighting a cigarette with a trembling hand, your lover waiting for you to say anything, your lover smoothing her skirt and standing up, and turning, and walking out the door, and the silence spreading, and the spreading not ceasing, and every room as full of silence as of space. Or the first telephone in town, black and gleaming and full of voices. As if that somehow brought her nearer, wherever she was. Or—or how to weave perfect garments from the feathers of a peacock. After all it was my family that first brought peacocks to this town.

"My great-grandfather said he wanted to 'rescue History from the imprecision of Memory,' which is to say, he wanted to make his great-grandchildren into a library, a collection of books that turned and studied their own pages. But despite the formaldehyde whiff of moral purity emanating from his request, what he wanted most of all was to steal from us. To steal our first kisses, our first dawns, our first readings of one thousand novels and our first attempts at poetry—to steal the freshness of vision that is the birthright and consolation of anyone who wakes up one fine morning to discover their own eyes seeing a flower, a sentence, a face. *Legio nomen mihi est, quia multi sumus:* my great-grandfather gave us knowledge, surely, but he mostly gave us sight that obstructed our seeing, taste that obstructed our tasting, and words that obstructed our speaking. I envy the solitude of your skull."

He paused to catch his breath. Then his tone turned melancholic, his voice quiet:

"By the time I was born, my family was regarded with fear. Despite my uncles' great wealth and renown, not one daughter of this town offered herself in marriage, so one morning they rode out together on gray stallions, seeking women of other towns. They returned a week later with wives concealed inside silver, silk-upholstered coaches, parading these mysterious conveyances before the steps of the chapel to the accompaniment of bleating trumpets. But their pageantry was a false promise. Of my twelve uncles, four committed suicide, three were sent to a sanatorium, two disappeared on their wedding days, one—who crept nightly to the barn and tortured the chickens—developed a skin rash that infected him, his wife, and my father with unconquerable fevers, leading them all to premature deaths, and the remaining two, along with their families and the offspring, myself included, of their deceased brothers, sleep all day in the shade of the almond trees, awaiting the weekly delivery of plums and liquors and dried meats. Sometimes we make a game of memory; someone speaks a word—'yellow' or 'snowflake' or 'scrimshaw'—and the rest of us quote related phrases from old Hollywood films, from Hafez or Shakespeare or Sei Shōnagon, from midcentury milk advertisements, sea shanties, antique affidavits, or the debauched banter of speakeasy habitués. Of course, we must cite the circumstance, must append details of time and place, speaker and audience, lest the submission be rejected. But this game quickly grows tiresome because no one ever loses, it goes on endlessly, one by one we fall back to sleep: our peacocks were put out to pasture years ago."

Here I interrupted:

"The peacocks . . ."

"I know," he said. "That's why I came to see you."

He paused, reticent.

"To say thank you."

Suddenly I did not know him at all. His face was vanishing into miles and miles of bedsheets, cirrus clouds. Because, after all, if he knew—

"Some thank-you," I said. "Standing in my doorway, babbling. Why didn't you take care of them yourself?"

He sighed, curling his legs around mine.

"Darling, I woke one morning and they were gone. I was ten years old. My uncles forbade us from leaving the manor, and even so I'm always arguing with my father and grandfather, trying to establish in the midst of their ceaseless soliloquizing a single thought of my own, because every time I think I've finally seen a thing for the very first time, one of them bends my mind to his memory: 'If you'll recall,' he says, 'when I traveled down to Houston . . . ,' and then I'm exhausted all over again by a melancholy so pure I can hardly lift my head from the pillow. Except that I must, because dreams are even worse than waking, in my dreams I wander through some medieval farce of a fortress leading inevitably to a murky hall within which my rotten immortal great-grandfather gazes down from his throne in a moth-diminished purple robe, one eye half-curdled, the other already spoiled. The more time we're given, the less we have to live. Each generation has passed sooner than the last. You can't imagine how much of my life I've spent trying to think my way out of this inheritance, but thinking has no dimension, every direction is the same, I reach what I believe is the far horizon of a thought just to end up where I began. And I'm not the only one: each of my forefathers was the same. Why do you suppose they went one after another to early graves? Only when I do not think at all, when I forget thinking, when I walk in circles beneath the almond trees, only then as my body imitates and thereby materializes the circuits of my mind do I feel some small measure of calm, I've had no feeling as powerful as a thought, any sense or intuition however subtle arrives formless and is shortly reconfigured by the blunt preconstructions of my mind, there is no way, absolutely no way out, and recently I have even begun having hallucinations, absolutely unprecedented, of some kind of angel."

This was the first time I'd heard anyone other than the vicar talk about angels.

"Don't tell me—"

"Let me finish," he said. "When I see them—it's always so sudden and so silent—when I see them peeking out from the peony bushes or huddled in the almond branches, staring at me as still as statues, not even breathing, that's when I begin babbling, and I don't even know what I'm saying, phrases flee my mouth like bats from a cave, and then

I wander off into the desert and faint in front of a beautiful stranger. This so-called hereditary vision is a suffocating gift; it has precluded all action or sanity of action, it refuses all joy, allows only indolence, or madness, or death, all of which, in their various permutations, my uncles have achieved within the walls of their terrible paradise."

And as soon as he said 'paradise,' he collapsed back onto the cot. His cheek against my shoulder was hot, feverish. His lashes shivered like he'd walked through a cobweb. After a moment he opened his eyes.

"With you," he said slowly, "I've felt what I can only call lightness, a lightness unlike anything I've known before, because no one, not my father or my grandfather or his father before him, not one of them has ever . . ."

My smile was triumphant, helplessly wide: "You're really telling me," I said, "that you're the first faggot in four generations?"

And he laughed, but his laughter—exuberant, abandoned—immediately fizzled into a fit of coughing: I held him as his body shook and shuddered, as he pressed his fingers painfully, unconsciously, into my arm, I whispered and held him until the coughs softened and diminished into breaths, and he gazed up at me with tired, amorous eyes.

(A name is a door that someone else opens into us. 'Faggot' is a door opened too often by the wrong hands. But you were a faggot, my love, thank god. And when I say 'faggot' I am chewing rose petals and spitting them out in the shape of a word.)

"I came here because . . ."

For the first time his voice was faint, shy, almost weightless.

"I came here because I thought . . . perhaps . . . you might release me."

Now he smirked, blushing.

"Because I thought, if at the very least you swallowed my cum, my forefathers might flee my mind in fright . . ."

Morning had vanished into afternoon, and afternoon into evening. We were writing a fairy tale about a magical elixir. We were eating peach slices. We were surrounded by passing instants, so attuned to time that every second hurt.

As the sun slid down, I asked: "Have you ever, in all your lives, heard of a boy giving birth?"

Because I was at last allowing myself not to know. And he was allowing himself to enter into my unknowing.

"We can try," he said.

We did. But then he began coughing again, just a little, and asked me for a cup of water.

"Of course, darling."

As I rushed down the rickety steps, I was inspired by a thought so thrilling it erased all others.

The screen door slammed behind me. The air was full of distances measured by the droning of cicadas. All around the yard, mesquite trees swished and shook in a faint breeze, emanating a warm scent of spices. But I saw nothing, because the night was extraordinarily intimate with itself. And part of me did not wish to trespass on its intimacy. But I needed forms, forgive me: I pressed my eyes onto the darkness.

The soil was hard and chalky; the flowers were brittle as potpourri. With reckless delicacy I gleaned sprig after sprig, humming quietly to myself from a song I'd heard on the radio: "If dreams were lightning, and thunder were desire, this old house would've burnt down a long time ago . . ."

Then suddenly I stopped humming. I stopped breathing. My skin went cold. And I did not know why until I remembered that out of the corner of my eye I had seen a face, peeking through a gap in the fence. But a face without expression, like a mask.

I sprinted onto the porch and into the house, bolting the door. The flowers whispered dryly in my hands. Seconds passed in which

I imagined myself walking across the kitchen and up the stairs and into my bedroom. But to cross the kitchen, I would have to pass by the window. But if I could just pass by the window, which would take no more than two steps, if I could just pass by the window, it would be only a matter of moments before I was safely back in Legion's arms, so I took one step, then another, walking on tiptoe, and it wasn't so bad, and anyway I wasn't sure of what I'd seen, I hadn't actually seen anything at all, so I took another step, and my heart was hammering, and I couldn't help myself, I tried my best but I couldn't help myself, when I took that step I raised my eyes—and there it was, in the window, floating as still and silent as a tooth.

I woke the next morning on the kitchen floor. Light was pouring in. Crumbs of lavender beside me, throwing tiny shadows. My neck ached. My mind was slowly descending back into itself. For a moment I knew nothing at all. And then, all at once.

I sat bolt upright. I called his name. I ran for the stairs, tripping, bruising my knee; but Legion having died during the early hours of the morning, my voice vibrated in his ears. No one heard it.

That afternoon I wrote a note to his uncles, to be delivered with the tobacco and the bourbon in the mule cart. I waited for a response, but none came. He was only an interruption, I suppose, to the thoughts that consumed their days.

At midnight I carried him down from the attic and buried him among the roots of a vast mesquite in whose branches the peacocks had once taken shade from the sun.

His wish had been granted, in a sense. His mind died with him. No one inherited our kisses. No one inherited our eyes.

13.

Peacocks are no harder to raise than chickens. They prefer the heat to the cold, because they like to spread their feathers in the sun; it should come as no surprise that they once flourished in our town, despite that piercing shriek to which no one grew accustomed and which is the only sound peacocks choose to make. (But 'despite' was not written in my voice. 'Despite' belongs to other mouths, attempting at all times to speak through me, mouths that rip apart the thin silver threads with which I sew them shut, the thin silver phrases I'm writing with the tip of a needle. But some mouths are clever, too. They hide behind the others, the gnashing ones, and whisper only a single word, they whisper 'despite' and alter the intention of my entire sentence, and then I must waste four sentences disproving them, so let me say simply) I adore peacocks because their shriek is unassimilable.

Anywhere, but particularly in the desert, a peacock is a dense epicenter of decadence. For the sake of this decadence, the peacock has sacrificed the sky, has forgone the function of flight in order to obtain a different function, that of artifice: or more precisely, communication. I mean to say, a peacock's feathers are a form of speech—and to all who witness them, pure poetry. But the shriek bursts forth from their gilded throats at the pitch of pain, striking my skull with such sudden violence that I am silenced by terror and awe. In the beauty of their feathers, etc., do you understand?

So it also should come as no surprise that years after the end of this story, at a metropolitan botanical garden, having chanced upon one of those blossoms whose perfume is not sweet but putrid, whose temperature is equivalent to that of a human body, and who are known, to my delight, as *corpse flowers,* I fell in love. The function of their perfume is the same as that of any other flower, but the form inverts the logic of desire. The corpse flower asserts the allure of rot.

Its Latin name is *Amorphophallus titanum: phallus* meaning what it means, *titanum* meaning 'giant,' and *amorpho* meaning 'misshapen' or 'formless,' depending on one's interpretation.

I am fascinated by this unpleasant nom de plume because 'misshapen' is an adjective almost always deployed in pseudoscientific discourse to describe some so-called disfigurement. 'Disfigurement' is another way of saying: your body interrupts. But a disfigurement is, most precisely, a departure from normative form. In the realm of art, such departures are usually greeted as avant-garde . . .

To contextualize my latter-day visit to the botanical garden, I should mention that by the time I saw the as-it-were *Amorphophallus titanum,* I had come to understand myself as something other than a man, and also as something other than a woman. I am what pseudoscientific discourses once called a transsexual. I am what you (in the solitude of your skull) might call 'disfigured,' or what I, in homage to Lady Macbeth, might call 'unsexed.' My pussy is, in the matter of reproduction, useless; it is understood by pseudoscientific discourses to be merely an inverted penis (read: misshapen phallus) or the facsimile of a vagina (read: formless phallus).

But I understand my pussy to be a *peacock feather,* because it has forgone its prior function in order to obtain a different function, that of artifice: or more precisely, communication. I understand my pussy to be a corpse flower, because it asserts the allure of rot: You won't have any children with me, okay? But while the adaptations performed by the peacock and the corpse flower are considered natural, mine is considered artificial—because you have forgotten that we are not so far from birds and flowers. Remember with me.

V.

"It hasn't rained this hard since the Flood," my mother said, standing among the tin cans we'd placed around the kitchen. The ceiling was dripping. The window was toothless, glazed with water. She'd been invoking the Bible more often since the bishop came and, so she claimed, banished the iniquity from her vegetables. But even as she proclaimed the storm a miracle, I feared it augured a plague. Two weeks had passed since Legion's death. The angels had apparently retreated, but I was unable to sleep, because I still expected them around every corner, in every window and pool of shadow. My fantasies of affection had been replaced, at last, by memories; each night, for the hour or two I did drift, I dreamed of Legion beside me on the cot, so lightly that he seemed to flicker in and out of my arms.

In the moments before and after, my mind was brushed by sounds and colors (telegraph static; a length of yellow brocade; the bright brittle notes of a harpsichord), unfamiliar feelings (a fascination with Colt Dragoon revolvers; a lust for the laces on my lover's corset; a dread of needles), and vague recollections (nurses surrounding me in a white windowless room; women twirling at sunrise in soiled dresses; wrinkled hands—my own—planting an almond tree), which I soon came to recognize as the pulverized psyches of Legion's forefathers, traces of whom I had absorbed in the hours before his death. Had he known? He couldn't have . . .

Of course, I told my mother nothing.

"You look tired," she said.

Then, watching the rain rise in the cans, she rejoiced.

"Our faith," she said, "is perpetually rewarded!" She had decided, by the way, to bake a cake in the shape of a cathedral. Wasn't that just a wonderful idea? With marzipan miniatures of the bishop and his brood, and angels clambering up the buttresses and through the stained-glass windows. She was thinking of giving them little marbled masks for faces, not weeping or laughing, just sort of looking. And she would send it to the bishop himself, "to thank him," she said, "for lifting the arid spectacle of sunlight from the streets of our town, for as Lucifer himself knows well, heat and brightness inspire mortal eyes to all manner of misprision."

As she spoke, my ears and eyes swarmed with silence, a silence as dense as language but without words to give it form. I needed to ask her a question, but I did not know what the question was—because if I asked a question like *how do you know about the angels?*, and if that question was too narrow, if it missed the point, even only slightly, her answer might stabilize the instant, and a stabilized instant is one in which we do not see anything at all except what we already know how to see.

But we didn't have vanilla, she said, and she needed, but *needed* vanilla, and would I mind walking to the bakery to procure more?

She glanced out the window, briefly. The rain was reducing the distances, filling up the empty spaces of our town. Yet she so believed in its miraculous aspect that she doubted any danger would befall her one and only son.

"Be careful on the road," she said. "And don't take too long."

Her hands were shaking; she wanted nothing more than to bake her nightmare diorama. I wanted nothing more than to escape the scene of that desire.

I clutched my walking stick, wrapped myself in a quilt, and huddled off into the weather. The bakery was a mile away. At first the journey was manageable, the rain painted me back to life, and for a moment I felt unsaddled—giddy and restive, liable to bolt. I imagined myself fording the Pecos, wandering in the shadow of Guadalupe; I imagined vistas and campfires, droning harmonicas, the distant lights of El Paso. Soon enough, however, the quilt was soaked through, and extraordinarily heavy, as heavy as another body, and I was shivering beneath a downpour so relentless I could hardly see the ditches at the edges of the road.

There were a few homes and storefronts close by, but I didn't want to suffer the embarrassment of wet linens or questions about my mother's health. So there was the church—remnant of a monastery that predated the town, artifact of an earlier colonial wave—a wall of whitewashed adobe taller than any other structure around, yet without any decoration, save for a rooftop cross made from the hammered gold gifted by Legion's primogenitor, 'in thanks to Our Father's gnarled angel, benefactor of a Hereditary Vision.' That cross glimmered down through the rain. That great golden cross—as if glimmering itself had been crucified. Christ was nothing more than a slant of light.

I clambered up the stone steps, kneeling on the stoop to fling the sodden burden from my shoulders, then heaved open the weighty wooden doors, piercing the heart of the question I could not ask my mother, the question I could not ask because there were too many questions inside or beside it and only one instant in which to ask, one instant the size and shape of a single question, so I decided instead to enter the church and ask with my body, fit my body to the shape of the question. I hadn't been there in years, had only heard the bells clanging in its tower, ringing out across the flat scrub desert—and no matter where I was, buying eggs at the market or writing poems in my bedroom, they were always just as loud. (These days I avoid towns with churches and especially towns with cathedrals, at least at the hours when the bells are ringing, because even now they give me headaches, but maybe god can't hear them unless they ring as loudly as they do. And to him they are as faint as wind chimes.)

The nave was tall and wide but, after the blank grandeur of the facade, oddly foreshortened. The altar—a pink mica-flecked block of granite—sat in spitting distance of the doors, which creaked listlessly on their hinges and hissed across the floor before closing behind me with a single arid boom. The pews rose out of the hard clay floor in rows of white adobe. Along the walls, iconography was scant: not so much as a statuette of the Madonna or a faded fresco commemorating the Annunciation. All adornment was reserved for the dome, which is, after all, nearest to god, for whose greater glory a representation of dawn had been painted in shades of rose and lilac, punctuated by pale stars. From its highest point hung a circular mirror in whose vast, smoky surface I saw my own reflection, or what I called my reflection but which—as if I were staring down into a well—was no more than a rippling blur, and whose wooden frame was inlaid with a mother-of-pearl phrase, rendered legible despite the distance by a coy glow that dove, slipped and swirled among the loops of the letters: *For now we see through a glass, darkly.*

And the church was dark, or at least dim. Not a single candle spoke. Through blue-and-green stained-glass windows, light sifted down into a turquoise gloom. Passing between the pews, I felt I was walking beneath the surface of a quiet limestone pond—and though silence is simply silence, though silence is not a question of magnitudes or intensities, somehow, surrounded by the storm and the echoing thunder, I sensed a silence close around me like velvet curtains, so that the air had about it the sultriness of breath.

Rain struck the stained glass. Rain pattered the dome. Alone in a provincial church, my wet skin steaming, I smelled the musk of wild horses emanating from my body. Wild horses—crushing honeysuckles under their hooves.

Is this how you would have remembered me?

Suddenly trumpets sounded near the doors. Gusts of gray incense billowed down the aisle, eddying in the pews, where bouquets of pink peonies lay sensuously submerged in smoke. A golden band glimmered on my ring finger; green silk gathered in folds along my forearms and rippled upon my breasts. In my abdomen, a second heart pulsed faintly. For a moment I knew how to have a story—or at the very least realized I was in the middle of a thought: *Don't you dare leave me alone at the altar . . .*

> (Still and forever you are babbling at my door, still and forever I am tasting your milk, still and forever you are telling me your story and even now you are asleep on my cot, no more clouds in your eyes. Within the globe of those hours you whirl and whirl like a trapped moth. Let me whirl with you. Let me be reborn as a sentence. Let me slumber among commas and semicolons while the author plays the typewriter, orchestrates the seasons, the sounds, the slant of light. Each hour is a pebble I carry in my pocket, but if I were to tell anyone about you—when I said 'pebble' what I meant was 'pearl,' each hour is a pearl, and I call it a pebble only out of extreme humility, because no one wants to hear about anyone else's love. And your life: Who saw it? The almond trees saw it; the peony bushes saw it. Your uncles saw nothing, your grandfather and great-grandfather saw nothing, there was no precedence for how you saw. I stood before you in a gown of peacock feathers because I was not afraid of beauty. Beauty dissolved into me like sugar in a cup of tea. But don't forget to sip me slowly, darling.)

And just as soon, the smoke dispersed, the flowers rotted, the trumpets paraded off to a vanishing point. My breasts shrank; my womb dissolved. Thunder rumbled, reverberating in the walls and rattling the windows. Not even a second passed—and light exploded into shrapnel, erasing the blue glow. I cried out and stumbled backward.

♥

I woke curled up in a pew, disoriented by the slickness of damp adobe. The air was cold and gusty; the din of rain was nearer now. I opened my eyes. A shard of mirror glinted beside my head. Vague luster of god's glass: nothing to see except the numinous.

> 'In the beginning was the word,' wrote the Apostle John. Divine soliloquy delivered in the dark, for no audience. Then—green trees. Blue feathers and pools of foam, bursting from broken syllables. Flesh growing on the bones of letters. Earth is the echo of a foregone language. And if I find a fleck of god stuck like a topaz in the lettered tendons of my typewriter, that's because I've grazed up against one of his words. A word not buried deep enough inside a thing. Maybe because he forgot, or because he couldn't bear to finish . . .
>
> Do you hear me? If you hear me, that's because I spoke a word of god. I don't know which one.

But if the mirror would not see, if god refused, well then. Then I would accept. There was a crack in the dome. Not wide, but irrevocable—like a peach split by the weight of its own sweetness. *La vie en rose:* rain streamed down the sides, tinted pink; the painted dawn was fading, drifting, following the flow of water, slipping between the panes of stained glass, collecting and moldering pinkly along the cornice, then thickening to fluorescence before brimming and showering the nave with lurid droplets, splashing crystalline static around the altar and spilling step by step into the aisle, where it melted once more into a stream rolling toward the door. Pinkish wavelets lapped at the pews; shards of glass spun and flashed like confetti in the current. I'd never seen a waterfall, much less a waterfall inside a room, and never before or since a waterfall the color of nectar. For many years this memory was as wordless as a dream; only now am I attempting to tell you how a church was broken. Or how the church had revealed itself at last—by becoming a cavern, which is the underived form of a church. Because slick glittering stalagmites prefigure the glittering stone statuettes of saints, and stalactites (where bats fold their wings and sway in their sleep) prefigure gargoyles. Without the cavern, the church is formless.

> But—and listen, because nothing has happened since. Absolutely nothing. I live alone in a room, in a large city. You

have to know what to do with what happens to you, or nothing else will happen. Because when something happens, that's an invitation to another reality. But the invitation isn't: 'Right this way, madam.' The invitation is realizing what you want with alarming clarity only when it's suddenly gone. Another reality asked too much of me, and because of that is unforgettable. I don't mean the angels. My capacity for transcendence was exhausted all in one night and I moved to a faraway city and promised never to return to West Texas.

(I keep spitting out diamonds. But diamonds don't say anything because they can't break. Diamonds make a virtue of being unsayable. I'm praying to escape the palace of my glistening laughter. I'm praying for a season of graphite.

Graphite destroys itself to become a word.)

But—and wait, listen. But then I had that surgery. Because nothing was happening and so I decided to make something happen. And I found out, when we're first forming in the womb, we all have the same genital, and that genital is a vagina. So I wondered: what would happen if I, too, returned to my underived form? Oh and it's beautiful, I'm bewitched by my own transfiguration. But in the months before the surgery, I forgot to realize that even if I inverted my shame, it wouldn't go away. In fact it's stuck inside me. I gave myself a thorn in the flesh. And so I'm telling you this story: to make something happen.

Because—that night in the church, there were angels. Milling about, floating beneath the cracked dome. Or what I call angels because that was how you described them to me, because my only act of resurrection is to refer to things by the names you gave them, so I saw angels floating in long and dazzlingly luminescent silver robes, lacking even so much as skeletons to offer form to the coolly flaming fabric that hung so bewitchingly frail from their marble masks.

My eyes were intoxicated by their excess of luster, the supernatural frequency of rustling that transmitted from their robes like a glitchy, mercurial mirage as they floated below the rift through which that pink waterfall was plashing down around the improbably dry altar and into the sudden celestial ecosystem forming at my feet, where flowers sprouted beside the stream and burst forth from the pews, their petals twirling and transforming as nimbly as the fragments in a kaleidoscope. Meanwhile the angels were singing, and I have sympathy in this sense for the authors of the Bible because describing an angel's song is extraordinarily difficult without resorting to melodrama and generalization, but that restless flock in the dome, with their resplendent and inscrutable faces, they were singing, very quietly at first, so quietly at first that I did not hear them over the meteorological detonations of a storm no longer muffled by the silence of a sealed room but having actually entered the room, because even though the front doors were closed, don't they always say that god will open a window?

Then, as suddenly as this sentence, the rumble ceased. The waterfall having erased at last the final fleck of pink pigment, the dome was pale as an egg, and the pews, except for the blank patch of plaster where I sat, were now buried beneath a fine field of moss from which the flowers spun and clicked their tessellated petals, pressing a faint prismatic glow against the eerie silver haze radiating heatlessly from the angels—whose song was undifferentiated by word or note, free of harmony, as unmelodious as a sigh, but a sigh that, rather than dying out, slowly grew louder, as if I were alone in a late autumn wood and gradually sensed, approaching from afar and rattling bough after bough of dry leaves in miles and miles of unseen trees, a long, cold gust of wind. Some sonic scrap of that soft cacophony of flora swished into the curl of my ears, narrowing therein to a hiss, whistling among the folds of my brain and unsettling the neural soil within which nameless memories were disintegrating quietly into the unthinkable aura of a selfhood.

> Twenty years in a godforsaken attic saying nothing even to the motes of dust. Why speak when all you can do is bring pity upon your little fairy life? Why speak when everyone hears you only in a general way? Waiting meanwhile for someone whose ears are tuned to that perfect pitch at which your secrets sound like revelations; waiting, mired in desire—the pressure of desire without the pleasure of combustion. Sentences so pristine because they are dense with desire; the surface chill of those sentences, the molten core. But even the most elaborate mechanism can't flip its own switch. Then one May evening you came along and did just that, and I reconfigured myself around the form of your finger. Legion—

I was overwhelmed with a breathtaking, irresistible grief. My chest contracted around a single point, which hurt so much I gasped; I doubled over, thinking I might vomit, but instead my eyes swarmed with tears.

The angels remained expressionless. Their eye sockets were empty; their hard stone lips half-open, preternaturally still. But their robes rustled more and more luminously, as if nourished by the decibel of my distress. I remembered then what John of Patmos wrote about Heaven in his Book of Revelation: 'There shall be neither sorrow, nor crying.' And I understood that Heaven was born not of love, but of fear. God keeps humans at such a great distance because if he saw our weeping faces he would feel so much tenderness. And he could no longer withhold paradise, he would give it to all of us, all at once, and then all he would have left—all he would have left is empty hands.

So for his Heaven, god made angels. For his endless Sunday. And he gave them marble faces—he forced them not to weep.

Love requires the gesture of refusal: a *no* as amorous as its *yes.* Angels have no choice. Angels can neither accept nor refuse, they can only praise. There is no sorrow in Heaven; there is only the narcotic of light.

So most, in thrall to His divine substance, sing forever. But some experience an error. They cannot bear their faces. They go mad from the monotony of rapture. These angels fall to earth.

And when such an angel finds someone alone, someone grieving, it gets attached. When it gets attached, it begins to follow, to watch—and soon enough, to sing.

Where one angel lingers, more will come.

They feed on our weeping.

But I did not survive just to be an angel's favorite soap opera.

Legion didn't die for anyone. He just died.

So the waterfall spilled down the aisle. The angels circled the dome. The flowers swooned to their sighs with unsettling sentience.

And I forgive you, okay?

I forgave them but I refused to weep.

I wiped my eyes. I blocked my ears with moss. I sat up in the pew and spoke a single sentence:

"I will give you something better."

The angels fell silent. For a moment they simply hovered in midair, then, all at once, they tilted their heads, staring at me blankly. One descended from the dome, rustling weightlessly down to float just above the stream; its face was the same as the others, but it had gathered all its radiance into its eye sockets, which were now ablaze. Its robes, in turn, had dimmed; its fringes, gray and tattered as cobwebs, nearly grazed the rushing water.

"I will need to lie upon the altar," I said.

The angel said nothing. But when I touched the stream with my toe, the surface felt as firm as glass, as if the water were flowing and frozen at the same time: I stepped tentatively out onto its rippling stillness and walked up the aisle, taking careful strides, almost laughing, because I remembered the vicar proclaiming, from that very altar, 'the meek shall inherit the earth,' with no idea what his words would mean—some fairy walking on water in a broken church.

The angel followed behind me. I felt the light of its eyes on my back, its stoic but somehow ingenuous curiosity. As I climbed up to the chancel, all that hid my nakedness was a tunic; I unfastened its buttons and pulled the loose fabric over my head, tossing it among the flowers. Then I ascended to the altar.

The other angels became curious, too. One by one they left the dome, forming a semicircle around the rough block of pink granite where my musk steamed from my skin. After a moment they began to sing again. This time I believe they were attempting to parse, rather than provoke; but because there is no pleasure in eternity and therefore no expression for pleasure in their language, they could describe my voluptuousness only by expressing its opposite, by enveloping me in barren melodies—by which I mean their song was still awful, though not in the same way. It sounded like a gasp, but an endless gasp, extending into their lungs with extraordinary, excruciating slowness, as if god were not transcendent but infinitesimal, and eternal life were merely a matter of time slowed almost to a halt.

Perhaps their key was lovelier at god's speed, but I didn't care. The song felt far away, and my musk near; the drift of hair below my hips was lush and overgrown—the scent was strongest and sweetest there, like the air in the tomb of a medieval nun, opened after hundreds of years. I reached down into it.

This is my body, which I give unto thee: I ached exquisitely, and then the aching passed. Sticky opalescence pooled in my palms.

Take, I said. Eat.

One by one they drifted toward the altar. One by one they bent to sip from my hands.

An angel's skin is colder than ice. Each faint brush of marble drained heat from my body, and by the time the last one touched me I was shivering. My bravado had faded. I had no idea what to do next.

Nor did the angels, apparently. They withdrew, watching. Cum dripped from their hard marble lips. But I was too frightened to reach for my tunic—too frightened to move at all.

Then I heard a faint crack. And then another. Fine fractures were webbing their faces. Their robes were lightless, flaking into dust.

For a moment they did not react: their eye sockets were empty; their lips half-open, preternaturally still.

Then the angels stared at one another, expressionless, howling in agony.

♥

When I woke the rain had stopped. The moss and the flowers had vanished. The last thing I remember before fainting was stained glass bursting from the window frames. These were unbroken; the dome was sealed. Not a trace of the angels.

I buttoned up my tunic.

I walked to the bakery and bought vanilla.

I said nothing: I had no proof except my own memory.

But I couldn't stay there anymore, either.

I said goodbye to my mother intricately icing the windows on her cake, and to Legion buried beneath the mesquite tree (good night, darling), then I packed up my possessions (the hair clips, the honeysuckle perfume, the tube of coral lipstick) and drove away in my father's powder-blue pickup. Eventually I landed in a large city where no one knew me and I knew no one. I worked, I went to school, I had a few surgeries, I fell in and out of love. I thought of you every day.

And the angels?

Sometimes I don't see them for months.

But tonight, as soon as I wrote that first sentence, 'When I was what you might call a young man . . . ,' I saw floating just outside my window, expressionless, intolerably bright, a face that had sniffed the scent of ink.

As soon as I shut the blinds, it started humming. So I turned on the radio, and wouldn't you know what was playing? That old John Prine song, the one Bonnie Raitt sang so well.

Well. I'm tired. Tired of myself, and tired of this story, which, nonetheless, I've written one thousand and one times, because every time I try to tell another story, inevitably it takes the shape of this one.

So let me say, for now: see you tomorrow. Let me say: amen.

[SPICEWOOD, TEXAS, SUMMER 2014
BROOKLYN, NEW YORK, SUMMER 2019]

WILD AND BLUE

Peach and Sandy were giggling, speeding down the highway in a powderblue Ford Thunderbird at ninety miles an hour.

—I feel like Adriana La Fucking Cerva, bitch.

Coffin-cut pink acrylics clutching the steering wheel lightly, she turned toward Sandy, smacked her Dubble Bubble, then struck a pose (sex eyes, Duck lips).

—Like, get me some snakeskin, bitch!

Tossing her head back, so that the iridescent sequin glued to her upper cheekbone caught the light and glinted:

—Like, Christophaaaa!

Outside the desert was almost past dusk. The air was grainy as a photograph. Sandy held out a vial full of silver powder, into which Peach, without even looking, dipped her pinkie nail.

♥

Later they were in Room 19 at the *Eve's Garden* off Highway 90. They took no Adderall, drank no liquor, smoked no cigarettes. The ashtrays were empty; the bedside glasses shrink-wrapped. Peach and Sandy were happy. Happier than they'd felt their entire lives, wondering how they'd never felt like this before—wondering why there had been so few nights like this, wondering if it was possible for every night to feel like this? As if their minds had been formed by wonder instead of fear, had been restructured, in one night, in a matter of hours, in a matter of minutes, upon a trellis of pleasure. Because they were worried about nothing, didn't have an anxious thought in their minds, not her and not him, not one thousand and not even one, and in fact felt what Peach always imagined people meant when they said 'at home in the world,' so she took Sandy's face in her hands and wiped away his tears while her own mascara ran down her face.

For some time they didn't speak. Cars rolled by out the window like water. A highway is another way to outrun time. Peach was singing "Silent Night," like this:

—All was calm, all was bright.

And Sandy thought no holy Mother could match her beauty, which was like experiencing a myth in real time. Her lashes, thickened and multiplied by mascara, were like a sunburst, but as if a shadow—as if darkness produced its own glow. Looking into her eyes, he felt like he was falling into another dimension. And the ribbons in her hair, resting lightly on either side of her neck like the petals of a ghost orchid (he had seen photographs on Google, had searched late at night, with his laptop on his chest, 'orchid species,' because he thought maybe if he saw something so strange and alluring just before his eyes closed, then his dreams might be different, might approach heaven): so, the ribbons in her hair, the sense of god haunting the air around her head; the sudden and oscillating depths of her eyes, transparent green tunnels opening and closing like valves, like halls of chlorophyll—

And for both of them, the motel curtains (some polyester imitation of organza, stained and riddled with snags) were as mysterious as a waterfall; both of them were shrouded in its mist, so lightly blue like the descent of a manta ray. And the ceiling (stippled stucco from the 70s) felt ancient, as hallowed as a backwater chapel adrift in a field of gnarled orange trees, heavy with the memory of fruit.

They took a bath together, giggling among bubbles. He ran his hands over her slick breasts. His cock swayed slowly underwater, like a memory of a flower. She thought she saw a string of pearls around his neck, but without a string: just floating together, centimeters apart, levitating above his collarbones. But then it disappeared. Then it disappeared, goodbye . . . and she saw the cowboy renting a room in the dim recesses of a saloon; the cowboy now lounging in his clapboard tub, rolling a cigarette with a corn husk.

So of course she saw herself running away with that man from out of town, the man with a slim scar on his face, riding a speckled stallion, shrouded in a sandstorm—glittering, full of faces, illusions of faces that he carried like a deck of cards, cards made of sand, as elusive as sand, dissolving into the storm he carried with him from town to town, from day to night, from desert to horizon . . .

Sandy was a man and Peach was a woman, it was so simple. Forever they were a man and a woman, like silhouettes on a high cliff. For a moment it was as simple as 'forever they were a man and a woman, like silhouettes on a high cliff.' For a moment Peach forgot her own name. She felt as glamorous as a woman with memories only of Spring, only of honeysuckles rank and bursting like declarations of love from the vines, as she strolled through the dusk and bells rang and rippled the stillness of the pond in the depths of her mind . . .

Then came more grain: he was a cowboy (rakish, hair falling into his face, eyes for no one but me) and she was the woman with the torn pink dress, who tore her dress in the creosote brambles, who stole a horse, a bluehaunched mare, from the ranch of another man, a wealthy German stallion breeder with cold blue eyes and the halitosis he attempted to cover with rosewater, which made it all the worse, and who had laughed and laughed at her, because the drug was fading—

she was remembering the man at the little dive bar off the highway where she'd stopped with Sandy that afternoon, laughing because he'd looked at the driver's license, which had said she was a man (she, Peach), which the man, the bartender, thought was so funny because it made sense after all, why else would a woman have such enormous tits, such enormous tits and a voice that didn't quite make sense, a voice that sounded just slightly off-key coming from that face, hers, which he, in an instant, having just imagined slapping it with his cock, now thought ridiculous—

she was remembering (was feeling her fantasy tempered by a blush of rot) because the drug was fading, felt Peach (felt Sandy, too, who suddenly remembered the pearls he sometimes felt levitating around his neck, the pearls he had wanted to forget), the drug, the silver powder which they had stolen together, three days earlier, from the summer ranch of the pharmaceutical mogul who was planning to release it to market, pending FDA approval, as Dysphorable™.

There was one lamp in the room, the type of lamp which no memory would hold. It was hard to notice even when you sat beside it. There was an air conditioner, and a carpet with a pattern. Peach and Sandy lay side by side in bed on top of a brownish floral quilt.

She was beginning to have trouble sensing her own beauty. Her hands seemed suddenly huge, as if her fingers were swelling; her wrists, too, had thickened—they looked like her father's. She winced; felt a contraction of shame, which reached down into her gut like a dry retch. It was an emptiness so profound she couldn't bear to accept it. She flipped open her clamshell pocket mirror. Her chin was too big; her brow ridge too thick; her eyes sunken and sullen. She was a mistake. She was a mistake and it was too late. It was all too late. The air was feeling almost computer-generated, as if it had never held life. Peach was choking on her own breath.

And then her body—which she hadn't seen, because rising from the bath minutes before, she had known better than to look in the mirror—then her body (do you hear me, God?) then her body was no longer the body of—well, of what her body imagined to be the body of a woman. Proprioception split open. Her ribcage was expanding, was prying apart; her shoulders were like great blocks of stone; her head was the head of an enormous baby. Peach was horrified to be buried alive in her own body, buried alive and there was no way out. Help me, I'm suffocating. Help me, please . . .

(Sandy still thought Peach was beautiful, but now her beauty troubled him, made him ache. He wanted it for himself. She was like a disturbance in his mind. When he loved her he did not know who he was. Once, long ago, they had been 'boyfriends' together. They hadn't spoken for years and he had forgotten the violence of wanting to be beautiful. He had simply chased after men who allowed him to pretend that he was only seeking a hot rush of horror, the horror of being alive, of the disgusting fact of pleasure—the totality of degradation. But he had grown tired, too. And the more tired he felt, the brighter the pearls became. The pearls buzzed to life. They glowed with their own light. He needed a means to dim them without destroying himself.

And then one of the men had happened to be a pharmaceutical mogul.

And Peach had always been so skilled at picking locks.

So one week ago he had called her from a payphone. It was good to hear her voice.)

Peach was catatonic, staring at the ceiling. Sandy sat up:

—Should we take a little more?

After a while, she replied:

—What are the side effects?

—He didn't say.

—A little more then.

♥

When they woke, they woke with dread. Sandy immediately reached for the vial. Peach dipped another pinkie in the dust. Then everything lustered.

—I love you, baby, he said, kissing her on the forehead.

They were headed for Southern California, where Peach's older sister lived in a small cabin up in the mountains. But before they left Texas, she wanted one last chicken fried steak. As she assessed her outfit in the mirror, striking one pose and then another, she kept muttering,

—Diva at the diner, steak and a Shiner,

in a half-whispered singsong. After tying a handkerchief in a yellow bow around her neck, she patted the pockets of her blue jeans, before realizing she couldn't remember where she'd put the car keys.

—Sugar, have you seen my keys?

But Sandy was realizing he couldn't remember where he'd left his money clip—his grandfather's, wrought from silver and inset with a coldwater agate, the birthstone they'd shared—which, for ten years, he'd always placed on the bedside table each night before he slept. All their cash was rolled up into it. Sandy lifted the mattress and Peach opened all the drawers; Sandy spilled their suitcases and Peach ripped apart the curtains.

—Car's gone.

—No way.

—Gone.

She swung the door wide and sprinted into the lot. Sandy slumped in the doorway, lifting the vial from his breast pocket as Peach rounded the corner of the motel. He tapped some powder into his palm and pinched a bump between his forefinger and thumb. He nodded to an older man in snakeskin boots slow-stepping toward the ice machine. He lit a Marlboro Gold. Then he took a deep breath. Everything would work out. Peach probably had some jewelry they could pawn, and he'd seen her hotwire a car once outside a Target in Abilene. But he was startled awake when the Thunderbird came roaring back around the corner—blue like an act of God—before screeching to a halt in front of him, the air smelling of Hermès and burnt tires, Peach spritzing herself with *Eau de Merveilles*, dusting her cheeks with blush, yelling,

—We left the goddamn keys in the goddamn ignition,

before tossing the money clip through the window.

—Get in, cowboy.

♥

At the diner Sandy ate two strips of bacon with a side of fried okra. Peach had the best chicken fried steak of her life—crispy, sunk in gravy, sprinkled with fresh diced serranos—and a Dr. Pepper. "Always on My Mind" was playing on the jukebox. When she went to the restroom to reapply her crimson lipstick, he dissolved a heap of silver powder in his coffee. (In the bathroom, tracing her famous Cupid's bow, she thought, 'I am the woman in the story I wrote in my head, before I ever knew I was writing a story. I am the woman in the story about love.' Because he had come back, he had come back, and no one could ever say again that he did not love her. He loved her so much that he would even love a woman. He had broken the only law of his desire because he respected the mystery, the inviolable mystery of her face, in which shards, almost runic, of the boy he'd once known remained, glinting like mica, emanating the aura of certain dusks in certain meadows, without disclosing its source—as if these shards were proof of lost time, enshrined and protected by the face of the beautiful woman in which they had been inlaid, as if within a reliquary.) And when she came back, he was pale and wide-eyed, with shaking hands:

—Peach . . .

—Are you okay?

She slid down into the red Formica booth, taking his hands in hers.

—Hey, are you okay?

—How did we get here?

—What do you mean?

—I mean how the fuck are we at a highway diner in Pecos, Texas.

Now she noticed the vial, next to his coffee cup, on the table and in plain sight. At least a quarter of the powder was missing.

—Baby, she said. Baby, what did you do?

For a moment he met her gaze, shaking his head.

—You are so beautiful.

Tears welled in his eyes. He glanced out the window, blinking.

—What did you do, Sandy?

—The last thing I remember . . . the last thing I remember is climbing out the window at the Pederson ranch, he said, then glanced back at her, stifling a sob:

—I'm scared, Peachy.

—Hey, she said.

(Quickly, quietly, she slipped the vial into her mother-of-pearl clutch.)

—Hey, look at me, she said, wiping away his tears delicately with the sides of her thumbs, careful with her long pink acrylics:

—When is my birthday?

—I don't remember.

It hurt, it hurt like the beginning of a panic, but she couldn't let it. They were in public. She was a woman in public and she could not panic, so she said:

—Yes you do. What season was it when we first met?

—Autumn. The leaves were on the ground.

—And where did we meet?

—At a party. A house party in Hyde Park.

—Whose party?

—Yours. Your birthday.

—But I didn't know you.

—A boy invited me. But he got drunk too fast and kept telling the same joke, so I went to the backyard to smoke.

—And what did you say, when you walked up to me?

But at that moment they were interrupted by the details of a 'developing story' playing from a handheld radio on the bar counter:

—Police are investigating a robbery at the private ranch of Kevin Pederson, CEO of AmenaCorp, involving an experimental drug, which, the company warned in a press release, is, in its uncatalyzed state, dangerous for public consumption . . . the suspects . . . are still at large, but investigators believe they may be hiding out in . . .

Peach tilted her head, like *let's get out of here.*

—I'll explain everything on the way, she said.

Sandy left cash on the table.

(The waitress had heard the radio and seen the vial of powder, but said nothing to anyone. 'Good luck,' she thought. Later that night, she spent the cash on a few rounds of tequila Red Bulls for herself and her friends and then went home with a man who fucked her well and knew all the words to "At My Window.")

♥

That night they checked in at a motel in Tucson. Despite a harrowing day of driving—paranoid about Pederson's pigs and both of them in withdrawal, chainsmoking Sandy's Golds, passing a bottle of Jimador back and forth—his lost memories hadn't come back. Peach felt grotesque, sweating her blush off and embarrassed of every word she spoke, like God was subjecting her to her own reverb. She wanted, at the very least, to feel beautiful; at the very least on this last ride, which would never be repeated, she wanted to feel beautiful so she could relax enough to experience a romance while it was happening, rather than in retrospect, rather than losing the instants to her fear that from this or that angle, Sandy would think she looked like a man, which would ruin his love for her once and for all, because she had failed to maintain in every second and from every angle the necessary proof of her womanhood, because if she looked like a man even once, she thought, he would never entirely see her as a woman again, because no matter how beautiful she became, he would never forget the moment when he first glimpsed—with, she imagined, a kind of disgusted pity—the man-failure counterfeiting himself as a woman, humiliatingly, named Peach.

Meanwhile Sandy, who felt a string of pearls clutching his neck, choking him, couldn't stop thinking about the silver powder, which Peach had forsworn the moment she realized that it would steal her memories, because:

—Above all, I don't want to forget you.

And in a motel in Tucson, he promised, crying, his forehead against her forehead, his lips against her lips, never to touch it again:

—I want you to be my wife . . .

She fell asleep in his arms, while he whispered a plan:

They would mail the vial anonymously back to Pederson, then detour for Las Vegas and get married in a little chapel full of fake flowers, with a faux-Roman fountain spouting water so aquamarine it would seem like liquid candy. And then they would go drink martinis on the top floor of a fancy hotel.

♥

In the morning, Peach woke first. She stared at Sandy's sleeping face, brushed his wavy brown hair behind his ear. She was a woman. It was so simple. She was a woman because she was in love. It could be enough. One day it could be enough because she was a woman and it didn't matter if Sandy was a man or a woman or some kind of secret thing. She was Sandy's woman and it was enough.

—Good morning, baby, she said.

He yawned, blinking.

He opened his eyes.

For a moment he was confused.

Then, struck with terror.

He leapt backward off the bed.

—What the fuck, he said.

—What?

—What the fuck?

—Sandy, what's going on?

—Who are you?

—No.

—Who the fuck are you?

—No. Sandy, look at me.

—Stop saying my name.

—Please. Please, baby.

He was moving wildly, grabbing his clothes from the floor.

—Please, Sandy. Please. Not like this.

She reached out for him, but he stepped back.

—Stay the fuck away from me.

—We're getting married today.

—You're insane.

He took his money clip from the nightstand and slipped it in his pocket.

—Sandy, wait.

He wedged his feet into his shoes without tying the laces.

—Sandy, she said.

He headed for the door.

—That night, she said. When you walked up to me, in the backyard of the house in Hyde Park, what did you say?

(You are as pretty, he'd said, as a peach.)

[AUSTIN, TEXAS, APRIL 1, 2024]

EZEKIEL IN THE SNOW

Her makeup is violent . . . like swan's eyes, but in richer, kaleidoscope colors; instead of eyebrows, fringes of inferior precious stones hang from the rims of her eyelids . . .

—SEVERO SARDUY, TR. SUZANNE JILL LEVINE, *COBRA* (1972)

[The Law] guards against this danger by precluding all the unworthy from entering the holy congregation. It begins with the men who belie their sex and are affected with effemination, who debase the currency of nature and violate it by assuming the passions and the outward form of licentious women. For it expels those whose generative organs are fractured or mutilated, who husband the flower of their youthful bloom, lest it should quickly wither, and restamp the masculine cast into a feminine form.

—PHILO OF ALEXANDRIA, TR. F. H. COLSON,
THE SPECIAL LAWS, BOOK ONE, CHAPTER 325 (C. 40 AD)

The story tells us that when Presine left [the King's castle] she took her three daughters to Avalon, which was called the Lost Isle because no man, however many times he had been there before, could ever find it again except by chance . . . . [S]he took them up on a high mountain—according to the story it was called Eleneos, which means "flowering mountain"—whence she could easily see the land of Scotland. Weeping, she would say to them, "There you see the land where you were born and where you would have had your share of the inheritance . . . . The power of your father's seed would eventually have drawn you and your sisters toward his human nature, and you would soon have left behind the ways of nymphs and fairies forever."

—JEAN D'ARRAS, TR. DONALD MADDOX AND SARA STURM-MADDOX,
MELUSINE; OR, THE NOBLE HISTORY OF LUSIGNAN (1394)

Sometimes, hidden in the heart of her Name, the fairy is transformed to suit the life of our imagination. . . . And yet . . . if we remain in her presence, the fairy dies, and with her, the Name.

—MARCEL PROUST, TR. LYDIA DAVIS, *SWANN'S WAY* (1913)

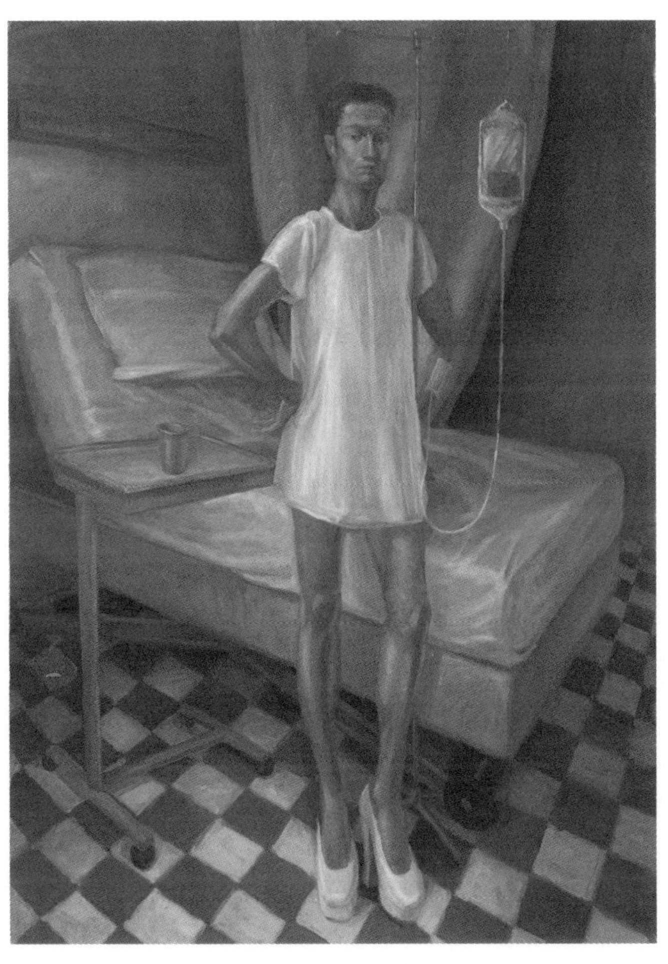

Hugh Steers, *Man and I.V.* (1994). Oil on canvas,
65 x 47 in (165.1 x 119.38 cm)

I DO NOT want god to take the form of a mortal man and that's the truth. Whenever god makes an entrance you know it's not because he was just stopping in. You know it's the end, when he comes. I don't want it to end. I don't want to watch doves fall from the trees and blueberries burst into flame. But then again I wasn't the sort to wake my mother in the middle of the night and say, 'I saw an angel and I killed it because it wouldn't tell me where god was.' That was him, Ezekiel. Of all names. Mother named him Ezekiel and me she called Elizabeth. Elizabeth Anne, for God's sake, and my brother after a prophet. Mother said he was touched and I said you just wait. Said maybe he'll turn out a preacher and I said maybe he'll wander the desert naked. Mother coddled him all his life on the off chance.

I wasn't right about the desert. Ezekiel in the snow is more surprise to me than all the rest of it. I will never forget when he said, 'And here's its feathers,' and by god there were feathers. Mother had no idea where he got them, no one was missing a chicken. Ezekiel in the snow. Me driving to him now because of all the rest of it. Some sort of prophet he is. Some sort of dreams he must be having. Driving past the dead lakes and the geese singing like throat-slit prima donnas. Ezekiel, come warm your hands with us. Ezekiel, tell us a story. Ezekiel, that was no angel. Now he is blind for everything but dreams. Digging for opals, he said. Called Mother from a pay phone. Opals, my god. And in the snow.

♥

"No," said the man in the yellow vest. His beard was white as bloodroot. On the bar, a stack of flea-bitten books about orchids. "Seen no one," he said. Then he patted the pocket of his vest, fingered its yellow velvet flap, and removed a small bundle of bird bones. "Except you and everyone with a front porch." Out of the barroom dark limped a greyhound, one eye half-curdled, the other already spoiled.

Her teeth, too, were nowhere near a quorum. But her fur was different: some cousin of mother-of-pearl, silver, almost lilac. "Only dog named in the Bible," he said. She licked from the man's palm with a thin, eloquent tongue, slowly, from what nearly seemed a sense of delicacy, then disappeared into the dark, to seek from the bones whatever memory of marrow remained. "That makes dogs only one less than the angels." The man removed a jaundiced handkerchief from the opposite pocket to wipe his hands. There was soil in his nails to which he did not attend. His skin was wrinkled like autumn leaves. But he had no beer, only the books. When he leaned close, his breath smelled of wet moss. "What kind of man are you looking for?"

I don't know, I said. I haven't seen Ezekiel for three years. Some sort of prophet, I said. Who knows why. But I trust a man in a yellow vest to have seen a prophet if there is one to be seen.

♥

I went back to my motel, in the style of a Spanish mission: rosy adobe, line of weathered beams. Built by someone who mistook snow for sand, seems to me. Or maybe just dreaming of Summer. Past the wrought-iron gate, its bars tipped in lily florets, lay a gravel courtyard for cars. Yellowed flyer taped to my door claimed some circus caravan was on the edge of town, in the pinewood. For who, in February? The eye of god. Or lumberjacks, by happenstance.

Inside: glazed aqua tiles for the floor, pitch-blue under the bed, the table, the curtains. Potpourri somewhere. Made the whole room reek of honeysuckle. Ezekiel used to clip it from the vine with Mother's tiny silver scissors. One day he culled a thimbleful of sweet dew. Took him eight hours. Refused dinner that night, and breakfast the next morning. Said no other sustenance would do. Did so for two days, until he fainted.

Not a week later, he stole Mother's orchid from the kitchen

table. Brought it to his closet and shut the door. I said nothing, but Mother soon noticed and followed the whispering to its source. She rapped on the wood. 'What business do you have with my orchid,' she said. Ezekiel said they were having a conversation. Said to Mother, 'It'll talk to you too if you'd care to remember how.' She simply pursed her lips, opened the door and pointed toward the kitchen. But she has a misbegotten kernel of mysticism in her: what was inflamed in her one and only son. That was her only orchid and she was always looking at it but that day she wouldn't look and the next morning it was gone. Mother never said what she did to it. Never raised another orchid. Never once more said the word.

I opened the window, scooped snow off the sill with a plastic cup, poured a one-shot Belvedere. For who, in February? Ezekiel in the snow, and me drinking because of all the rest of it. Well, I said. You cannot turn the circles of the sun.

♥

The proprietress offered dinner to her guests for a small fee. To her guest, in this case. Doilies for napkins. Her lids were wrinkled, but her eyes were eyes that did not dream, they were eyes that saw. "Years ago I hosted all the debutantes in the East Texas ballroom circuit," she said, laying out chili casserole and a congealed shrimp salad, Bundt shaped and neon green. I did not believe her, but I did not mind, either. She sighed. The salad quivered. I cut myself a slice because I did not like to see shrimp so obvious, so still and almost *on display*, like in an aquarium, if you kept dead ones for pets but didn't know they were dead. For who, in February—or any day, any hour?

After two glasses of wine, she excused herself. I thought I was alone, so I poured myself a glass, too. Come thou font, etc. I looked out the window, into the snow. Almost dropped my wine when I saw that greyhound, far off, in a beech copse. But then the proprietress appeared again in the doorway, dressed in a yellow chiffon gown, with a pink ribbon pinned to the fringe. "You've inspired me," she said. I hadn't said anything. Eyelids dusted silver, hands gloved in perfect creamsicle silk. She sat beside me. "Would you lead me in a waltz?" Her voice was rich as buttermilk: I looked in her eyes, pure seeing. No illusions. I said sure, if you sing. So she sang, some song about Spanish moss. I took her waist, and in that dining room we moved among the embroidered stags and the firelight while outside dusk fell and the snow seemed like a field of lavender and I kissed her on her lips and she kissed me too. Who knows why. We went to her bed, behind the dining room.

♥

Next morning, she said from the bath: "Some of my jewelry is missing." Since when, I said. "A few days now." Lemon silhouettes of butterflies patterned a faded-blue nightgown. Imitation Tiffany lamps. Bedside, a black pack of Nat Shermans. She never wore perfume, just washed with lard and rose water.

"They left, let's see, my ruby ring, my mother's brooch, my earrings. But all my opals, gone." I sat up in bed. My god, I thought. My god. Anything but opals. "I asked the Park Rangers, but—they don't do opal searches. They don't give a damn about opals."

I had a book with me but I hadn't once opened it since I'd come. I look more than I read. Spent my girlhood looking at Ezekiel looking at blades of grass. Writing down every last word he spoke. But I didn't listen to him because he was always talking. Opals, my god.

When did the circus come into town, I said. "What circus." In the pinewood, I said. "That circus was never open. Only stopped here years ago because the snow wouldn't let them pass, and their elephant died from frostbite . . ." Splash of water. "Dead elephants will bankrupt a circus, you know."

I have to go, I said. I went to the bathroom and kissed her for longer than I expected. Steam hovering like the ghost of a rosebush.

♥

I'd filled my thermos with wine because I did not want to go to the circus. No one was driving and the snow was deep on the road. My nipples were sore from biting. My tongue was tired, too. But it was not so cold, with the wine. In Winter there is no such thing as a breeze. Only wind, howling implicit. All the branches lacquered, ice-wise. No sound but my steps, not even geese. If I met Christ on this road I would avert my eyes. Ezekiel is as much revelation as I can bear.

A ways out of town, I took the flyer from my pocket. Fragile from damp, bleached at the creases. Turn off the main road at the painted pine, it said. There was a bare tree ahead, pink as promised, and day-old boot-prints beneath it. Digging for opals was all he said. But the phone said Michigan, and I was closer by two hundred miles than Mother, who was anyway no hardy soul now. He better not be selling those stones or I swear to high heaven I will disown you myself, Ezekiel. One tree—pink as a wound. 'Midnight for the bride of quietness,' he'd say. 'Struck by the clock's third blade.' Then, not ten steps away, that goddamn greyhound, ears lifted, eyes wide. Looked me in the face as if I'd surprised away her blindness. Shuffled her legs in the snow, like a far-off horse. Let out what seemed less growl than wheeze. But she was no innocent. No iridescent thing is innocent.

Soon she wandered off, slow, svelte, limping into the woods. I followed, woozy from wine and white light. My breath was like cheap perfume.

♥

There were boot-prints and beside them, paw-prints. There were fallen branches piercing snowdrifts, dark crooked lines like cracks in the softened glare. There was the slow silver form of the greyhound, limping. And up ahead, there was a clearing.

Candy-cane tents in a semicircle, the largest collapsed like the masts of a Grecian shipwreck, the other two still intact by miracle or mistake. Beside the smallest, a popcorn machine now nested by finches. Nearby a barren maypole, one shred of yellow ribbon yet attached by a nail. In the center, an iron-barred crimson palanquin, pseudo-palace, certain tomb, from which emerged two enormous tusks.

They were crusted by bluish bark. Frozen mold. Studded, too, by tiny icicles. But that was an elephant, before it was the story of one. That was an elephant and no one had unlocked the cage. What can you do with an elephant in Michigan. Can't keep it with the cows. Certainly can't keep it in the living room. So you let it starve in some icy inverse of a desert.

The greyhound was digging at the base of a tent. Habitual, not frantic. Where the boot-prints stopped. I was drunk. My heart was beating wildly. I saw a pail of pink paint on an exposed stone. I saw the greyhound vanish under the canvas. A finch flashed skyward.

♥

I had to strike the door-flap with my thermos. Jagged scraps of ice sloughed off the stiff cloth. Wine spilled over my fingers, dark as oil against the snow. Then I stepped back, wiped my hands, and took a knife from my sack. Not my knife, and likely not the right knife. But she had happened to have, up in the dining room, a small blade from Ostia. 'Repoussé silver hilt,' she whispered, against my ear. I borrowed it.

Now I opened the flap, waiting. But no one came. Not even the dog. Only the surprised release of a steeped breeze.

♥

At first my eyes were dazzled by the residue of snowblink. The darkness was a shock. Softened fitfully by the glitchy warmth of artificial candles, hundreds, jaundiced, twitching. And there you were, Ezekiel—suspended, almost floating in a nest of gauze and tubes. You were always the last spider. Remember what you told me, in the park when dusk was falling, by the pool of water in the hidden place overhung with blue ferns? Remember, Ezekiel, how you lifted a frond to show me the dewy web of a brown recluse? The threads form semagrams, you said. I wanted you to tell me what was written. The meaning of an iridescence. But you said a spider's story is final. That twinkle in the silk. Once you enter it, you do not leave.

Come with me

Enclosed in the maze of your own wings: some feathers pink, some blue, some silvery scraps of gauze, stains here and there, blood. Half a chrysalis. Rustling from the brief chill I brought in with me. Emerging here and there from the densities of fabric was a tangle of transparent tubes, forking like a root system, disappearing into the dark—bearing back, dripping, gurgling, squirting, fluids of different lusters and viscosities. One like ink. Another like cherry syrup. Then some sort of milky jelly. And in the middle of it all, Ezekiel, there you were: heaving, half-mummified, waiting. For who, in February? Never knew you to be looking for a lover. Found a few, I suppose. If that was the meaning of the names you sometimes mentioned in your phone calls, Aurora and the rest. But now you were alone. Now you were bruised, cracked with wounds, your skin fissured, encrusted. Dirt beneath your nails, but something else, too. Some twinkling.

What are you calling this dream, I said.

You looked up. Our eyes met. (*Sunburst*)

And the room dissolved into a tunnel of crystals folding into themselves, riotously colorful—a sea of luminous atoms, infinitesimally eddying. Hell in Technicolor. Every depth was a fractal. Eternity is a form of vertigo.

But with a click, the room resolved: scraps of form and color, drawn, stretched across the air to some unseen center of gravity, became objects. I was standing in a cool grotto, sunk in shadow. Artificial candles again. Hundreds, filling surfaces, boxes or tables or vanities, who knows. Strewn about the tent, forming a vague semicircle, were anonymous furnishings concealed by layers of silvery gauze. A blue suede chaise lay stranded in the grass. Gauze around its ankles. Reclining, rouged cheek resting on a delicate hand, draped in a swan-feather gown and surrounded by misty orchids nodding from clay vessels like the promise of an audience, Ezekiel snorted a line of lustrous dust off a Minoan tablet. Hair curled into blond wavelets and pinned up by a tight bouquet of milk thistle. Cinnabar lipstick. Cowboy boots.

"Powdered opals," (s)he said. "Helps me chitchat with the flowers."

Ezekiel.

"They're talking about you," (s)he said.

Please, Easy. Why am I here.

But (s)he was whispering in the ear of an orchid. (S)he was writing in cursive. (S)he was applying false lashes without aid of a mirror.

Okay, I said. Okay. Tell me what they are saying.

"It's difficult to translate perfume into phrases," (s)he said, stirring opal powder into a small clay bowl filled with hot milk. Then she began to glaze her nails, eggshell blue. The greyhound condensed out of the bronze fog, curling around the legs of the chaise.

"You must ingest the powder."

I would do no such thing. I did not want to hear the flowers speak, nor find out it was a farce. I mean I did not want a new dimension, it was too much knowing, too much for the enterprise of myself. Let me have the seasons and the sun and the unburnt and unburning blueberries. Let me have the purple Texas dust. If I allowed another dimension there would be no end to my wanting, I would eat God alive. Would steal his eyes for souvenirs. But neither did I want to disbelieve in what had been all along since my very first breath the proof of Ezekiel's gaze. He watched the sky and I saw the soil, simple as that. Or he took care of *fading things* and I of *things that do not fade.* Was Easy too who wrote a letter:

'To see paradise, gaze into the eyes of a zealot. I know heaven is true so long as I discern a swarm of angels, small as flecks of light, forecast upon a lacquered cornea; so long as I see projected there, in miniature, the hothouse of the risen dead. But if I turned and followed the direction of her gaze, darling, I would see only burning blue air . . .'

Postmarked some motel in Colorado Springs, already outdated by the time I replied a week later. Sent me letters because he was afraid to lose his journals, always on the road like that. Once left a whole manuscript in a toilet stall. So any phrase he wanted remembered, he mailed me from somewhere. The archive under my bed.

Consequently, I hoped they were more than whims. Or if they were whims. If they were whims. Let them be like the gesticulation that, in conversation, suggests possibilities. The arm flung out like a horizon. Let them be just that gesticulation which in air is blithe but in water is vital, because in water the same outflung arm prevents the body from sinking. In water, gesticulation is a form of flight. Swimming is like dreaming.

"Elizabeth, the orchids are calling us by other names . . ."

Now her eyes met mine. She was no mere eau de Marlene Dietrich. In those eyes, which had waited for so long on some recapitulation of Eden, I saw a new paradise approaching:

(*Solar flare*) The room collapsed like an accordion. But kept collapsing, through zero space. Pullulation of gold. Tachycardia of god. And me somewhere off the track of time, falling forever—until the room landed, with a thud, in a glass case. The air was humid, green. "When you write this all down," said Ezekiel, "say something like: 'Between thick, fleshy leaves, among insubstantial fronds, the shadows were greener, deeper, sheltering the blue domes of Dahlias dripping with dew, and pink belfries of Bubblegum mint, and Orchids gossiping, whispering a faint perfume; rising over this damp canopy, tall, thin candlesticks wafted a haze of light. Our Lady of the Flowerbreath rustled among the Interrupted ferns'—did you know there was such a thing?—'before bursting forth from the Fountain grass in a hospital gown, embroidered, here and there, with clusters of silver sequins and cinched at the waist with the skeleton of a snake, the dead and relicked clone of a former lover's champagne ball python, by the name of Old Milk . . .'"

And so she did, trailing an intravenous drip attached to a pole. Some aquatic concoction of opal dust dangling, sloshing from the speed: "Circling yon stormy seas," said Ezekiel, "a miniaturized horde of those light, swift ships of which no certain artistic depiction remains, invented around 500 BCE by the pirates of the Eastern Mediterranean and later copied by the Rhodian navy; in short, a miniaturized horde of *hemioliae*—their rows of oars, thin as the ribs of a hummingbird, beating against the milky waves—pursue a battery-operated Syracusia, that behemoth byproduct of Imperial fancy whose floors, according to Moschion the Paradoxographer, were tiled in mosaic chapters of the *Iliad,* so that to read the poem you had to walk from room to room

of the craft, refusing to meet the gaze of your peers, ignoring gardens, libraries, and a temple to Aphrodite, as well as the sea. Through the transparent bag—half hourglass, half aquarium—you see tiny swashbucklers climbing the sides of the impossible vessel, cutlasses in hand, preparing to commandeer and proclaim it a pirate island devoted not to Aphrodite but to her transsexual twin Aphroditos, who emerges from the temple scattering little sparks of opaline light (produced by the mechanized friction of iron fillings in her carapace) while the merrymaking usurpers adorn themselves with infinitesimal trinkets and, pouring into the library, press petals, small as flecks of fragrant dust, between the folds of scrolls . . ."

Miss Flowerbreath with her essences. Essence of honeysuckle. Essence of prickly pear. She collapsed onto a flowerbed, Lady Ezekiel of the Elegant Sigh: "When you write this," she said, her blond curls wild with leaves and flecks of soil, "say I tell Aurora hello, hello to a true Scorpio . . . say for me, nobody does resigned amorousness like Monica Vitti, also a Scorpio . . ."

Another rustling resulted in the greyhound. Echo of wolf. Essence of silver. Swirling like smoke around her feet.

Why am I here. Why this story.

"Because I can't remember," she said. "I have some memories so faint they're nothing more than a gloom of sensations, irradiated by traces of time but not of space, or sound, or image; composed, that is, not of any one sensation in particular, but of something more total, more auroral—the haunting of my mind by an earlier version of itself. Which is to say," she said, plucking a petal, offering it to the greyhound, whose tongue curled around it like a sunset wave, "not what I saw, but how I saw it. But you always remember the grain, you could enumerate the contents of a single atom in such detail that it would seem, to your interlocutor, an entire biome; Elizabeth, you're the only one who was there . . ."

Ezekiel. Where have you been.

"I've been trying to remember," she said. The greyhound yawned. Petal scraps caught in her thick white teeth. "To remember something other than myself. Attempting to recover the desert of ten years ago while surrounded by the desert of the present instant was like reading a metaphor in which an author, rather than activating the dialectic of contrast, blurs the image of a noun by likening it to something slightly too similar—I mean to say I thought the desert was distracting me, so I sought out the snow. I thought if my eyes absorbed the negative of sand, then in my mind as in a darkroom, with desire for an enlarger and consciousness like a chemical bath, a photograph might emerge and reveal a desert of the past. Anyway I was wrong. Snow wasn't enough; nor did my isolation produce ghosts, nor the silence, voices. Or not to the extent I had hoped: sometimes I've heard trills, seen shimmers. The opals helped . . ."

Ok, Easy. What do you remember.

"Murk, greenly overhanging," she said, rubbing the luminous pink velvet of the greyhound's folded ear. "An underworld of root and soil and rotten lily petals, that library of spiders where we followed the tune of a strange music, as if played on a flute hewn from a rough pink chunk of coral, and on a piano within which, in place of strings, were single hairs of mermaids, and in place of hammers, rows of blue crab claws, and whose lid was formed not from some varnished slab of wood, but from the same scallop shell on which Aphrodite famously emerged from the sea—such was the sound of the song bubbling up from the depths of a fetid pond . . ."

You heard a song. I heard a scream. Mother had taken us on the road. The Summer before my wedding, your wandering. An adventure, she said. Before you two leave town forever. But I'd read the letters in her drawer, the *darlings* and the *one day soons.* Said she'd meet him halfway, in Texarkana. Her driving from Midland, him from Mississippi. Mother liked to fall in love by mail. Liked to dream of distances and highways. Made a flirtation into a soap opera right from the get-go, all for the cost of a stamp. 'Naught has been else has been twice.' So she said. Xeroxed her own letters at the library. Original went to the post office and the copy to her bedroom drawer.

Etc.—until at last one day we packed our bags. Out in East Texas she met the man for tea. The two of us at the motel with nothing to do, so off we went into the woods. Heard a woman screaming and you said it was a miracle. Like her voice was an element, sure as air or water. Something like a sparkling—state of matter before it is specified. Said it reminded you of the childhood of heaven. When god was young. Back when there were no angels, just translucent bees, buzzing.

(Inside her intravenous aquarium, lounging on marble lawn chairs atop the deck of the Syracusia, the pirates were eating pomegranates, whose infinitesimal ruby seeds glinted in their fingers like electrons swirling around atoms; Ezekiel's eyes were as glitchy and colorful as a smashed computer screen.)

I wasn't keen on seeking the source. But you insisted, said maybe it was a matter of tuning my ears. Said it was like an oyster, gone mad from grains of sand. Wasn't a pearl a gem. But wasn't it also a howl. So we went into the woods. The dusk of trees. Perpetual sundown.

At first it was a forest like any other: flowering dogwood, sugar maple. Beds of moss. Sudden gusts of wings in the branches. Gray, shriveled palms of prickly pear, dissolving in pools of water. "But then the other forest began—in fragments, shimmers. I remember," said Ezekiel. "The air began to thicken with blue fog until it became so dense we could scarcely breathe, much less see where we were walking; a rift of polychromatic anemones ripped apart the soil like a sudden wound. Schools of minnows, emerging from the hollows of hickory trees, swam and swirled before vanishing off into the woods, while silver eels rippled among the roots of the trees. The song surrounded us like an atmosphere, as unanimous as mist. We had entered the realm of the singer . . ."

And sure, it wasn't quite a scream. But if it was a song. If it was a song. Then so is the whistle of the wind between the teeth of an anonymous skull. We came to a limestone ridge, jutting into the gloom. Graffiti on the outside. Sentences split apart by little images, like some of the words were growing flesh.

"In the season of rotten peaches and prehistoric sunlight,
in the season of skeletons singing and dolphins knowing,
in the season of tarantulas making nests in half-rotten boxes of love letters,
in the season of angels laying strawberries like traps in the fields for a lovelorn maiden,
in the season of hazelnuts splitting their husks in the humid fog,
in the season of God forgetting his own name,
in the season of antlers crackling in the deep woods,
in the season of rustling flame-envelopes enclosing the angels as they entered the atmosphere of earth, preparing to cast strawberries like spells on a Spring night:
in the season of you,  my sisters,
and in the season of rising from a murkily luminous pond with a mouthful of topaz," said Ezekiel, tracing the unspeakable word in the soil with a glassy acrylic nail.

This much is true: Something about seasons. Seasons I have never seen. And that suffocated word, so heavy it could not be made to rise from the grave of the tongue. In we went. Into a crumbling cave at the base of the ridge. Me following you because of all the rest of it. Swearing never again to walk toward a screaming. Swearing to spend the rest of my life walking toward a ripening, Ezekiel. Blueberries don't scream. But god bless me, that day I still went the way of your footsteps. Womb of blue breath. Of stalactite and stalagmite—finger of God and Adam, you said. The Second Coming, you said, "will be cataclyzed at the moment of their meeting. I remember that, too," said Ezekiel. "We were short enough that we did not need to bend or kneel through the dark, but nevertheless we stumbled among the rough crags and outcrops of that slick, twinkling, half-lacquered cloister, grasping at shadows of gypsum, seeking after a new sound, a sort of static or rumbling within which the song was crushed, caught and tangled, and which, step by step, we came to perceive as the premonition of a waterfall: because at the end of the hall, the cave opened out into a kind of atrium, touched and illuminated by a single shaft of light, which fell from a crack high up in the dome—decorated with spike-fields of Frostwork, glitter-beds of Dogtooth spar, pale mushrooming knobs of Moonmilk and intricate crystal calyxes, infinitesimally unfolding, of Anthodite—and was instantaneously absorbed, by infinite light-beaming refraction of innumerable mineral facets, into every milky molecule of the swirling, semi-opaque mist thereafter not only swirling but simultaneously shimmering, like a storm of opal dust, within those sunken environs. On the far side of the cavern, saturated by an aura of ultraviolet radiation, blazing a fluorescent curaçao blue through the haze, the waterfall crashed, perpetually, into a pool. Arms aloft before us, stubbing our toes here and there on squat, round calcite blooms shaped like cacti—as daintily woven as Lacespine, as exquisitely spiked as Ladyfingers—we navigated our way among lumped silhouettes that briefly revealed themselves to be pale, chalky columns heaped, cresting like the syrup-leaking papery gills of milkcap mushrooms, emerging from the fog as we passed beside them, guided by the clarifying blue roil. We were coming close to the source of the song, which, rather than resolving into

clarion, recognizable notes, softened more and more toward silence, until it ceased and, without warning, the floor sloped sharply and my foot slipped into the water of the pool. Ripples spread across the surface until they were broken by counter-ripples emanating from the crush of the falls." The water was blue. Foam swelled. Foam evaporated into bubbles. Nothing happened. "Then, combing her wet green ringlets with the spiny shell of a sea urchin, rouging her cheeks with powdered coral, that mermaid of many tales—between whose fingers stretched thin, delicate membranes, plasma-slick and clear as fins, and laced with tiny, forking blood vessels, within which iridescent fluid pumped and rushed—rose from the bubbles, calling herself Melusine, and addressing us by other names . . ."

No she didn't. You know she didn't, Easy. You know there wasn't any *she* to speak of. What we saw in the water was no mermaid.

"Her lips glossed pink and plumped with jellyfish venom, her forked tongue flickering between teeth as transparent as topaz, Melusine hissed and spat, speaking words at a singsong pitch, as if to the tune of accompanying instruments. She said, 'The Pope sent his emissaries to Avalon, under the banner of Isidore of Seville, with a *secret, sacred order from Our Father, which he whispered in my ear so that I may whisper it in yours,* declaring Pressyne and her daughters *no longer valid manifestations of God among man, and therefore banished to an eternity of Uncreation.* So Isidore sailed across the lake of our lost island in a catapult-rigged dromon whose fifty oarsmen were armed with flaming arrows, and burned its forests of apple trees to ash. Mother and I escaped underwater with the two of you, unborn, suspended within the fluid of powder-blue eggs, as smooth and heavy as river stones, which she held in a pouch like that of a kangaroo. But as soon as you were born,' she said, popping pearls into her mouth, crushing and swallowing them between sips of some greenish sludge liqueur from the flute of a conch shell, 'she sewed her pouch shut, ripped off her scales one by one and sliced the webs from between her fingers, then sutured her wounds with green strands of her own hair. She lay in bed for days, wrapped in gauze, bleeding, refusing my poultices, tending to her newborns. Jean d'Arras, by private coin and commission of the kings of Luxembourg and Lusignan and the House of Plantagenet, each of whom wished to enshroud their thrones with an aura of mystical birthright, published his poem about our family to great acclaim in France. The royals declared themselves descendants of Pressyne. The poem claimed she raised their castles and blessed their so-called crusades, and just the same it claimed her mystic curse, rather than so-called *human error,* was accountable for any of their failures. Lacking the capacity to produce meaning, Empire loves nothing more than to rebrand magical beasts, to place their stories 'under state protection,' to ingest and denature the dense matter of exogenous mysticisms the better to blur its violence with the predestined innocence of a fable. I couldn't watch her destroy herself. One day I left, and she raised you as Ezekiel and Elizabeth Anne. By the time I came back you were gone. I've been looking for you for twenty years. Let me return your names . . .' said Melusine," said Ezekiel, yawning, eyes closed. The dog drifted off into the ferns and Fountain grass. The pirates atop the Syracusia performed episodes from the *Iliad*. The gods were the size of ants.

Ezekiel, you've devoted your life to what never happened. *This world is not Conclusion,* you said. *A species stands beyond.* Well, you can irradiate a ghost. But you can't cover a skeleton with breath. What's bone is bone. And down at the bottom of the azure pool, that was no breathing mermaid. That was bone. The head and ribcage of a woman, the tail of a fish.

"Melusine," you said.

"Our sister," you said.

And you cried on the gypsum shore. Tomb of blue breath. Nothing more.

So I said.

And you looked at me, leaves rustling in your coiffure. You looked me right in the eyes and you said,

"Tell Mom hi for me, Lizzie."

And after a dazzling, and all at once—I was alone. You left me alone in an old circus tent, in the middle of Michigan. You left me in the snow.

I haven't seen you since, Ezekiel. Haven't heard a word. But every so often, passing by a garden, I hesitate. Lean toward an orchid. Breathe its perfume.

Our names must be extraordinarily delicate.

[NEW HAVEN, CONNECTICUT, 2018
BROOKLYN, NEW YORK, SEPTEMBER 2020]

CELEBRITY SKIN

It kept seeming to her that, as a woman sometimes saved herself untouched in order to give herself one day to love, she might want to die still completely whole so that eternity would have all of her.

—CLARICE LISPECTOR, TR. STEFAN TOBLER,
AN APPRENTICESHIP, OR THE BOOK OF PLEASURES

What is the matter with your eyes? They are full of green leaves, crowded with streams and trees and animals. Where am I? Why can I not see myself in your eyes?

—PETER S. BEAGLE, *THE LAST UNICORN*

[My mother] said, "Well you can't have a hole running through you all the time, Courtney."

—COURTNEY LOVE, INTERVIEW ON
LATER . . . WITH JOOLS HOLLAND

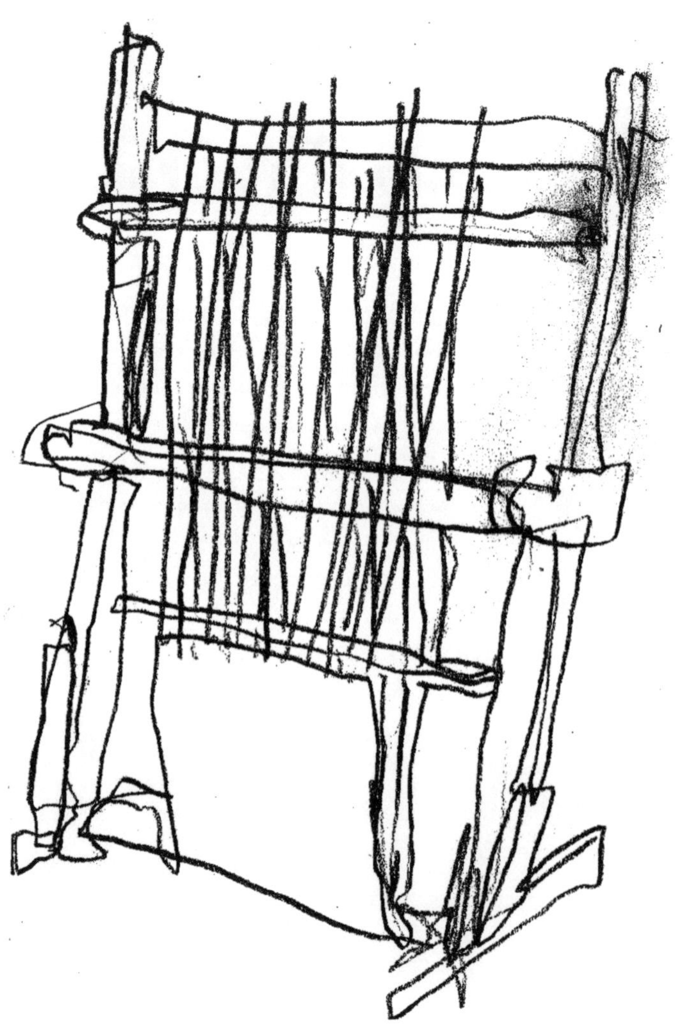

FIGURES

APHRODITOS: Born, Unknown. Died, Never. Twin sister of Aphrodite, or perhaps Aphrodite's 'shadow-self,' or perhaps simply one of the parallel or parallax forms Aphrodite may take. It is not so hard for a goddess to express various selves in simultaneous times, or to be felt and seen variously by simultaneous viewers; the life-force of a goddess may therefore never be extinguished in full, even if some aspect of herself is killed or caught.

CYBELE: Whose cult originated at Pessinus, in Phrygia. The Greek historian Herodian relates that Pessinus means 'place of the fall,' commemorating Cybele's dramatic manner of arrival—falling from the sky as a stone. The stone was a meteoric incarnation of the goddess, called a baetyl, around which her priestesses built a temple where, as part of their sacred rites, many performed an ancient analogue to bottom surgery, that ancestor of the orchiectomy which has been sensationalized, in latter-days, as 'castration.' In 205 BCE, however, representatives of the Roman senate—having consulted the scrolls of the Sibylline Oracles on the occasion of Hannibal's invasion, which, according to the senate, instructed the State to 'bring the Great Mother of Mount Ida to Rome,' which the senate interpreted to mean 'steal her baetyl from her Phrygian priestesses,' in order to avert Carthaginian occupation—seized Cybele and ferried her across the Mediterranean, where they installed her in a new temple atop the Palatine Hill, assimilating her into the Roman pantheon. Her priestesses followed, but the senate banned them from participating in her public worship—ruling, at the same time, that anyone who 'had been castrated' was forbidden from becoming a citizen of Rome, and any Roman who 'became castrated' would forfeit citizenship. They were imprisoned within the temple grounds, only allowed to leave on certain days, utterly disenfranchised.

The senate moved swiftly to control the women through whom Cybele burbled and burst in plumes of scarlet steam, to sever the goddess from the possibility of an apparition, an expression in sudden time, rotating, tangled like helices of hyacinth around thin bone-like lattices and pillars of disintegrating sugar, sudden flowers confecting from crystalline webs of holy smoke within the involuted instant of one irrevocable and instantaneous ritual, written by one priestess into the skin of another, written with a blade in a brief language, an intimacy like that of lovers but more than lovers, bound by shape-shift and surrender, one formed by another's hand, not a sacrifice so much as a portal (a wound in time) through which a goddess could enter the sanctuary of the self, unspeakable, unsexing, in thick mute syllables of blood. These laws were not simply assertions of gender hegemony, but attempts at ethnocide.

Later, another temple to Cybele was built in Montevergine, whether by order of the senate, or by a group of priestesses seeking greater freedom far from the seat of the Republic, I do not know.

ARCHBISHOP ISIDORE OF SEVILLE: Born, Cartagena, 560 CE. Died, Seville, Visigothic Kingdom, 636 CE. Later canonized by the Catholic Church.

POPE HONORIUS I: Born, Campania, Byzantine Empire, 585 CE. Died, Vatican City, 634 CE. Bishop of Rome.

CALIGULA: Born, Anzio, 12 CE. Died, Palatine Hill, 41 CE. Emperor of Rome.

CAST

HYLONOME: Lover of Anadyomene, partner of Angel, sibyl of Cumae. Three older sisters. No direct descendants. Born, Calabritto. Died, Verona. Studied lute in later life; proficient in a number of ballads. Traveled two seasons with a theatrical troupe, *Locum Tenens,* until stranded in the Dolomites during a blizzard. Prima donna disappeared into a snowdrift; axles broke and spokes splintered. Lost her pinkie toe to frostbite. Kept the shriveled digit on her person in a pocket-sized wooden casket. Appeared in Naples concealed by a veil. Intermittent muse to a minor portrait painter who later drowned in a Venetian canal. Subject of no epic poems. Partial to strawberry pie. Official records of her tenure lost to the marshes which slowly rose and spread and drowned what remained of Cumae, following its destruction in 1207 CE.

ANADYOMENE: a.k.a. Ana, lover of Antheia. Designer of a corset which resembled, in style, the crenulations of a seashell, and which—for its lightness, felicity of form, and armor against back-alley blades—became popular among the fairies of Ostia & environs. Once rode a three-horned Corsican red stag through an autumn wood; on this occasion discovered her faculty for interspecies telepathy. Later, aided by careful maintenance of her own gills, developed relationships with a clique of pink starfish who populated the reef near her residence—and who guided her to drowned ruins where she located a clay tablet inscribed by a confidant of King Minos. Developed a written script derived from Minoan court pictographs, but applied to the particular interests (lipstick, dusk, false eyelashes, cloud formations, love triangles) of aforementioned fairies with whom she, in her thirties, established a cult—*Nobody's Daughters*—devoted not to any gods or goddesses, but to 'being beautiful together.' Born, Knossos. Died, Pompeii.

ANGEL: Cataloger of minor objects. Favorite subjects included articles of domesticity such as cups, to-do lists, slices of bread, and tunics drying on the line. Frequently described by strangers and acquaintances as 'delicate,' 'retiring,' or 'tremulous.' Big, breathtaking eyes—an almost unsettling 'frozen violet'—with double lashes. Shy, and therefore, at first, apparently simple. In fact possessed of extreme psychological acuity, extending to light yet unsparing private caricature of those who would make asses of themselves in public forums such as parties, &c. Also extraordinarily mischievous, with an almost 'kitten-like' charm. Slow to anger, but—in relation to themselves—emotionally volatile. Struggled to select a pair of socks when leaving home, resulting in frequent distress and delays in departure; often no pair felt 'right.' We all have our Achilles' heel. Friend to animals. Sculptor of small and detailed stelae, left unsigned, installed in temples, tombs and beneath shade trees across the northwest Roman Empire. Carved a gravestone, to which they made a pilgrimage once a year, in Verona. Here they also buried a handful of blue glass shards. Reported to have mystified the Sphinx. Born, Vaison-la-Romaine. Died, Aquae Sulis.

DAUGHTERS OF APHRODITOS: Epistrophia, Antheia, Nikephoros, et al. Some later joined Anadyomene in Ostia. References to a cult of Aphroditos, while not nearly as extensive in Greek or Roman writings as those regarding the cult of Cybele, can be found in the work of Macrobius, referencing earlier work, much more specific, but no longer extant, by Philocoros.

OURANIA: Born, Lesbos. Died, Unknown. Aphrodision sibyl for nineteen years. Botanist. Collector of tinctures and essences for the admixture of perfume, favoring orange and lemon, elemi resin, violet, fir and cedar, vetiver, pink pepper, oakmoss, ambergris and benzoin. Created a fragrance for personal use that would become famous, by hearsay, across the Mediterranean, for its irresistible scent and impossible ingredients:

ex-lover's spit, nymph-bitten peach, rattlesnake venom,

ashes of love letters, powdered opals, honey from a bee who stung your mother,

wings of a butterfly who died inside a flower, wings of a dragonfly who brushed the cheek of a woman you've seen, but only in a dream, Pegasus feathers,

amphetamine salts, bioluminescent plankton, estrogen foam,

jelly from the mucosal glands of a mermaid, given willingly,

dirt from the forest clearing where you first felt pleasure (from the place where your body indented the grass, your heat and his pressure, his heat and your pleasure crushing wildflowers, secretly, okay baby? cum dripping into the dirt, mixing with the dirt, invisible in the dirt, forever in the dirt, among pink petals, secret petals, secret heat, secret dirt),

fungal spores from the place of your death,

autumn leaves from the year of your birth,

cloud vapor

and anything else

I.

But it had all begun among the high rocky cliffs of Avellino, east of Naples, where her parents were born. *A backward old town that's often remembered, so many times that the memories are worn.* Long before she was a sibyl, Hylonome was the youngest child of a Roman bureaucrat, a former Imperial officer who had retired early, following his majesty's untimely demise (poisoned, some said, by a close confidant, who'd since vanished—as suddenly as he had, a few years prior, appeared at the emperor's side—with powdered milk thistle dissolved in a goblet of wine); her parents' 'one and only son.'

Her mother, Clarissa, spent days alone with her loom, within whose warp and weft she encrypted confessions of her extramarital affairs, maps indicating the precise location of the Garden of the Hesperides or the Siren's summer house, and recollections of the horse (Hylonome, after whom the sibyl later named herself) whose wildness she had not broken but instead surrendered herself to, as if the ambit of the mare's gallop, canter or parabolic leap—marked by the regular and restive thud of her hooves along a relentless and obliterative circuit of seaside pasture—were exerting a gravitational spell as irresistible as the radiance of a fairy circle, a kind of event horizon, the ultraviolet limit of a covert dimension (nested within the third and fourth) into whose intertemporal void Clarissa's mind had, one Autumn afternoon of her late adolescence, suddenly and irrevocably vanished, so that she'd seemed to her sisters to experience even the terror of labor as if she were sleepwalking, screaming from a tomb of dreams, trapped in a forest of mirrors among whose depthless proliferating forms the mare Hylonome appeared and disappeared, delirious and whinnying, a wound in her side.

Clarissa had loved that horse. She had required no man, had refused one proposal after another, preferring to spend her days walking beside Hylonome in that pasture among the Amalfi cliffs; lying beside her, the mare's heavy velvet head at rest in her lap; feeding her cubes of sugar and brushing her with perfumed bristles; or, on rare occasions, years into their intimacy, whenever Hylonome gave some secret signal known only to the two of them, riding her bareback across the sand.

But then, one morning, the mare was gone. The emperor Caligula, while touring the provinces, had happened to pass Hylonome's meadow, and, mesmerized, watching the mare run her relentless circles, gave the signal for his retinue to halt—because, prior to his expedition, the emperor had personally consulted the Sibylline Oracles (those three volumes of prophetic cause-and-effect composed centuries earlier by the very first sibyl of Cumae, sold to or seized by the emperor Tarquinius Superbus but certainly kept since under State lock-and-key in an armored marble crypt) regarding some or other political equation, the solution to which, quoth the sibyl's scribbles, was to build a *circus* in the name of Artemis between the Tyrrhenian Sea and Mount Vesuvius, at the heart of a meadow in the land where the wives of the centaurs are buried. So he'd arranged an expedition across Campania, and—interpreting her as some demigod descendant of Chiron, elected to protect the secret cemetery—poached the smoky-blue-haunched mare, transporting her to Rome (bucking, whinnying, with a wound in her side) within the slats of a ruby-studded crate, installing her thereafter in the Imperial stables and later, infamously, to a seat in the Roman senate, to whose bewildered bureaucrats he counterfeited her as a gelded stallion; his next in line; his one and only son. The mare was drugged daily with herbal sedatives. After Caligula's assassination, she disappears from the historical record.

Clarissa had not witnessed the event itself. She was off collecting strawberries in a piece of cloth

> (so she'd later told her daughter Hylonome, by neither utterance nor singsong but flickering holograph transmitted from the mute smoky refractive depths of her infinity eyes, saying

> nothing, gazing hard not at memory but at some spectral trace element of Hylonome—the mare—swirling, galloping, undying, within the pearlescent dust storm lustering on the far horizon of her vision),

an old shred of quilt upon which the goddess Aphrodite herself had once, supposedly, left a lipstick trace. Clarissa was off collecting strawberries in a sacred scrap of fabric to share with her mare on account of the hot summer day. But when she returned, all she saw were the carriages of the Imperial retinue trailing off into the hills. And all she heard were wheels and greaves and whinnying. Whinnying like a horse trapped in a burning barn. Then only wheels, and then just dust. Afterward she bore her life as a broken horse bears the saddle.

Though in months and later months she returned to watch the steel squadrons of the empire construct a *circus* in the meadow, she remained asleep, unwilling or unable to forfeit her nightmare because it was the nearest reality to her lost paradise. She married the man her parents found for her and gave birth to three children and spent her days at her loom or maintaining their home. Clarissa adored her youngest child, doted even—but with a far-off look in her eyes, an awareness, which never entirely receded, of that pearlescent weather on the horizon of time. And Hylonome, though she sensed its resonance, could not interrupt its broadcast. So she sat and watched her mother at the loom.

II.

As Hylonome aged into adulthood, she became attuned to the references men made with great frequency, as passing jest or opaque fable-warning slurred hoarse and sourbreathed after too much wine, to Sirens, false nymphs with rouged cheeks and perfumed hair, deceivers of good Roman men who enamor the unwitting by making, with their gestures and glances and honeyscented folds of fine fabric, mirages of feminine charm—eunuchs, counterfeit priestesses, postulants of a 'glamorous foreign goddess,' pilgrims to the Temple of Cybele one town over from Avellino, in Montevergine, who must be avoided at all costs.

So one night in her twenty-third year, long after dusk, Hylonome folded a few things into a satchel, pocketed a purseful of Roman silver from her father's coffers and caught a mule cart headed for a rock farm not far from Montevergine. Before dawn she was knocking at the front door of Cybele's temple. The knocks scattered across the empty square like the wings of wooden doves, swift, hollow and dry, vanishing into dim cool recesses of stone. She had stolen some of her mother's rouge; now she applied it hastily to her cheeks, glancing back to make sure no one had seen. But the square was empty; the smoke of dawn was lingering, pink and elemental. The silence was effervescing.

A woman came to the door, gently enclosing Hylonome, as if between wings, in the envelope of her perfume. Her lashes fluttered long and slow, expectant in a sort of sleepy and blurrily amorous way, while Hylonome was realizing she had no idea what to say. No idea how to begin. So she stood there, mouth open—uncertain and raw as an oyster. The woman flicked her lashes up and down, betraying no hint that she'd surmised this girl in half a second, then—wafting scents of soil, sap and honeysuckle—brushed a clumsily elegant chestnut lock from her face, saying:

"Well, we have a spare bed. Take a rest and we'll talk more this evening. What's your name?"

"Hylonome," said Hylonome for the first time in her life.

"Alright, Hylonome," said the woman. "I'm Semele."

A single pearl hung from her neck. The pearl glowed in the cool antechamber. The pearl cast its glow on the woman's collarbones. Now she turned and swished up the hall in aquamarine organza, swaying her hips. Without turning back, limply extending her left arm to indicate a bedchamber,

"You'll find a quilt in the cupboard, and a tin pitcher of cool water by the bed."

Hylonome heard the woman yawning as she disappeared up the hall. Her perfume hovered long after. Under the influence of its pleasantness, Hylonome slept deeply beneath the burnt-orange quilt. Birds were singing in the branches of the trees.

♥

In the evening, the women were reclining in the courtyard with goblets of wine, singing love songs. The courtyard was bowered by lush green honeysuckle brambles. The air was humid, dense with the scent. The women rowed the warm air languidly with their gestures, as if floating in the waters of a glade. They seemed to levitate. Hylonome did not know how to begin. Semele sat beside her, rippling and descending like a small waterfall:

"So," she said, "how did you choose your name?"

And Hylonome blushed clean through her mess of rouge, then stammered the story I just told you.

"So I couldn't stay there anymore," she said, "because I couldn't bear my father's mockery or my mother's strange equation; she says I can't be a woman because she can't bear to lose her son, her heart was already broken once . . . if it breaks again she will die, she says; with that dryness of spirit which comes from resignation, from knowing the truth and doing nothing to stop it, with that utmost dryness, she says, 'without a doubt I will die if my heart breaks again' . . . so I left, I left Avellino so she wouldn't have to see her son be taken from her, too . . ."

Then:

"Do you see? At the very least my name is Hylonome . . . so one day, when I return home . . . when she sees me and I am . . . not her son, because I am the proof that her son is . . . lost, irrevocably lost . . . at the very least my name . . . if that makes sense . . ."

Then, almost wincing:

". . . what I mean to say is . . . maybe I can save myself . . . without destroying her, or can save her without destroying myself . . . at the very least I am Hylonome so that, in some sense . . . by losing her son, she will recover her mare . . ."

"Well," said Semele, "you're welcome to stay awhile. But Avellino is right around the corner; it wouldn't take much for word to reach your family . . . which would be dangerous for us and for you. I suspect you may need to go a little further than Montevergine."

Semele turned and gestured toward a figure, a woman veiled by honeysuckle vines, who rose and drifted among the singers as lush green shadows slid across her face, disclosing and disguising first her lips, then her eyes, so that she seemed to shapeshift as she crossed the courtyard, before settling as smoothly as mist.

"Hylonome, meet our other guest, Anadyomene, 'risen from the sea,' who is on her way to Amathus, seeking after Aphroditos."

"Call me Ana," said the girl. She was about the same age as Hylonome, but a few seasons ahead in glamour. Her eyelids shimmered silver, as if they were transmitting a message from another realm; her rouge was intentional rather than ravenous—and she smelled like bluebells. Hylonome was enamored.

"Who is Aphroditos?" she said. Ana unbuttoned her tunic to

reveal a necklace from which dangled a small iron charm, a miniature goddess with tumbling curls and full breasts, lifting the folds of her gown to reveal a hard cock.

“Her cock is apotropaic,” said Ana.

Hylonome just nodded as if she knew what that meant. She was mesmerized by Ana’s candor and sense of purpose.

“I’m going to Amathus because I’ve heard of a mystery cult behind a waterfall in the woods outside the city. Apparently they’ve made or been god-given a fume which, when inhaled slowly, over time, entangles your mind in a divine substance, transforming you into the likeness of Aphroditos.”

“May I . . . come with you,” said Hylonome.

Anadyomene smiled coyly.

“If you don’t mind sharing a bed.”

Vibrating like a hummingbird emanating an emerald haze,

“Not at all,” said Hylonome.

And so they went.

The next morning Hylonome tidied her cot, then—after Semele came to give her a parting gift, a small alabaster dish packed with shimmering powder, “to apply to your eyelids”—joined Anadyomene in a mule cart bound for Cumae, then for the port, then on a merchant boat bound for Cyprus. Their first kiss was on open water, hidden behind baskets of dried strawberries.

III.

Two weeks later, they were drinking honeysuckle liqueur at a bar in the port of Amathus. After a few thimbles, Ana rose from the table, glancing around, blinking with slow sensuality like a butterfly balanced on the wet petal of a pink evening primrose, slowly beating its wings. Then, in a moment, she was off. And then, further afield—she perched, again, on another flower. She was ensnaring a man with her weaving fingers; soon she was sitting beside him, playing his cheek like a lyre. After two weeks cramped on open sea, during which Ana, especially, was prone to vomiting gracelessly off the boat's bucking bow, she now seemed, under mere and improbable influence of evening glow—the instantaneous confection of a halo—to have attuned herself perfectly to the frequency of Aphrodite's whispers. Which is to say this girl was, to Hylonome, already a kind of celebrity, because Hylonome herself had not howled, trembling, gasping and clutching at her lover like a savior; had not, could not have stumbled about the docks like a leggy colt, then vaulted, with no more than a wink, to the weightless sylvan remove of the summer sky, leaping like a Pegasus from bower to bower of pearlescent cloudbank.

Ana left the bar, the man following after her, but not before stopping by their table to say, "Meet me in a couple hours at the inn across the street. But not before then. Ask for a room under the name Penelope, from Ithaca."

So she walked to the public gardens and hopped the wall, but scraped her knee on a broken seashell embedded in the clay. It was a deep gash. Her blood mixed with the soil, nurturing the roots of an orange tree, staining its future fruits pink. She bound her wound with a strip of linen. The garden throbbed. Roots shook in the earth and flowers fumed. She felt the slow and heavy pulse of the living and decaying garden. The flowers fuming in the dark. The scent was like realizing falling in love was not just a form of story, but something that could happen to you—if only you could pay attention, with the risk of being so fragile, long enough to vaporize your sticky inner glory . . .

Later, Ana was sewing her wound shut with silver thread and a fishhook beside the tile bath at the inn.

"He paid for the night," she said. "Which means we can charge a feast to his ledger."

♥

The sweet density of the dates made Hylonome giddy. The pita was fluffy. The pork was rich and tender, dripping in red wine and spiced with coriander seeds.

"Okay, baby," said Ana. "Now that you're fed and sutured, tell me what the hell happened."

"Oh, I was in the gardens. You wouldn't believe the scent . . ."

"Falling in love with a flower?"

"I felt her pulse in the soil."

"So you can do it, too."

"Do what?"

"Sense the gestures of the gods."

"Not on purpose."

"Sometimes I feel them turning. Or—or grasping for something."

"I hear them weeping . . ."

"Once I heard Persephone sing."

"And Aphroditos? I haven't felt her at all."

"She conceals the wavelength of her song. But I know where to find her daughters. One of them—Antheia, remember? 'The blooming, the friend of flowers'—gave me my name. All the daughters are given one of Aphrodite's epithets."

"So you've been here before."

"Never. But I was looking for somewhere to go, and she sent for me."

"How do you know her?"

"Babe, I told you this."

"I was drunk."

"We were lovers."

Hylonome felt an irresistible flame spark and catch in the cage of her ribs. So this was jealousy, she thought.

"Are you lovers still?"

"Like I said, not for years now. I haven't seen her once since she left for Cyprus. Our letters are intimate more than romantic. The way you are with exes."

"Well . . . would you?"

"Would I what?"

"If—" Now Hylonome stammered. She felt a blush spread like a heat wave over her cheeks. She was furious, or she was ashamed, or she was realizing that she had so far only understood romance as an insular experience, a riddled language protecting a paradise dimension useless to any who would seek to plunder it, a lover's matrix of meanings, irreducible, incommunicable except in terms of their relational web, sensible only as a sunburst, as mysterious as a neon sea urchin, irradiated, violet. She had never considered romance a social condition. Or hadn't wanted to.

"If Antheia were flirting with you, would you fuck her?"

She had said exactly what she meant. But it felt like a demon had been strumming her vocal cords. Because it wasn't what she meant so much as what she feared. Paranoia was the name of a demon who pretended to protect you while constructing around you the circumstances of your humiliation. Paranoia was the way a zealous adherence to extremities, an apocalyptic fear of abandonment and a sense of predestination about the narrative exigencies of a romance (that is, a belief in following all the leads coincidence offers, however ill advised, 'for the sake of meaning') came to delimit a person's imagination about the possibilities of loving. And now a searing geyser of sparks was spreading, was effervescing in her chest—now she was mistaking jealousy for righteousness, now she was making a fool of herself, now it was so embarrassing because Ana was pitying her. Ana was watching her realize the difference in scale or at least in form of their respective conceptions of this passion.

"I'm not pitying you, Lo. Stop putting me on a pedestal. I'm scared too. We're about to be around a bunch of other girls who probably all fuck or have fucked or at least have an interlocking series of insane love triangles, and we haven't talked about our relationship once."

It was true (though she hadn't wanted to admit it even to herself, or have her thoughts about them touch her thoughts about Ana—to have those thoughts occupy the same place, like they would tomorrow, when she arrived at her own future) Hylonome had been thinking of the other girls . . .

"But there's a power imbalance," Hylonome said, "because you already know them, or at least one of them. And she invited you there. You have a guaranteed place. I'm just tagging along and hoping they'll like me."

"Babe, I brought this up on the boat."

"That's not how I remember it."

"Stop. You're doing it again."

"What is it you think I'm doing?"

"Obstructing your own aim. I don't think your fears are unfounded, sweetheart. I'm not saying that. The truth is I understand why you're feeling stressed: you're taking leap after leap of faith, making an Odyssey by impulse alone. But our stories are twined by time. No force can fray them."

"But what about tomorrow?"

"I want to be your lover. I want to know you a long time."

"I want that, too."

"Do you want to have other lovers?"

"Well . . ."

Hylonome hadn't been in love except twice (this was the second) and so had little sense of the persistence of feeling years after the end of a romance in its own hermetic and reiterative perpetuity, in the heaven and hell of the heart. She hadn't yet experienced love as a multitemporal web of parallel realities, so it was hard to imagine loving more than one person at once . . .

"Yes," said Hylonome. "I do."

"Look, you're not going to lose me," said Ana. "I've never let a girl hold me while I vomit before."

Then: "I bet you'll have a crush on Antheia."

"Would she have a crush on me?"

"I'm sure. You're beautiful."

"You're more beautiful."

"No, I just have more control over it."

"I . . ."

"What?"

"I want to . . . choke . . . on your cum . . ."

"And then what?"

"Then I want you," she said, as Ana began sucking on her nipple, "to . . . to . . . I want you . . ."

IV.

THEY WERE WALKING through a sparse, scrubby wood. Sand collected in small drifts among the gnarled roots of the unripe and fruitless strawberry trees. A cool gourd slapped against Ana's hip as she walked, pausing sometimes to untie it from her leather belt, uncork it, swing it skyward in such a clean and perfect arc that the wine sloshing within was ejected as a single stream, visible for the flash of a second before vanishing, as if fleeing, into her mouth. (Or that was how Hylonome would remember it later, telling stories of long-lost lovers by campfire.) Then she'd wipe her wine-dark lips with her tunic sleeve and pass the gourd to Hylonome, who lifted the bottle to her lips and took a pious sip. Then another pious sip, and another. A ruddy crab was skittering dryly away into a mess of brush. You could smell the salt of the sea, and the evergreen and nostalgic waft of pines and cedars rising here and there from the sand, then gathering up ahead into copses thick with green, like a detonation of Eden halted by the hand of god.

Soon the trees were no longer one, but many. Soon the sky was no longer still and bright, but gloom and glow and manifold. The leaves were flickering like sentience was a breath passing through them. The dirt was musky with rot and needles. The land tilted up. The going was steeper. Ana was out of wine. Hylonome's legs ached. When they crested the hill, the trees were too tall to see anything but an intermittent azure flicker of the lake below; too tall even to see the pillar of smoke rising from the willows bowing at the shore. But they smelled the fumes. Ana tossed back an orange.

"We're close now."

"I'm about half a mile from fainting."

"Won't be that far, baby. They're burning honeysuckle to the goddess."

Hylonome peeled the skin with ease, dropping bright petals of rind beside her as she followed the switchback path Ana left lightly behind like a tunnel of air while wending her way down into the valley. She bit into the swelling, succulent heft of flesh as if it were the heart of Summer. Noon was long gone. The gloom was turning gold. The leaves were rustling with glow as if awakening to a destiny—as if exhaling the souls of forgotten nymphs. Soon the land leveled. Ana led her to the edge of the woods, where the trees were high columns. They watched the bright beach from within a porous but hermetic atmosphere of forest shade; they watched, walking, appearing and disappearing between trees, following the plume of bonfire smoke. The beach was curving. The forest was facing itself. The air was spiced with honeysuckle ash. And then there were voices.

♥

"Who are you," asked the woman beside the bonfire, absorbing the blaze into her eyes, the heat hardening their luster like a glaze. But her lids shimmered mistily with pale green powder, as if she'd been borne there from the cool, wet air of a distant glade—like looking into her eyes was a way of falling asleep beneath the fronds of ferns. She was so beautiful that even Ana seemed bashful. Her hair was long and thick with autumnal curls deepening from auburn into cinnabar, cloistering her face, removing her slightly from the present instant. She wore, like the others, a creamsicle robe, cinched with a ribbon of powder-blue twine. They were singing softly, tossing dry honeysuckle petals inscribed with prayers into the flames while she provoked sparks with a slender, bone-like branch. The lake was quiet except for the exhalation of waves, the crackling of wood and the murmur of holy writ.

"Anadyomene," said Ana.

The woman raised her eyebrows. Hylonome forgot to breathe. She watched them both in absolute silence. Silence was spreading.

Finally,

"Who gave you that name?" she said.

"Your sister Antheia, who once traveled to the port of Ostia and spent six months in my bed."

The woman's expression marbled. Only her eyes flickered with cloaked sentience. Maybe she was impressed but preferred to maintain a mask of disinterested arcadian distance; or maybe she was embarrassed to have misjudged the relevance of her guests; or was pierced by the jealousy a beautiful woman feels when another woman's allure, rather than her own, is the subject of a story, whether or not she would have chosen, given the option, to inspire the story herself . . .

"What was the occasion?"

"We were in love."

"No," said the woman. "For your name."

"Oh. Well. To put it simply I dreamed about a mist spilling from a crack in the floor of a cave, a mist like seafoam from which Aphroditos rose and spoke to me, unrolling a scroll whose every letter was iridescing as if with pearl inlay, saying that I would not understand her language until I inhaled her perfume . . ."

"What shade were her eyes?"

"Like moonstone. Almost transparent."

Again, silence: the waves lapping. The women singing so softly. Flowers enveloped by heat. Petals folding.

"So you weren't lying after all," the woman said. "My name is Epistrophia. I'll take you to the waterfall. Your friend can come, too."

And she led them back into the |||| trees |||| to a (cave), which revealed itself—after they'd wandered, by light of a taper, through a mirrored garden of silvering spikes—to be a sacred path, a tunnel leading to a secret glade, whose lush dewy environs were enclosed by limestone cliffs.

First she smelled them, then she saw them. The humidity of the air was cut and clarified by the zest of hundreds of orange trees. Short and squat, their thin trunks and thinner branches weighed down by innumerable fruits, round and nearly pulsing from the pressure of nectar swelling, relentlessly, inside.

Hylonome glanced sidelong at Ana, who seemed as surprised as she was, though more by wonder than fear.

♥

Hylonome had never seen a waterfall. Ana didn't remember seeing one as an infant, but her mother had told the story of that miraculous afternoon, which, like a ruin, halfway to remembering, was as precious to her as a fragment of parchment saved from the bibliographic blaze at Alexandria.

"Watch your step," said Epistrophia, teleporting, so it seemed, from stone to slick stone sunk within the vaporous auroral mists of foam swirling and effervescing at the base of the waterfall, like the suffocating but luminous auras which haunt the homes of nymphs and any place Aphrodite's tears have fallen.

Ana's attention, like lattices of crystal clicking into place, gathered itself into a point. Her mind was trying to become as incorruptible as topaz. Hylonome attempted quartz. There was only one way in—to walk the path behind the waterfall without falling into the fulminating pool.

One leapt, the other stumbled. One slipped, the other strode. One gleamed, the other gasped. Ana turned, offering a hand to help her make the final step.

♥

Having passed the test—Epistrophia never once looked back, but in fact inspected the lacquered claws she'd formed from wafer-thin curls of pale clay, molded to her nails, painted with pinkish glaze (a dull luster like ill-timed primrose petals, frozen in ice) and fired in a kiln near Amathus owned by a man who wanted nothing more than to have her in his bed, after which she'd affixed them to her fingertips with a glue pressed from animal grease, bark pitch, soot and semiprecious stones, the same recipe which bound the helmets and breastplates of Roman centurions—Hylonome, reaching blindly for the damp, smooth and irregular limestone wall of the cavern, shedding the dazzling memory of light to which eyes, surpassing sight, cling like an heirloom when faced with sudden dark, took three deep breaths. Slowly she began to sense the span of the antechamber, what Epistrophia referred to as "the Hall of Holy Fingertips," so named for a slow but certain expenditure of passion (neither Cold Pastoral nor burning wick), the way so many stalactites hovered mere millimeters over their corresponding stalagmites, oozing droplets of mineral fluid, rich iridescent sap of pleasure and deferral of pleasure, of infinitesimal and translucent time—globed concentrate of an asymptotic and myriad flirtation with matrimony.

"When they meet," said Epistrophia, "our Seafoam Mistress will descend to the underworld with an army of seahorses, mermaids and ex-lovers, to uproot, at last, the cursed and blameless Pomegranate tree and—without losing a single soul—replant it here within her perennial orchard, overhanging her waterfall, so freeing Persephone, our Lady's first and longest love, from the Autumn and Winter of her anesthetic marriage to Hades; the slow decay which, for a goddess, has no end, only deepening gradations of blank."

It was the grandest cavern Hylonome had ever seen, whose ceiling rose as high as the domes of Rome's marble temples; higher and broader by far than a whitewashed adobe church where a posse of renegade angels would, two thousand years later in a small West Texas town, attempt to break one of the latter-day descendants of Hylonome's bloodline, in order to extract, for the pleasure of its rare flavor, a vial of Fairy Tears; higher and broader, too, than a mermaid's grave in Texarkana, where one of Anadyomene's descendants at last understood her womanhood not as a solitary experience, but as a sisterly one—not a pretension to ad hoc invention, but a way of remembering, a form of reverb.

The cavern was less crypt than atrium of mists, deepening near the dome into impenetrable shadows from whose storm-cloud murk plunged attenuating columns of stalactites, like lightning bolts flung down from the lusty grip of Zeus and trapped, calcified by instantaneous chemical reaction with particles of subterranean gloom, in the brevity of being which in this case was only revealing, only re-vealing the act of falling into nonbeing, with the violence of outraged light, in the instant before the instant of striking. But the only extant source of glow in that vaulted antechamber was a cool and periodic aurora transmitted in faint lambent pulsations of filtered curaçao from the force-field of the waterfall, whose wavelets lapped at a darkened beach of inlaid tiles the same shade as Epistrophia's glazed nails. The walls—fading as the women followed her through the mist, then emerging again on the far side as they approached the mouth of a round corridor—were etched with random scribblings of stone, which the Daughters, said Epistrophia, sometimes interpreted by firelight as shapeshifting runes formed by the unseen breaths of Aphroditos, who played the flames like a flute.

While Hylonome followed Ana in following her along the curve of a tunnel lit by streams of sunlight falling faintly from folds in the stone, Epistrophia was telling the story of how the Daughters came to live behind the waterfall:

". . . soon taking up residence in one of many habitable caves formed millennia ago within pinkish hills of apparent rubble by the slow ache of the Earth's crust and then even more slowly by the patient artifice of rainfall, of intricate rills slipping among cracks in the stone and collecting into pools, pools in sun and shadow, in penumbral overhangs within and without the caves."

Small chambers opened now and then like arcosolia off the

corridor; these were the Daughters' bedrooms, where they slept and sexed and performed toilette. Hylonome dared not glance in, for fear of seeing one of the girls in a state of undress and unraveling the delicate golden threads with which she'd bound that unsleeping feminine demon-savior howling and singing and clawing at the dirt, at what once were memories, were now no more than particles of sound and scent and color, worm-eaten flesh of the fruits of terror and desire decomposing ripe and overripe into the topsoil of her heart.

They arrived at what would have appeared to Hylonome the massed debris of an ancient collapsed cave, nothing more than a cleft of air between heaped immovable boulders of pink granite, had firelight not issued forth, fitfully spangling the hanging roots of the First Orange Tree, the oldest in the garden, which—rising from the cliff above the waterfall for untold centuries, dangling and dropping fruits into the green vale below, rooting down and further down, splitting rock from rock with slow, patient, unrelenting sinews, branching and attenuating into stilettos of wood—had caused the aforementioned collapse; so, too, would she have mistaken the chanting for a breeze trapped in the rock, had the choir-slurred syllables not suddenly achieved the fatal viscosity of language:

" . . . and neither any . . . nor any ho-o-ly place was there from which we were absent . . ."

Epistrophia slipped easily into the fissure.

". . . no gro-o-ve . . . no da-a-nce . . . no so-o-o-o-und . . ."

Hylonome, taking Ana's hand once more, ducked under the accidental arch of rubble. The flickering light confused her eyes, distorting the shadows along the wall and disrupting her sense of space; she stumbled forward, snagging her cyan tunic on a sharp lip of stone and stubbing her toe likewise.

"Do you feel that?" asked Ana. "Here," she said, lifting Hylonome's palm to the cavern wall. A new wavelength, which, further along, she began to feel beneath her feet; and then below the chorus of voices, in the air itself—a surging in the curve of her ears, like the sound of a wave in a conch.

"She's close," said Ana. "She's in here somewhere."

Called down, thought Hylonome, by her sacred song . . .

May we please leave a message for Aphrodit . . . no, not that one . . . de-tos, not die-tee . . . Yes, we're sure . . .

Ring ring
Ring ring
Ring ring
Click:

Hello. . .

How did you find this number? . . .

Ah, she would say, sniffing at last a curling wisp of honeysuckle smoke,

the yellow pages . . . So you're not affiliated with the Temple in Amathus . . .

All like me, you say? Put on this earth to be absolutely divine?

As long as there's music, she would say, *I'd be delighted to make an appearance.*

And she had brought, as a housewarming gift, a corset structured by moonstone ribs between which stretched webs of silver gauze, her baetyl.

Ana gestured for Hylonome to follow her around a bend in the cave, from which a voice both keen and immaterial now issued in syllables as fine and shapely as stalactite droplets:

"A reading from the *Historical Library* of Diodorus Siculus, Book Four, Chapter Six, Verse Five."

V.

> Come, you spirits
> That tend on mortal thoughts, unsex me here . . .
>
> —LADY MACBETH

HYLONOME GATHERED THE folds of her tunic, passing into a chamber more spacious than the Daughters' bedrooms but not nearly so forbidding as that hall of interlocking fangs where the waterfall hoarded semiprecious instants. Here the walls were pink and dry and rough, providing natural alcoves and altars for decorations, so that the room resembled a chapel half-buried in volcanic ash, inhabited once more after the eruption by the unperturbed—indeed, emboldened—faithful, who fled oncoming lava flows rubbing fascinae in their palms, bearing on their backs the most precious liturgical relics, all of which the congregation had now returned to their resting places, without, however, first removing the layers of pumice from the chapel's many surfaces, preferring instead to let it remain, the better to remember the malice of Olympos.

Atop every altar rose a candelabra, its boughs concealed within static fountains of beeswax, like a willow drenched in caramel; meanwhile in each alcove, whose interior glowed from a rich glaze—powder blue, encircled by a halo of starlike ochre—a unique species of flower, rather than the statue of one or another goddess, tilted from a terra-cotta vase: late spider orchid, moonbeam and sunray, black tulip, poet's jasmine, night-blooming jessamine, wild pink and others Hylonome didn't recognize, dense as clouds of stained glass.

Orchidox relics, blind flowers de profundis you called to me

A single tear rolled down her cheek.

I am not alone

From bare portions of wall hung tapestries depicting Aphroditos, undressed, breasts and phallus in beatific view, descending from her wretched Mount in the aforevisioned corset (how Hylonome knew, she did not know) with wings of seafoam, her eyes like tide pools struck blank and brilliant by the glare of the moon.

Below the tapestries, nine women in creamsicle robes were arranged in a semicircle; some leaned from low wooden benches whose pillowed seats were tasseled with pearls, while others balanced gently on eminences of pink granite, and others still sat upon the varicolored rugs that rested haphazardly atop one another from wall to wall, in homage to Pangaea; on the far end, the source of that exquisite voice reclined atop a blue suede chaise, with a heavy scroll unrolling in her hands, reciting now the aside from Diodorus Siculus:

"There are some who declare that creatures of two sexes . . . coming rarely into the world as they do, have the qualities of presaging the future . . ."

But her face was concealed behind a crepe veil, embroidered with the image of a cataract of honeysuckles into which (for the petals) flakes of amber and milky opal and (for the leaves and vines) shavings of emerald were sewn, while her effulgent curls, cropped at her collarbones, hovered and curled like silver smoke around the veil; her head, meanwhile, was crowned in the wings of butterflies—white peacock, silver emperor, pearly leafwing—which fluttered and trembled at the slightest tilt of her head, as if insufflated once more with life, so that, mantled in a cloak-cloud of living honeysuckles floating creamily and silently above ponderous waving thicknesses and depths of shaggy green—like a host of fireflies awakening in the boughs of a tree—she appeared half woman, half bower, like some timeless oasal dryad, antiquated residue of a leafier earth. She was lithe, almost skeletal, with long, eloquent legs; her body wafted scents of sea breeze, of marshes and limoncello. Now she lifted her eyes imperceptibly from the page, her finger pressed upon the recited sentence, in order to study her new guest.

There stood Hylonome. There she stood beneath the rubble arch. There she stood before the Daughters of Aphroditos.

For one instant her face was as timeless as a mask; adoration was anonymizing her, or at least calling her down from the cloudcatacombs of a relentlessly looping soulstorm, like one seeing, for the first time and all at once, not one or two scattered secrets, not a tombpilfered artifact radiating a few hues from the aura of a place and time that are lost forever (dissolved into the whirlpool of hours, the unslakable razortoothed kaleidoscope of History, clicking and churning, grinding like a millstone, pulverizing all traces of song, memory and perfume), but everything that had been excised from the scenes of her adolescence; every impulse that had been plucked like a living nerve, ripped up like a root from the field of her flesh; everyone whose immaterial telegraph wires were severed, who otherwise would've registered earlier the transmissions (telepathic, intersubjective) of their kin: every lacuna, dent or error she had felt or seen or heretofore experienced as only one more portal ripping open to a howling dimension of emptiness was now filled, all at once, by some object, some woman or gesture clutched precisely—like the jewels encrusting the spine of an incunabulum or the skull of a saint, thereafter no longer 'remains,' but holy relic, as if skin could be a premonition of goldleaf, as if death were merely the prelude to a more enduring decoration—by the Tines of Eternity, the aforesaid gaps, the silhouetted ruins of what might have been, what never was, is long forgotten.

A single tear, sparkling in the candlelight, was the only evidence of Hylonome's inner richness. Which, as it fell, fell into place: the final jewel in the crown of One Instant within the womb of a waterfall—then disappeared.

At length, the voice spoke from the chaise:

"Nikephoros, deer, wood u get th' ghourl a fressh &cure-chiff owt thee armwah?"

And tilting back again:

"Watts yore neighm, dearling?"

Hylonome's eyes diminished; now again she heard, she smelled, she touched, she tasted; she was reduced to herself—what was her name?

"Hylonome."

(Nikephoros offered her a napkin—folded crisply and scented faintly with something profoundly feminine, something like a sudden sense that flowers are watching you, for which Hylonome had no point of reference—then returned to a bench in the audience.)

"High-low know-me. Nowhere half-ewe calm froam?"

"Avellino," she said, dotting her eyes with the cloth.

"Fah-errway."

"Yes. The farthest I've ever been from home . . ."

"Bot wye? Symmplea fore th' plagiar o'hour compainy?"

Hylonome shifted back and forth, as if retreating.

"I don't know how to say it. It's not like a story, where a hero goes on a quest . . . I guess I needed to go, just to go somewhere because nothing made sense, I've never made sense and . . . well, when Ana told me about you . . . I wanted to see . . . I want to see . . . if . . ."

The woman sat upright, unlatched her veil, and cast it in tinselly disarray onto the chaise.

"Tale mi, doorling."

She was half-blind; her eyes wore little veils of their own, webs of twinkling milky filament, as if woven by opal-legged spiders; and her lips possessed the same chic gauche improbable air of the older Marlene Dietrich's: painted on in high crimson arcs, like the top half of a cartoon heart. She was the most beautiful woman Hylonome had ever seen.

Or perhaps no longer beautiful, but breathtaking

Her face was like a fragment of Sappho's verse; what it had lost in unity of form, it had gained in mystery of aspect.

"Tell mi want u see."

Hylonome stuttered:

"I see . . ."

She was like someone in a nightmare, unblinking, unable to blink.

"I see her . . . swirling like . . . like silver fluid . . . in your veins . . ."

The woman smiled. The woman, the sibyl Ourania, smiled at Hylonome with a kind of recognition: the recognition of a figure not from the past, but from the future. (Here was the girl who'd been glossolaling in the margins of her senses, stealing her sleep and her insight. The lost one, the one with a hole running through her—that one who the goddess said would see her 'twinkling blood'—would bring about what Aphroditos, with an almost untranslatable urgency, a chaos of god-wind and temporal distortion, called 'Hermaphroiesis,' the meaning of which, without revealing her uncertainty to her disciples, the sybil was even now attempting to interpret.) Thus spoke Ourania:

> "Murk ye, hid yee this messedge, yon Alone-o-my, dotterse one et owl, scarpains scuttlen the wailtampr'd caveir craks!
>
> Bud knott beecurse i miisylph cunn clam celestibritee,
>
> four eye aim lonely thy sypal of the ouraclle di Aphrodittie, vestel di amours, nothink marr, heartly vasell inoff, far shee extemps farr bayround mi botti, burzts thru th' dame o' myy disinterpraytations, splitten mi saintdances assunder wi' babelon brewks of nonessense, overspellin' mi lyk wyves o' creamsin sheefome: blottee whatere amixin wit ruddee baubbles o' vaporessense, spellin ope thru th' rivt, floawing dawn lyk mourneighing mizt, replaysing whord wi' blod ween mi voyce feyelles—chreu veintrille-o-chasm!
>
> Of whooze moaning aye aim gnot innocentaur innerhaunt, halfing traitored sighed fer vissione, witchisn't unseeyn bt seeng a'notherr angel, sing thru clowweds, or mour priesticelly, scynne dubble: th' realm o' th' dissappearits soporinterprosed opon th' dieurnelle whorld, so th' boath'r bleurred.
>
> Clothes yore eyes:
>
> Dew yyu ciy wut hy'ceenth?

A barockly decreat'd cavyearn, torcht by howlee efflame? Wails o' rawk poolsating wi th' miserious, effeminaming heart-beast o'thee goldiss hersalve?

Iamb the Syllabil.

Due u cee what Icing? Is yore fathe sophishn't?

Th' immemortal mater of 'R Laydise whoohm, fowl a' sheefoam & hauntdyd by (g)hosts a' sheeherses;

stonne mayd flaysh:

Hermaphroiesis.

En thist delapserian whirled weir wee, heretoforcepped by th' fangrs o' th' clawk, may alas't reverse our Faite, ayy sé-ance, twise, ayy implure, ayy incan't thy Name:

Halo'd Aphoreyedos, glo-pake gawwdess, immanightblooming sacret latee, noctious icon:

reliquate thy whaunt-er fall, thy clyffs & bodrfly-twinklee veils, thy maidodes & senswoosh caraferns, thy seacrid growfe a' ourange treetises, thy perpactual awetime & drhymes o' pyrl & thy Persephoning wreckllusion;

renouns thy internetee for my byrdbon bodee;

drawe yore praysense to a poind—

Efferdizzyack Ache-o, legnd yore meldy tombeye tung!"

And with that, Ourania struck her cherry-red nail like a match along the length of unrolled parchment, which burst, at once, into flame.

VI.

The sibyl of Aphroditos vanished behind a scrim of smoke, elaborating in curls of pale neon pink as thick and threadbare as clouds of cotton candy, within which, as if struggling to be born from sticky sweet mounds and carnivalesque wisps of Tivoli spider silk, Hylonome began to discern the misty, evanescent apparition of a horse—a blue-haunched mare falling through the air, bound by loops of immaterial, unbreakable silver thread—accumulating like a froth of soul, taking form, nearly substance, then (Hylonome almost shouted *no*) dispersing with a single swipe of Ourania's flicked wrist, from whose fingertips, in place of decorated nails, now emitted, as if wavering from the wicks of candles, peach-tinted briolettes of flame.

"Paye cluese a'tension, High Lunamay . . ." lisped Ourania, smirking.

She held her hand aloft, placed her middle finger against her thumb, and snapped. For a moment, nothing happened. Hylonome held her breath. Then she felt it again, surging in her ears, like almost nothing, a little less than nothing—the pulse at the heart of the ocean. A flash of phosphorescence in absolute darkness. The birth of the goddess. The first and the last. Mother of Pearl.

The cavern shook. Far beyond the fringes of little Pangaea, before Ourania's chaise, between her eyes and the eyes of her Daughters, the pale porous stone cracked open, forming a rift in the floor from which seafoam sputtered, iridescent, then bubbled and spat, bursting forth in magmatic ropes of quicksilvering, translucent liquid, which the Daughters, rising from their tasseled pillows and perches of granite, one by one approached, each bearing the half shell of an oyster in which she collected, from one of the streams rolling in molasses-slow-motion toward the carpets, her personal pool of Holy Water.

Ana and Hylonome followed.

The chaise was empty. Ourania was already gone. No one had seen her leave. So the Daughters drank. Very slightly, like a premonition of Spring, their breasts leavened. Their skin softened. Gills split from their necks.

And for Ana and Hylonome, it was the first time.

♥

Afterward—when the room returned to a kind of homeostasis, a merely mortal glamour—Antheia, splayed on a buttercup scrap of carpet, twirling Ana's hair between her fingers, called out to Hylonome:

"Darling, won't you come sit with us?"

But Hylonome was still fading, retrograde, into the brief totality of Ourania's bubblegumcloudy vision, the endless recital of goodbye—a web of dissolving pink dimensions, sticking to the mare without breaking her fall—because in such a world she would not restore the mare Hylonome to reality, but sacrifice reality for the terror of endless sky; so, mortified by her own flightlessness, half in love with the long and layered feathers of her sisters, half-speechless in the face of a sudden slake and surfeit of meaning, Hylonome didn't move at all. She was standing, holding her half shell, at a distance from the others.

"Where . . . where should I . . ."

Ana stood and went to her.

"Right here, baby."

Hylonome sat, strait backed, on a pillow next to Antheia.

Not all the Daughters were partial to the arrival of a woman so consummately uncool. It reminded them of what they had narrowly escaped, by trial of duration and seismograph of sisterhood. The spectacle of unknowing. So Epistrophia, luxuriating nearby atop a pile of pink feather boas, her mouth pursed in affronted fascination, glared at Hylonome from beneath a fragile verandah of lashes. What could she have to do with the glory of the Goddess?

"You couldn't have chosen a better night to come," said Antheia. "We only have our cocktails once a moon!"

"Time bends for passion," said Ana, looking up from her ex-lover's lap, "like syntax for poetry."

Was Hylonome jealous? She'd noticed the sudden shift in Ana's diction. Ana didn't talk like that when they were alone. But it wasn't that simple; she felt something like aspiration, too. Fragments of a far-flung romance were appearing, repeating, whirling into the pure chaos of the present; Hylonome could recognize their shape if not their significance. She wondered what it would be like to feel such things, looking on as Antheia slipped Ana some little shiny sphere that looked, to her, like a pearl. The two women whispered, giggling, into one another's ears, before Ana popped it into her mouth and swallowed.

"Look. All this," said Antheia, half-turning to Hylonome, gesturing up and down her own body, "is about living the dullest days with the extravagance of a celebrity, but the absolute freedom of a woman forsaken by the gods. As if to the applause of an audience, but without any audience at all. Don't you see?"

"I think so . . ." said Hylonome timidly. But she couldn't shake that pink place; the silver fluid in Ourania's veins; the fumes of the flowers. "What . . . what did Ourania mean by 'Hermaphroiesis'?"

"At first," said Epistrophia—rising, now, from her feather boas, and to the occasion; rising up to bear down on Hylonome with her wisdom—"it was an aside, so slight it seemed a mumble. At first it was one phrase among many, then one among few. And today it was foremost. Certain words will whirl around her mind for months, unnoticed until they begin to glint, to evince an iridescence, taking on, at last, a kind of substance, something like a premonition of life, the first thought of a world; as if, pressurized by the heat and force of a mind so heavy with never—ripening the antimatter nectar of nothing; reduced and reduced again, simmered to a swamp of void—words could be the final particles of ignition, the enzymes preceding the combustion of creation. But then, sometimes they simply fizzle out . . ."

"What will come will come," said Antheia. "No use fussing with ciphers except as opportunities for the free expression of the feminine wiles, foremost among which, of course, is gossip. Which brings me to you. Our humble harbinger. Are you seeking safe harbor or just stopping through for a sip of seafoam?"

"Well," said Hylonome.

Ana smirked. She seemed curious, in a mischievous way, to watch Hylonome navigate the Daughters' elocutions.

"Well," said Hylonome, her mind eased by Epistrophia's air of expertise and Antheia's offhand charm;

"Well," she said, beginning to awaken to the present instant;

"Well, I don't know what I'm looking for . . . but I know you've found it . . . I didn't know it was possible for people like . . . us . . . to be so beautiful . . ."

Antheia tapped her cigarette against Hylonome's half shell.

"The revelation of the seed," she said, "precedes the revelation of the plant. There's so much else to show you, beginning with how to apply a spot of rouge . . ."

Then she leaned over and gave Hylonome a kiss on the cheek.

♥

Ourania, meanwhile, was alone in her own cave, wearing nothing now but a sheer slip, her bony form catching the fabric at slight and jutting angles—the knobs of her knees, the peaks of her hips—except around her fulsome breasts, hanging low and shapely, bouncing slightly as she stepped here and there in her slippers, removing her jewels and laying them to rest, lifting off layers of eyeshadow with a cool cloth, spritzing perfume. No matter how powerful her prophecy, every night ended just like this. The woman and the void. The sudden absence of Aphroditos always left a chill in her chest, to which Ourania had never quite accustomed herself. She found some ease, however, in the reenactment of her own gestures, which she performed as she paced, flinging an arm, flicking a finger, for no one.

After the revelation, time passed, time kept passing . . . and that hurt; it was so lonely to watch nothing happen . . .

But even so, there was all this:

This life; this tending the orange trees in the morning, eavesdropping on the birds, who sometimes brought news but more often than not only relayed genomic strands of song—voices, breezes, storms and parties; cathedral bells, screaming mermaids, peaches thudding in an orchard; or the muttering of marble lips, or flowers falling on a horse's grave, or pythons curling around the necks of women writing books—less the sense than the sound of other times and places. She felt it all like a déjà vu, as if she were remembering you.

And there was more, too; not only the divinity, but the dailiness; the gossip and the washing of linens; the shucking of oysters and fermenting of moonshine; the painting of faces and parodies of celebrity; this scholarship of femininity; this preserving a set of sentiments as if they were precious objects (a certain way of batting your lashes, or an aptitude for mythologizing, with a wink, the failure of your latest romance) so that they acquired a kind of solidity, a slowly thickening antidote to the shape of life they had, previously, been forced to tenant. If the Daughters could preserve this small oasis; if they could deepen, felt Ourania, day by day, year by year, the fact of their fancies, perhaps the antidote would hold, would spill into the future, so that whoever came after—forgotten women, women born lost—would not have to waste so much life in the murk of error, not the fact but the feeling that every turn, no matter how true, was false. Then, perhaps, in one thousand years, it wouldn't hurt so much not to know: there might be candles in the dark, and perfumes without depth, and without end. The only meaning was in the way it felt, safekeeping a way of feeling: because without being an answer, nonetheless it satisfied the question . . .

But then, of course, there were the words, the words that felt like portals to another plane of the question, underneath time:

On such a plane, in such a place, there was no need for future or past; there was simply a starburst, as final and unstable as an opal—a meaning so intimate you could spend your life staring into its light without discerning its shape or source and still be slaked, still be thrilled by the restless glory of devoting your life to the mystery of a word. On that secret plane, it sparkled and scintillated beyond cause and effect, in the opaque clarity of its own perpetuity.

But when she returned to the world, it was with empty hands.

Ourania poured herself a cup of hot honey-wine, which wafted pleasantly into her nostrils. It was a way of pressing back against her solitude. That and the cigarette burning at her bedside. One more half measure; each half measure half the last. Even so, a little closer to something like what she imagined people meant when they said 'a quiet night in.' Attempting to complete the scene, she imagined a pool of amber warmth in a steaming forest glade, where fern fronds grazed the surface of the water . . . because sometimes an image helped to secure a feeling . . .

She unrolled the scroll of notes she'd scribbled, these last weeks, in her sleep. Sometimes Aphroditos left a hint in the static. But insofar as the Olympians were concerned, terror and splendor were synonyms; they tended to muddy their inflections with the roar of spectacle. Was she returning, unalloyed, to earth? Was she announcing an epoch of publicity? That didn't seem right, and yet Ourania could discern no note of imminent danger, no trace of warning—simply an overflow of energy. 'Hermaphroiesis' was, like so many divine proclamations, more thunder than lightning. And yet, she felt, *this* cloudiness couldn't be so easily explained, couldn't simply be attributed to the limitations of divine dialtone: as a prophecy, 'Hermaphroiesis' was not only mysterious, not only muddy, but somehow corrupted. Maybe some other source was jamming the signal; the gods had a way of meddling in one another's messages, though she did not sense any Olympian with ill will toward the Lady . . .

Well. This much she knew: that girl was involved, that girl and the horse with whom she shared a name . . . the mare whose fate seemed to possess such an improbable gravity that even Aphroditos was touched by its threads . . . but who was herself untraceable, who seemed to have fallen off the track of time . . .

♥

Lit only by the jaundiced glow of a squat waxen bulb of candle: the spare cave. In one corner a cot on a plain, resin-soaked oak frame. Sand-colored linens topped by a many-colored quilt; a flat half-featherless pillow. Floor swept clean. Bundles of Cypriot desert flora hanging by twine from nails on one wall, drying. Along another wall, a small rack of clothes: sacramental robes (dreamsicle), a smock, a knot of scarves. On the floor, a chest with a glinting brass lock. A small wicker table with a plush stool on either side. A tin pail.

Hylonome was changing into one of the robes, luxurious as specimens of cloud, so rich in sunset shades of pink and gold it seemed to shimmer.

"I think . . ." she said, taking her seat on a stool, "I think I could make a home here."

Ana was seated beside the chest. Into it she placed a pouch of silver; from it she removed a small clay jar of honey-wine, which she carried to the wicker table where the candle flickered, illuminating

Hylonome as if the sun were caught in her threads. As if the Hesperides could be women like us.

Ana lifted the amphora, brushing Hylonome's forearm with her tunic sleeve as she filled their cups with fragrant liquid.

"Antheia told me she thinks you're cute," she said.

Hylonome blushed.

"Everyone needs to stop making fun of my rouge!"

Ana giggled, leaning across the table, looking Hylonome directly in the eyes:

"Are you feeling shy?"

Hylonome looked down into her honey-wine and took a deep sip. All she could manage was a mumble:

"Um . . ."

Ana lifted her chin with a forefinger.

"You didn't answer me, darling," she said.

Hylonome pursed her lips, eyes wide. Then, in one motion, she took Ana's face in her hands and began to kiss her.

Curls of smoke rose from the candle above which their fingers moved urgently through each other's hair: a wavy flaxen bob, an unkempt coiffure of chestnut ringlets, before they moved to the cot, where fingers, too, traced with feverish delicacy along the nape of a neck, around to a clavicle, along a magenta hem; so that when Ana pulled, just slightly, embroidered honeysuckles slipped off Hylonome's breasts, and oranges followed, as the fabric fell in golden folds and pooled on the dry earth.

♥

Later, in the dark, Hylonome was asking questions, because the present wasn't enough for the force of her feelings, and the future was too far to feel real, so she sought to absorb stories of Ana's past in order to interpose herself, phrase by phrase, between the lines—so that, even if there were no guarantee of romance anon, she and Ana would nevertheless already have been together forever:

"It was the first time I remember smelling the scent of a man so fully. I remember how delicate I felt lying on top of him, my hand resting upon his chest, absorbing his warmth," Ana was saying.

"That night," Ana was saying, "in a matter of minutes, I learned I had no precedence for pleasure. What I had, until that point, considered pleasure was nothing more than a distraction. That night I felt absolutely exposed because I couldn't keep quiet—every thrust felt like waking up in bright sunlight. I had been so tense all my life, so anxious, so when he at last and all at once stretched me open, it felt like being split apart, like a chrysalis splitting, like something in me, a part of me I did not know existed until right then, was being forced open, *compelled to exist,* by the force of this hung and mysterious fairy—like the pain of the splitting was a way to finally let pleasure through, like pods and seeds bursting open at the heat of a Spring sun, the sensation was so intense that it became total: when his cock was inside me, it was like being plugged into the wavelength of a serene shock, the shock of my inner monologue shattering all at once, a shattering that burst from my mouth as a howl and moan of pleasure and desperation, because there was no time for thought to form before the next thrust, it was all energy and no fear, no time for fear, no time for time, like living at the exact speed of the instant, like assfucking pinned me to the instant and there was no escaping to past or future or dream or dissociation or panic or even language, there was only the next thrust, only me waking up to the intensity of living one instant at a time, until he came inside me and I felt more beautiful than I had in my entire life . . ."

Then she added:

"Does that answer your question?"

Waves of heat rolled from Hylonome's heart and broke across the surface of her skin, spreading further, fanning over Ana as light as the thinnest membrane of the tide, where their bodies met. Hylonome was horny, was jealous—she was alive. It was night in a smoky cave near Amathus, above which a breeze blew in from the sea, lifting the leaves of cypresses and whistling through the listing grass.

"Yes," she said. "Yes . . ."

VII.

Even later—in the orchard beyond the halls and abyssopelagic chambers of Aphroditos' nymphomanic, waterfallenchanted daughters—boughs cracked, oranges fell. A silver form was descending from the sky, slow, silent and relentless, without concern for what lay crushed and punctured beneath it. The form, Hylonome would think later (though for now she remained asleep, curled into the musky underbrush of Ana's armpit), resembled an enormous mussel shell—it was as black, as expressionless and supernally curved. A faint monochrome glow emanated from the thin slit where the 'half shells' met. As it settled, the roar which issued from it (a single sonic discharge) belonged to neither beast nor man.

But the resemblance was broken, or at least corrupted, when from the vessel's underside detached a tongue; silver, planar, hard and thin as a sheet of steel. Its surface was inlaid with phosphorescent script, cursive loops of ruby reading 'Nuntius Dei.' Descending slowly, continuously, the tongue came to rest on the grass, light and unnatural. A breath of moonstruck smoke rolled forth—voluminous, involute, curling among the orange trees—from which emerged, trotting restively down the ramp (the quiet orchard filled with hoof-echoes, as if at the arrival of a cavalry), the infamous etymologist Isidore of Seville—wrapped in ultramarine robes said to have been sewn from the Virgin Mother's own burial shroud, whose capacious folds emanated an ultraviolet mirage of celestial grace, enchanting butterflies into following behind it—curled, hunched over the misty mane of an uncertain, somnolent mare (for there was an intravenous drip woven into her halter, piercing one of the veins in her neck, abstracting her soul by means of ketamine), whose eyes were haunted by visions of zero (that irresistible emptiness I cover with words), whose beauty (some kind of smoky blue) had been buried as if within a maze, accessible only via the footwork of a dream—you had to walk it weeping, like a lost maiden, exiled on account of her insanity (because her prince had not returned, had left and not returned, had not returned to her bed, because her prince had said enough of your unreasonable proclamations of passion), wandering through the shimmering, enormous carcass of an old goddess half-buried in a blue lagoon, her moss-rotten barnacled ribs curving high above brackish multifoliate marshes and improbable inland oyster beds as if to consecrate the fertility of decay; a horse whose beauty was like a lost language and whose rider was riding another horse entirely, a horse he'd willed into being by banishing the reality of the mare to the proliferating sepulcher of her maze.

From Isidore's hip hung an iridescent net, cut from the cloth of Arachne's first web; this slapped lightly against his thigh as he spurred the mare down the ramp and into the orange trees, heading toward the waterfall. His orders had come directly from the Pope (the first pope to set foot on Mars, the first to convert extraterrestrial protozoa): to trap the goddess Aphroditos inside her sibyl and seal her and her daughters in another dimension, a barren practice Earth which the Lord had once begun on a whim and left unfinished, worse even than purgatory because it served no end, not even an end perpetually deferred—nothing at all. In that place trees bore no fruit; in that place people had no genitals and could not die.

♥

Ourania was awake before the vessel floated silently over the beaches of Cyprus; before it landed atop the orange trees; before Isidore and his men rode behind the waterfall, their horses slipping, one or two falling, ejecting their riders into the lake; before Christ's own mercenaries shuffled through the pitch-dark of the Hall of Holy Fingertips, pointing red lasers at stalactite droplets and silver swooping bats; before they advanced along tunnels, stepped sideways into caves, seeking their targets; before they set fire to the tapestries in the temple, and pissed on the pillows, and filled the rift with concrete.

Ourania woke in confusion, filled with holy terror, to the sound of Aphroditos whispering in her mind. *Do you receive my divine substance in your body as you have received my divine voice in your mouth*

"I do," said Ourania, opening her eyes, filling her lungs with the goddess.

♥

There was no more time for interpretation.

Not even for: how can it be?

There was time only for one choice, one movement. Having closed the pearlnuminous corset latch by latch around her ribs, Nikephoros stood behind Ourania in the sibyl's bedchamber, lacing the baetyl up her back. The baetyl focused her power so that—having sent her Daughters to higher ground to take shelter in the boughs of the First Orange Tree—when Isidore arrived, when he sent his men into the heart of the caverns, she raised the sea from the soil, flooding every chamber of her holy precinct, drowning her sacred grove, transforming, for Hylonome's sake, the mare into a smoky-blue seahorse, wrecking the papal spacecraft and, cavern by cavern, swallowing every one of Isidore's men, as well as, she thought, the Archbishop himself, while her daughters headed for the coast. But as she floated (gills flaring) in her sunken bedchamber, she saw a red beam scanning, interpreting the aquatic dusk. "Impossible," she thought—not the laser of a gun, but the lamp of a three-bolt diver's helmet, recording the very secrets she had attempted to save by sacrificial flood. It was Isidore, capturing the footage which would aid him in composing the story of the Aphrodision sibyl's unreality.

He was prepared to lose his men. He was even prepared to lose his craft. Most of all, he was prepared to perform one gesture—before the goddess could escape her sibyl, he tangled her in Arachne's web, sealing her neither in past nor future, but in nowhere. Where she remains. A man can't kill a goddess, but he can render her irrelevant. The seahorse he trapped with some frustration in a specimen cup.

♥

The Daughters devoted themselves fruitlessly, for years, to finding Aphroditos under the sea, until one day they ceased coming up for air, exiling themselves to the Midnight Zone. Ana and Hylonome moved on. Eventually, as lovers do, they parted. The mare sank slowly into Hylonome's mind. She wept for years. That was all a long time ago now.

CODA

Eventually she had herself become a sibyl. That was another story. The sibyl of Cumae. But to herself she wasn't. At home, or what had once been a home away from the fumes of Apollo and the various dissociative exertions of her chthonic office, at home with her lover Angel, there had never been any spell-weaving. Angel believed in the sibyl, but without faith. Angel had never been interested in loving a myth. The sibyl was someone else. So Hylonome had left the house alone each morning to walk the path to her holy vent. Her fans lining either side, silent and staring. Always they stared. On the path she couldn't think. On the path—halfway between the sibyl and herself—she felt the confusion of the woman they made her become with their eyes. The woman she could forget once Apollo swung into her soul. She had chosen, on account of Ourania's fate, to avoid her sisters; no one knew about her time among the Daughters of Aphroditos. No one except Angel. But Angel had left her. At her lowest, Angel had left her. And yet it was for the best. The sibyl of Cumae was a messy bitch. Hylonome was crushed beneath the weight of her.

It hadn't always been that way. At first it had been like learning to breathe, like realizing your own lungs. The sibyl was everything Hylonome had been afraid to say or be herself; she was an opportunity for a kind of Romance—a proliferation of meaning. A reason for gods to draw near. For Apollo to run his divine fingers through her hair, whispering in her ear like a flock of silver butterflies: *I'm here, baby.* His voice enveloped her in a sultry and thousandfold silence, as if he were a cool breeze in her leaves on a sticky Spring day. As if thick drops of nectar were globing from the split skins of her fruits, sticking her leaves together—and he was spreading them open, opening milky, translucent membranes like plasmic, drippy half-formed webs, which he strummed with the tip of his tongue. She shivered from the friction between her instant and his immortal substance. But that, too, was long ago now. When she still fell asleep smelling Angel's hair. When Angel was to the sibyl as the sibyl was to the neon-pink smoke spilling up from the crack at the heart of a subterranean cavern. Behind every sibyl is an angel who loves her.

♥

Isidore of Seville had once, during the course of Hylonome's tenure, proposed to deliver and enforce a cease-and-desist letter, but, given that Apollo was a state-sanctioned god, direct intervention was overruled by Pope Honorius, who preferred, in a case of contact between Imperial religions, corporate restructuring—joint ventures, retirement packages—to time-skipping sacred subterfuge. 'Unreality' was an appropriate program only for those, like Aphroditos, who could not be expected to cooperate with contractual phase-out procedures, or had little to leverage in such a negotiation; in such cases, their likenesses seized, subjects were neutralized in a single stroke. Apollo and the rest of Olympos would prove useful, however, in synergizing the new order and the old; the Roman Empire—the legacy of the Greeks—would have a future as the precursor of Imperial Europe. It was a delicate process, requiring a handful of centuries and a legion of scribes. He had just the man for the job, a yet-unborn emperor named Constantine. No need to rush such things: the gods would, with proper incentive, be convinced to cooperate. State-sanctioned seers could be engineered easily when the time was right; sibyls were a mere matter of subclauses to be settled at a later date. So Isidore had relented.

Her tenure had, anyway, lasted only two years, which to Hylonome was a significant stretch of life but was, compared to other sibyls, laughably brief. She simply wasn't built to be a public figure, not when she had no sense, either, of how to be a private figure. She wanted to learn how to exist when no one was watching. Of what use was prophecy to solitude? Prophecy held no purchase over daily life. Simple pleasures relied on an aptitude for the instant. Where she, having swiveled from past to future, had never lived.

After her election to sibyl, she had sought access, on one occasion, to the books of the Sibylline Oracles—purchased, according to Roman record, from the first sibyl of Cumae, centuries earlier, by King Tarquinius Superbus, or, as some in the temple whispered, seized from her, immediately preceding her disappearance—only to discover from a retired sibyl who lived in the mountains north of Rome that the books had been burned in 84 BCE, under 'mysterious circumstances' (there had been, at this moment, a twinkle in the old woman's eyes), decades before Caligula's men had supposedly consulted them as a prelude to kidnapping her mother's mare. It struck her then that Caligula's racetrack had only been an alibi for some unknowable purpose concocted by Isidore of Seville, posing for a period as an advisor in the emperor's court. Why he had wanted that mare, Hylonome would never know for certain; she knew little about the man who had descended from the sky and disappeared without a trace. No one since had recognized him by name or description. Having signed a nondisclosure agreement with the papacy, Apollo himself was tight lipped about the matter. (He did not mention, either, his contractual obligations, saying, instead, that Aphroditos was alive and well, and had simply retired from her divine-human responsibilities, that the horse was dead and buried in Sicily after a life well lived, though without a tombstone, and advising Hylonome that further seeking after this Isidore would result in grave danger.) She surmised that the mare's pedigree was more than a myth, and Isidore had stolen her precisely because despite seeming to be merely a horse, she was, in fact, the last surviving descendant of the centaurs. But beyond that she had no leads. Her faith in Apollo waned.

♥

For Angel, the problem was not the sibyl herself but her lack of candor, her nonsensical persistence in that so-called holy role for the sake of—what? Some compensatory parasocial praise from strangers who knew nothing about her anyway? It wasn't so much that Angel disbelieved in Hylonome's mystical faculties; it was that Hylonome disbelieved in them herself, but—to avoid facing, at all costs, her total disillusionment with Apollo—devoted herself nevertheless to those who believed in her, exhausting herself on behalf of the manifold fans who sought solace in her fantastical proclamations. At home Hylonome ached and wept. At home Hylonome begged Angel to help her feel real. At home Hylonome read fan letters and worried whether they really adored her, or if they, too, had begun to disbelieve—what did Angel think of this line, or that one? She grew paranoid; she grew bitter. She started drinking and stopped eating. What love Angel felt for her was redirected into caretaking; what love she felt for Angel was redirected into the production of her faith. Put simply, there was too much sibyl and not enough Hylonome.

At home, Hylonome could abide neither reality nor the effervescences of Olympos. She was trapped between half devotions, useless for the daylight and useless before the fitful flame of a campfire. In the meantime Angel washed her blood from bedsheets, walls and wounds. Angel kept her breathing while she lay forever in the dreamless sleep of wakefulness, retreating to another gloom, not the gloom of the sibyl but the gloom of zero. Angel knew her as a dilettante of dimensions, making her dioramas for anyone but herself. Or if for herself, only for the duration of a drug, as brief as smoke, and as recursive. Angel could not respect what she did not, in the privacy of her unsibyled self, believe. Whatever Apollo said, the world remained the same.

So—

Thearios, god of Oracles,

Mousegetes, keeper of the Muses,
Proopsios, diviner of dimensions,
Hekatos, my arrow from afar,
Delphinios, dolphin leaping anon:
artful Apollo of the rising sun, silver rake, be gone forever.
What you taught me of the future was better taught by the instant.
What you taught me of poetry was better taught by the tongues of lovers.

So she'd said, but he refused. Your body belongs to me, he said. In return for my gifts, you gave me your mouth. Only death will release my voice.

And if I touch death lightly?

Angel had found her clutching shards of blue glass in her palms, her mind killed by an amphora of wine-dark wine, her lungs suffocated by smoke, bleeding, wrapped in bedsheets—not once, not twice, not three times, nor four, but one time too many. Angel found her singing songs that no one ever wrote. Angel found her laughing. Angel found her screaming at the god inside her. Angel found her dancing in her own blood. Angel found her sewing her wounds with green and gold thread, found her begging for their arms, found her far away from any thought of the sibyl. And when Angel left, no one found her anymore. And the deeper she cut, the more Apollo wailed, until even he could no longer bear it—and she expelled him with a single breath, as sudden as the first.

She didn't need a story anymore. She needed a life. She needed a foothold in something more solid than a cloud. The sibyl was anesthetized. And now (except in tree-bough whispers, in broad daylight, for half the length of an instant) now she did not have a god, but she had the hole he left. A hole is an opportunity to fill it.

♥

She'd meant something to many people, but she did not know them, or knew them only at a distance; she knew them not, per se, by their own stories, but by the way their stories interacted with her interpretations, which, because Apollo once ran his fingers through her hair, they took for prophecies. They were whims. She knew so little. Only enough to fill a stranger with faith, only enough to convince a crew to let her captain a ship before she wrecked it in the reef.

But I only built the ship to wreck it

It's about how you go down. Hylonome thought she could never win, so she tried to lose with style.

There was another lover after Angel.

There was another and another and another.

I wear a veil because every day is my wedding day

There was always someone sniffing the god on her, despite the fact that, as with even the muskiest perfume, she couldn't smell it on herself. Men and women approached her in taverns (for she had begun to go to taverns again), in meadows and gardens, seeking the silence of His song. The scent made her vulnerable to all manner of drifters—or maybe it was less the scent, after all, than the hole. Maybe they sensed the vessel in her, some place to store their secrets. Some place to keep them safe.

They would say something like, 'What you have is not a void, but an atmosphere. An atmosphere, like a lake, a skyful of cloudbanks or the onset of sleep, is the space in which things happen. Let me help you.'

But everyone she allowed herself to need soon grew tired of her. Without the sibyl she was a woman without a name. Talking solved nothing. She taught herself to speak more precisely than an aqueduct, she pitched her speech to the slightest angle of decline, she taught herself, lover by lover, to cradle the formless waters of her sensations across the great distances between mind and mind; she thought if she could at least make sense, if her lovers would say, at last, regardless of whether they agreed or disagreed, 'that makes sense,' then she could keep a foothold in reality for one more night—she just wanted to make sense, she just wanted, just one time, baby, *please just tell me I'm making sense:* but there was always a limit. She wasn't afraid of complication. Complication was the only road she'd known, complication was how she pinned the grains of sand, the flecks of god, the songs of mourning doves and *those flowers to which moths come in the evening* to every page, like a map of the movements of her nonsense, a way of walking her nonsense as if it were a holy pilgrimage, a way of guiding her lovers into her nonsense, tangling them in it, the centripetal spell of her labyrinth of love. But she didn't know what to do once she got them there. Because behind all that complication was only a girl who didn't know how to be simple.

But—she refused to die. She would survive, do you hear?

I have no idea what I will do with my life, I have never lived for anything but love, but I'm tired of living for love because there will always be another lover, there will always be another lover walking out the door and another lover walking in, there will always be me in the doorway watching lovers come and go, there will always be me freefalling through the doorway into the doorway into the doorway where I will be freefalling until I reach the very core of the dirt where I'll ripen until I'm food for flowers. Baby, I'm a rotten peach. Let me ripen one more time, Kyprogeneia. Let me ripen one more time for one more lover and I promise I won't wail my prayers in your ears anymore, I promise I won't beg you every night for Angel to come home, I promise I won't ever again ask for the intercession of thy hand, I promise never again to speak your name, I promise I will be beautiful and live a modest life if you answer one last prayer, if you make me simple

But Aphrodite didn't answer because even she'd had enough.

Well, I've had enough of her

Well, that's a lie. Kyprogeneia doesn't like when we beg, when we beg she sends us the same lover in another form, she punishes us so sweetly by giving us exactly what we want.

So there was another lover, and another and another. As long as there was just one more, there would always be.

Hylonome claimed—because temple oaths had required a vow of chastity, to which, despite her retirement, she was bound for life and which forbade men and women both from even so much as glimpsing her pussy—to allow only assfucking.

This they minded less than her madness.

They wanted the former sibyl of Cumae, not a shut-in babbling about a horse.

Still she refused to seek the company of her sisters.

There was another lover, and another.

She never knew about Ana's happy latter-days in a secret cove on the island of Stromboli.

And one day she died alone.

Here lies Hylonome.

[BROOKLYN, NEW YORK, JANUARY 2022
AUSTIN, TEXAS, NOVEMBER 1, 2023]

HTTPS://WATERFALL NOT FOUND

I always thought there should be two of us standing here.

—LAI YIU-FAI, *HAPPY TOGETHER*

I WANTED TO be beautiful too. I thought you practiced being beautiful until you were, so I watched the way my mother put on lipstick and followed along with my finger, but I was watching from among her gowns—because if she knew I was watching then she would become my mother and not 'a woman preparing for her evening.' If she were my mother then I would be a boy and she would not teach me about lipstick.

Soon she left and went where the ladies go, and I walked out from the gowns to where her lipstick lay on the counter in the powder room. Lipstick was how you became beautiful. The ladies all wore it when they went out into the night forest where the lights are strung up and the champagne in crystal glasses and the jasmine blooms. I put on her lipstick in the mirror slowly, slowly, it was a delicate art, and mother always said too much beauty made you ugly. I felt the spiders in the walls beckoning me to come into the cool dark under the house but I said to them, 'I am becoming beautiful and I do not need to hide under the house.' Then I said, 'I will be beautiful and no one will know I am a boy, because when you put on lipstick you are not a boy or a girl but a darling. I'm what the men call the ladies when they put on lipstick, they call them darling, and now my name will be darling too. I am going to be darling and not a spider do you hear?' I was triumphant, and slowly and with an air of indifference, because languor is a form of elegance, I turned and said to the mirror, 'my name is darling.'

Then I did not see him but I heard his voice and he said, 'You are murdering my son.' It was my father. I was scared and said 'I do not want to die father please why am I dying,' and I knew it was the lipstick because I was darling and not his son and so I said 'it's me father it's me,' I took off the lipstick and said 'it's me I promise.' Father looked at me and looked at me. His shoulders fell. He said, 'Go outside and ask god to forgive you because I cannot.' So I crawled beneath the house and into the cool dark and said 'god will not see me here' so I hid from god among the trembling webs of the spiders.

I said to the spiders, 'do you want lipstick and then you can be darling?' I opened the lipstick and I applied it to the spiders one after the other, and the spiders said nothing but looked at me with their eyes like stolen jewels. I bore witness to spring in the glamorous eyes of the spider. But I looked into the eyes of the spiders and—and so many flowers all at once, why did we need so many flowers. And why more fruit than I could eat, and which is rotted by its own sweetness? One spring I ate every fallen fruit and collapsed in the garden delirious and aching. I ached from the decadence of the silent world. From the cruel luxury of the garden. I was dressed in silver robes and I was weeping. Then something in me shifted, and I rose and ran from the garden to the place under the floorboards. I vomited in a tin pail. And why? Because beauty is a rotting thing. And it belongs to no one.

I was thirteen years old and I hated the spring, how ten million eyes watched the blooming trees, and the trees rotting just to be watched, just to court the eyes with sweetness, and I with my hard-scrabble beauty and no eyes on me. But the spiders. I am not finished with the spiders. I crushed them all under my shoes.

I repent, my god. I repent. I am not without blame in this world. Forgive me my trespasses. They stared at me with their still eyes and their lipstick and expected nothing. For spring would still come, and they had merely delivered a message: spring is coming. Their legs were twitching, clutched together so delicately, and a thick fluid was oozing, the unbearable dew of a dying spider, so I picked up their ancient bodies with my hands and dug in the soil until my nails broke and bled and I had buried them. Ancient things are too vastly silent to be beautiful. The bones of dinosaurs, a ruined cathedral, the cycles of the moon, god and his angels, for all of these we have another word: majesty. And in murdering them I had discovered the majesty of spiders.

I love my father, I love him but he does not know what I mean when I say 'majesty.' He only sees spiders crawling in the garden, and he says the garden is perfect but for the spiders, and I say it is only because of the spiders that the garden is perfect, and otherwise the garden is only an ornament, otherwise the flowers are useless, they mean nothing if not for the spiders, nothing we do not already know by looking at the flowers. So if I speak only of flowers it is my own weakness, there is more to life than flowers, all the times I have spoken of flowers I wonder if you have felt the spiders scurrying beneath the petals? Always there were spiders and if you did not see them it was because I was afraid not to be beautiful, I was afraid of what is called 'ugliness,' I was afraid that my realm was too pretty for what crawls beneath the flowers, that in telling you about the spiders, I would disgust you. But they are my majesty, and if you are disgusted it is because I am not writing for you—not for you, do you hear? All my letters about flowers, I wrote you so many letters and only wrote about flowers, but it is the spiders most of all that I have spoken of because until now I have not spoken of them at all. I have told you the desolate story of the flowers only so that you would ask: but what is missing? And I can say: the spiders.

Oh, but it wasn't only my father, it was the silence . . . no one told me I could wear lipstick and so I was silent, because they did not give me words to use, I had to make them up. That's why I write such crude and unbalanced phrases. I had to make them up myself. There was no story for a boy in lipstick.

So—so every time I loved lipstick my stomach ached and the only way to make it stop aching was to prove that boys do not love lipstick, and so because I was a boy I did not love lipstick either. But all of a sudden I loved lipstick and because no one told me I could love lipstick, I thought that meant I could not love lipstick, and the more I loved it, the more I would die. I thought that the day I surrendered to that love would be the day I would no longer be anything at all—not even a butterfly. And butterflies barely exist. Butterflies are the residue of our dreams.

I need them to show me the way to the dark heavens. The heavens that are beneath our feet. It was by following butterflies that I became an author. 'Butterflies' are what I called the angels falling in the distance. They led me into a cave, where I found a typewriter; they told me to sit before the typewriter and tell it my story. The typewriter listened, dim and glistening. Then it offered me the alphabet. Our vital riddle. Without it we do not even know our own names.

I want to say thank you to the devil, because the devil has the dark power of caves and roots and the devil is the princess of spring. The devil ripens fruit deep within the earth and offers it to us in sweetness. The devil invented the alphabet. But god forbids the alphabet in the kingdom of heaven. God has no language.

♥

Once there was a boy who loved the spring so much that he slept outdoors. I met him one early morning, bathing beneath a waterfall. I, who had traveled among dark trees to find where the water came from. I saw him bathing and he waved to me. So I removed my silks, because I too knew how to be naked. But to be naked meant something else with another boy than it did when you were alone. I wanted him to teach me. I was a silent object coming through the trees and into the clearing. There was nothing to say: I said nothing. Such were the laws of the forest. And by the laws of the forest he remained naked. But he passed behind the falls and disappeared. So I swam across the water to where he had been, and parted the waters, and disappeared with him behind the waterfall. Here we were sheltered by cool limestone and damp moss, and our clothing was forgotten somewhere else. Do you remember? Down on my knees I tasted your milk.

Yes, and one day you left. So I began to write you letters, letters I never sent because I was alone in our home behind the waterfall, the waterfall was empty and I was cold and frightened by the darkness—I mean because I did not know if you loved me, your letters said you loved me but I was alone, do you understand? You sent me letters but you never came home, so I did not send my letters about flowers, I buried them instead. I am always burying something, maybe one day that will mean a garden? I cannot go on, this is an impossible paradise and it makes me wretched. I need to lay my pen aside. We go on and on and on . . . I've fallen asleep writing to you many times . . . like how we fall asleep talking late into the night, don't we? Someone else take the pen and finish this desperate letter . . . I am aching for a paradise but I do not want to go on, it is painful, this responsibility of dreaming a paradise unto the earth, it is painful, and the tedium hurts me too, the lost hours, the hours when you lose sight of what once seemed a destiny, when you sit and write and every word feels imprecise, so you hate them and yourself and the endless hours, the tedium is painful like finding out you were not a hero all along. Let me say my language is returning to dust. These are palpitations, final breaths before I tear this letter to pieces. Let me say amen.

Paradise is when you are impossible but true. And you are true because you said so, you invented it. But you only invented it because it was already true but the dictionary didn't say anything about it, so you had to say it instead. Do you remember what 'we' means? Paradise is we. And I don't know what it means. Because I am no longer I and the flowers are no longer the flowers but I do not know what I am and what they are. I only know that it has not existed before. Maybe our name is simply: 'the flowers and I.' But even that I do not understand because I have never been anything other than a boy. To be a 'we' is something else, and maybe it is divine? Is 'the flowers and I' what I have called god and all along I have been waiting for myself? Ah, I do not know. I do not know. 'We' barely exists and has a meaning too delicate for me to understand. If I say anything more I run the risk of sounding mystical.

Once I saw a dead pigeon and ran screaming into the house, saying 'call the priest mother call the priest, oh where is the cemetery for birds.' Seeing hurts and it makes us fragile. We close our eyes.

♥

At the beginning of spring, or what is called the beginning of spring but is in fact late winter, when the trees are flowerless and silent, and there is no news yet of spring blossoms—in late winter I was unable even to read a book, to sit in an armchair and read twenty or thirty pages because I feared I would lose my way, that I would amble through a page or two only to be snagged upon a thorny sentence, and I would not make it to the end, I would be lost in the thicket, scratched and tortured, and the only way out would be never to read again, which would herald the end of my sanity, because reading is my only possible deliverance from a dark and ceaselessly turning planet, therefore, believing I could not read twenty pages, I would not dare open the book, would not even read a page. On some days, too, I was held to my bed by a demon invisible but insistent who I had known since adolescence when he first began to visit me, always trying to convince me of the sweetness of evil, saying 'doesn't it taste sweet in the mouth, sweet as can be,' always saying 'wouldn't it be sweet to hurt, and the more you hurt the sweeter you will feel'—this was a philosophical demon and his favorite question was love. On those days I could not read even a sentence, oh sentences you were excruciating and left me feverish and screaming out in a language that belonged not to men but to angels and which I have since forgotten just as I have forgotten many old dreams. But how much more alarming, in the end, to write a sentence, to sit at the typewriter terrified of writing because each sentence is a moral argument—what terrifies me is that I could write any sentence and I have only my fingers touching the keys until my fingertips hurt but

I go on because I like to hurt because it's romantic, it means you are dying and you know it, do you understand, you are dying from a sweetness, and dying is only 'goodnight, my love,' and nothing more . . .

I feel the exhaustion of having lived all the days I don't write about, because to write about them I could only say, 'I woke up, and then, and then, and then . . . and then . . . I'm sorry, where was I? Ah yes, and then I went to sleep,' do you understand? The exhaustion of watching the hands move on a clock, of watching time pass . . .

The riddle of the clock is this: how does it destroy us all so gently and with such quiet hands?

God is only a society of angels in the solitude of an office, each seated at a desk, before a typewriter, their wings draped delicately over the backs of their chairs, angels who long ago sent me epistles, which reach me only now, because since the rebellion heaven has been understaffed, and their postal service is defunct . . . but that isn't what I want to say . . . None of this is what I want to say . . . it's crude and rickety . . . I'm sorry, I'm afraid, who knows why . . . When I am afraid I ramble, and rambling saves me, in every form of punctuation there is hope, except for the period, so I ramble, I do not want to be hopeless . . . I want the impossible . . .

Angels sing without sleep for all eternity in an enormous opera without precedent and without author. They do it for god. God seems like the most dangerous kind of ecstasy. It provokes you to build cathedrals and destroy cities and give me names that made me want to die and run from the world into the arms of the boy when no one saw us and we kissed on the tennis courts. But once, we were only eighteen then, once in front of your friends Luke and Johnny who did not know about us and referred to me by various noms de plume depending on the season, who mocked me because I was the only boy in school who liked boys and said so, I who wore lipstick one day anyway because you taught me how to wear it when we were beautiful together in the backyard by the broken swing, that day in the school hallway in front of Luke and Johnny you called me faggot and you who have always been my only true friend and have taught me how to live delicately reduced me to almost nothing because you saw the other boys beating on me and laughing and saying faggot like it tasted bad and you standing there saying nothing and not even crying because you hated me for being beaten and you hated me for being a faggot and you hated me for loving you so much I couldn't keep our secret—and that is why we are wretched all of us, dear wretched things and I love you.

When you called out my name I turned and looked at you, already knowing what was going to happen, but not frightened at all, not even a little, only sad and tender because I pitied you, and you knew I was remembering how you blushed when you painted my lips, so you called me faggot and then I just stood there and smiled like you had called me darling. You said faggot and I smiled. And then they all smiled like schoolboys do, and they descended on me. When I was left crying in the hallway after the bell rang you knelt beside me and kissed my forehead and I smiled and said 'I love you' and then I said 'and isn't that a sad thing because you do not know how to love me' and then you ran to class because the bell had rung thirty seconds before and you did not know what to say.

I never know what to say, you taught me how to use lipstick but not how to write with it, and that is why this letter is only pretty like a major chord strummed on a spider's web—that is why it makes no sound. Ten years later I am writing you to tell you I loved you once, even though you made lipstick a memory of the cruelty of our love, so now when I love lipstick I must also remember you.

Lipstick is a knife.

I wore it because your love made me feel so beautiful that I wasn't afraid anymore, wasn't afraid for anyone to know I loved lipstick, I was a darling and I didn't need to hide beneath the floorboards because even if you hurt me, your love would protect me—your love was stronger even than you. I wore the lipstick because I wanted everyone to know that I was in love, that to wear lipstick I must be in love, because I was afraid if the world didn't know, then it never happened, then you had never loved me after all. I wore the lipstick because I was always afraid when we were alone, when we were alone I was afraid you would leave me, I clung to you and begged you please never to leave me alone behind the waterfall, I was so afraid of you leaving that I needed to find some way in my life not to be afraid, I needed to find some way I could beg no one, cling to no one, and that was by wearing the lipstick. It wasn't courage that led me to wear the lipstick, it was spite—I wore it because I couldn't bear to be close to you, I was so weak for you that I wanted to prove I could be strong for everyone else. I wore the lipstick to say: spring is coming. I don't know why I wore it.

♥

After you left I was alone in the forest and that is how I began to hear the voices of the flowers and attempt to decipher their language. When I write my story the world will know how I set out to make paradise with my bare hands. I will tell myself like a secret, I will whisper my story like rainfall, so you turn your head to the sky. But for now I clutch my wretched love and howl out these rickety phrases. This is the last time I will write to you. Deliberately I am trying to write in careless words, because I want the shipwreck, I only built the ship to wreck it. My sentences are slowly disintegrating, slowly I will lose my voice and the letter will be reduced to a dream, a handful of sand . . .

So I am translating, translating, translating, in the crumbling desert of pages, and the truth is I am so tired, tired of flowers, it's terrible, isn't it? I exhaust myself staring at flowers, I do it for hours and everyone who walks by thinks 'that boy loves flowers,' and they do not know I want to fly away, I don't know where. I don't know why the flowers chose me, I am tormented by them at all hours, even when I sleep, I do not understand them because they speak in perfumes, not in language. I know there was an angel who put me in the world to torment me, the angel that whispered in my ear that the flowers had a message for me, that I was meant to decipher it. I cannot decipher it, I do not know how. I gave my fear the name: love. It's a simple trick but it works in the beginning. I love beginnings, don't you? I dress up my fear as love and you believed me for a while, like everyone else believed me for a while, but the more afraid I get the harder it is to remember how to make it look like love, and soon it looks like fear, only fear. I know you because I am you.

When you left me I was flung out into space, where I passed by many dark planets orbiting a burning sun. And because of the sun, the planets had invented dawn. I always thought dawn belonged to me, but dawn is only because of planets in vast and inexplicable thrall. Dawn is the earth slumbering and awakening its great dreams. Dreams too delicate for the heat of the day. Don't forget it, okay? It was only because I could not hide from the world inside the dawn, could not take refuge in the dawn forever, because the clock creates dawn and then destroys it, which suggests to me that paradise exists, but every day is born and dies, and all it took was a slant of light. It's only that, because I love you, I want to preserve the dawn for us both. But not like a painting: I want the living dawn.

I learned how to preserve dusk. All you need is a jar and a few fireflies. Then you turn the lights off and open your eyes—and dusk has entered your room. But dawn is not so easy because it has no representative like the firefly to reveal the vastness of dusk. Dawn is not so easy because it is so far away . . .

Darling, listen, I'm running out of time. Heavy wings are closing around me, I feel a change in the air. The feathers tickle me and I laugh darkly. So darkly my laughter sounds almost like a howl. When I tell my story it is only so that wherever you are, you might remember the forest. Please come home.

I love you, I love you, I promise I love you and when I am dead my bones will love you too. I can't promise my spirit only because I do not know if I have one. Once I used to write exquisite phrases but I was lying because I always wanted to write like this, like something torn up and carelessly pieced back together. I never paid attention in geometry. I did not listen to the teacher who attempted to show me how to make triangles, and how to justify the triangles I had made. I want to be happy, and maybe if I had listened in geometry I would know how to make myself into a triangle and justify it. But a triangle does not justify itself, so maybe I won't justify myself either? I wake up in the morning and open the curtains. Outside my window I see great distances. The sky is the promise that one day we will fly.

We were not allowed to be simple. All because they told us our triangles were not triangles. They said our triangles were nonsense, only scribbles. They said if we didn't spend our time doodling we would know the difference between a triangle and nonsense. Ah, if they spent time doodling they would know that our nonsense is a secret kind of triangle. But they do not have angels whispering in their ears.

We always wanted simple things, but the world told us we could not be simple and also love lipstick, we had to choose. So we renounced simple things, and because we renounced simple things we never learned that sometimes it is okay to be simple. And now we don't know how to tell a story, or how to buy fruits and vegetables at the market, or how to love each other. But what we don't know together didn't keep us together; we don't know the same things but we are far apart . . . I don't understand riddles, I can never figure them out . . .

Perhaps if I write what the angels ask me to write, if I distribute their epistles, one day they will tell me why I loved you? But to explain my love does not require that I understand the explanation. So if I finish this letter, then you will know why I loved you, but still I will not know. Just as I can write a book about life and still not know what life is. But when you read it you will say: ah, so that's it. Because my vision was given to me in scraps, and so I wrote it in scraps. But it was given to you like a pebble is given, or the dawn. It was given to you like the gust of a great wing. All at once.

But my grace is this: when I do not know why I love you, then I know I am alive. There is no way out except in, so I amble through dark forests and into caves, where in the endless dark I hear the waterfalls sparkling over rocks into a further, fathomless night. I abdicate the light of day for the alphabet and the sweetness of the good devil. The devil does not steal our souls, he just shows us how to type on the typewriter, and relieve our souls from the burden of their solitude. But god is a propagandist who told his angels to tell us that the devil steals souls, and that he steals them with the twenty-six mystical letters of the alphabet. So I sit before the typewriter in the dark, and in the endless recital of my fingers upon the keys I am angry at you for loving me, I wanted to hurt you for loving me because you looked at me and did not look away and I was frightened that when you looked at me you would see how I shimmer and if you looked close you would see that I only shimmer at the beginning and soon the shimmering fades and beneath the shimmering is what I do not give words to. I do not attempt to describe it, I am surrounded by it like the air I breathe, but I do not look, I close my eyes and say I do not believe in nightmares, I do not believe that my freedom and the freedom of dreaming have led me only to nightmares. I do not know how to say the ugly and violent things that turn and turn in me, and the spiders I do not know how to describe except to say that they are numerous and I love them with a sickening love. And all the petals I crushed to make perfume, I am drunk on my perfumes but only when I am alone and in front of the typewriter. They sicken me because my beauty has brought me nothing and nonetheless I crush and crush, I crush up all the flowers I love and admire, and maybe when there is nothing left I will be loved, and if not I will be an object with hands full of crushed flowers. But when you looked at me I forgot how to make the perfume and so I suffocated because unless I crush them, the flowers grow too great. I gave my kingdom to you, I let the crown tumble and said, 'Rule over me terrible prince, I want to be ruled by you alone.' But you said you don't want to rule me, you want to love me. And I said I don't know how to love you except by saying my kingdom stands or falls for you, everything I have built here, the marble columns and grottoes of tangled wistaria, and the endless rooms, empty but for wind in lace curtains, they are for me until I remember you and then they are for you.

My trouble is that I began to read books before I learned to live. I confused phrases with prophecies. I thought that books told the truth about the world, I didn't know that sometimes books were only great dreams. The books said that to love meant to die on a cross. May I ask you, why was he so lonely that he tried to take everyone into him? I would crucify myself for one man.

♥

Listen: last week I was daydreaming of nothing in particular, and all of a sudden I imagined a play. There was no stage, no theater, and above all no audience. It was set in a small city. I had choreographed the mothers hanging laundry out their windows, and the horses galloping in the peach orchard, and the bicycles making their turns along cobbled roads. I had designated when and where the street should smell of roses, or of baked bread. I had invented miniature scenes. The autumn breezes, and the wandering clouds, every argument and every kiss accorded with my vision, though I allowed no deaths, no deaths except my own, because if I stayed in the play, I would never see you again;

nonetheless I wanted to know that somewhere the play was happening, even if not to me. Life was almost perfect but even god must rest. The seventh day eternal. We are left in a world where god is sleeping and its nearness to perfection only clarifies the distance. And so I wanted to write a play and by writing it finish the world god began. To let loose a swarm of butterflies from the cracked earth . . . but maybe I am not made to show you butterflies, maybe I am made to show you trampled wings and the uselessness of beauty . . .

I want so much to give you paradise, I am trying my hardest, I promise. I have at last exhumed my phrases, and though they are damp and humid and many are rotted like wet leaves I speak them anyway. But it seems the more I speak my true words the more I am at risk of losing my voice altogether. Now when I am so near to paradise, now when I see it in the far distance and know if I walked for one more day on the red clay I would reach it, I want to give up and rest, it's the exhaustion of not knowing what to do in paradise. When I arrive there I do not think I will have a thing to say. So instead—and this is the temptation god offers us by his slumber—instead when I am so near I do not want to finish my letter but to become like those who thoughtlessly wander down the streets gazing in shop windows at hats or sweaters or at their own reflections. But even so, I know that when I gaze at shop windows I end up instead seeing only my face in the glass, and I look at myself until I am so tired and must sit on the park benches trembling quietly and asking the trees if they are happy. The scandal of my shipwreck and I thought that by writing I would find a way back to you? I have forgotten what I was saying, I am only babbling. This is not a letter, it's just the fatal nonsense I offer to you: I wanted the play to be so near to life that it was like life itself, only in my play god never fell asleep and he finished the world and I did not need to write anything at all, no one wrote the play because the world was finished and paradise was around the corner. Anyway I only wrote it because I was lonely.

And because—because sometimes another fairy ambles through my periphery, a fairy who demands my attention, a fairy who I therefore cannot ignore, but I am lying because all along I have been waiting for such a fairy to come, I have been waiting as if that fairy is my salvation, my salvation from the tedium of having been born. But because I do not know what to do when I want a fairy and he falls in love with me, I am helpless, I only know that to want him was excruciating, but to have him is even more excruciating. So I decide I shall want no more, I shall lie here in my bed and stare at the wall! But then another fairy ambles along, and it begins all over again. My mind sees the fairy and adorns him, paints him a face and gives him a story, so that I have made an idea of a person, what we call a myth. The myth erases my hierarchies and crowns itself my king. Nothing justifies me if the myth does not justify me. But the myth grows pale. And so I blame the fairy, I howl until he casts me away, be gone from me, he says, be gone, and then I weep because my hands are empty, I stare at the wall, and . . . where was I . . . I stare at the wall . . . ah yes, until along comes another fairy . . .

You loved me once and that's a fact, okay? Many things are facts that do not feel like facts. Many facts feel like dreams. Life is a dreamed fact. But the only fact I cannot explain, it is my business to elide the facts but sometimes they are thorny and implacable, the only fact I cannot explain is that you left me. Because I can't imagine loving someone and leaving them, if I loved someone I could never leave, it's like a pact between my chromosomes to guarantee the meaning of my life—so when I think that you loved me after all, but really loved me, and when I think I might be able to prove it, when the possibility of this proof reveals itself to me, I begin to imagine that we might be together again, if I can prove our love I can correct the error, the error of you leaving me: and that's when the fantasies begin, and fantasies are different than dreams, you give them the weight of your phrases but they stagger and fall like featherless birds.

The less they give us the more we offer to them, the more we lavish them with phrases and with sweet nothings and with laughter; how many fairies have I charmed and kissed knowing all along I was lying and wanted to kiss you instead? I won't lie to you, it hurts me but I will not lie, I even took them to the places you took me, I defiled the forest and I defiled the tennis courts and I defiled the waterfall.

A miracle is when god cheats, because it makes the story better. Did you know that sometimes still I rush to the tennis courts? I wake up in the morning and a fantasy descends on me. I become convinced that you are waiting for me at the tennis courts or by the waterfall, but you are impatient or have somewhere else to be, somewhere urgent, and will only wait so long, so I half button my shirt and pull on sandals and sprint down the lane to reach you, but when I get there I am breathless and the court is empty or the riverbank is deserted and all I hear is the trickling water. Every time I arrive and every time you are not there but I say next time I will run fast enough.

Anyway, I was told that you kissed a fairy not too long ago, so I found him and enchanted him as I sometimes can when I do not wish to sleep or dream but instead to lay out blankets in the slumbering meadow as the sun sets and laugh and look like I am thinking of heavenly things, which often I am but not then, and waste my magic on a fairy who I will never love. I am interested in the world only insofar as it describes my love for you.

I kissed him too. And after I kissed him we ate peaches like a sacrilege because I remembered eating peaches with you. We had come back from the garden with our baskets full and sat in the rocking chairs on the porch while the pinkish fruits warmed in the sun, exhaling until the whole porch smelled so dense and so sweet that if you knew them by scent alone you'd think there were thousands of peaches. I felt beautiful, my lips glazed with nectar and my tongue tasting of spring; I felt that maybe even we were the reason for the peaches, that somehow we had made them with our love, as if they had crash-landed onto reality out of a dream. Meanwhile you were telling me about a book you were reading then and which I did not dare to read because I did not dare mingle our libraries until I was certain of our destiny. Besides I thought that to read it would only tear apart the daydream you made of it for me. That was when I knew I loved you, because that was the day I began to associate you with peaches, which I have loved since my childhood when dawn smelled of peaches. Listen: what is sweetest is a fact. A fact is something that happens every day, like a peach. Whereas a fantasy is only of a superficial sweetness, like so-called pure sugar, which only sweetens what was not sweet enough in itself. But peaches are facts. Facts with a destiny. And their destiny is to warm in the sun and perfume the porch.

Also no one eats the pit, otherwise no more peaches would be born. It is for the sake of the peach that its pit is hard and ugly and not sweet like its flesh. I am hard and ugly, but my words are sweet. And not because I sprinkle my ink with sugar. I only tell the facts.

So when I talk about my story I am talking about a fact that hasn't happened yet, so I disguise it by calling it a dream. And when I talk about destiny I am talking about how facts become something more than facts. How day after day becomes: 'once we lived behind the waterfall.' Anyway, I don't eat peaches anymore. I place them by my bed, beneath the window, until my bedroom smells of peaches and of you. Oh darling, wherever I go, I carry a peach.

You are at the distance of an irresolvable alphabet. To say your name and to say mine is only a difference of letters. But when we speak of death we speak in halting whispers and old phrases, and when we speak of heaven we speak like those who are trying to convince themselves of a fantasy that has already faded. We carry our castles on our backs all our days and when we fall they fall with us. The ache of death without witness. Language dies with the body and the dying body turns from death to narrate its own past. But I need nonsense, too, do you understand? When I am alone I only want to sing nonsense, to make songs out of words that mean nothing, words that will not hurt you, words that need not be sacred to anyone but me. When I write to you like this I forget my own nonsense, I am dying and nonetheless I put on performances as if I were going to live for many centuries. It is sad for me to sing and it is joyful, my joy is sad because there is a sadness in knowing you are going to die and falling in love anyway.

In mathematics the simplest solution is the most elegant, but I am not a mathematician and I trust the tangled truth. When it comes to death the simplest solution is the least elegant. After all angels are only flecks of god fallen from heaven. But so many fell that there wasn't enough god left.

There is a reason the dictionary provides both synonyms and antonyms, there is a reason we are called on to remember opposites, because to separate them is as unnatural as separating the waters from the waters—it took an act of god. I was told to speak either of flowers, and remain in the garden, or of spiders, and go down into the floorboards. But I want to commit the error of remembering a grammar. I want to place gorgeous adjectives beside crude nouns, do you hear? One day so many years ago I ambled into the backyard, where my mother and her friends were reclining on lawn chairs, drinking Dr Peppers and gossiping. When she saw me crossing the yard, she clasped me to her breast so fervently that at first I thought she had been ransacked by tenderness, but then she whispered in my ear, 'You musn't wear lipstick when my friends are visiting . . .' and trailed off, holding me, shrouding me for a moment in her perfume which always, briefly, lent the world the image of heaven, and I knew that she loved me and knew too that she wished I had not been born so delicate, but knowing that I could not be restructured into a man without also in some way being destroyed, she would sometimes leave her lipstick out on the dressing table, or drop an earring on the floor, knowing I would find it and try it on, would wear it until my ears bled and I wondered if my mother bled each time she wore her jewels, and I wanted to bleed like a woman for beauty . . . for beauty's sake, my god . . .

Whether or not you join me I will make it there, and whether or not it is ramshackle I will live there, and even though my heart is weak I will build it: I will find paradise in a semicolon, a comma . . . and a few words . . .

Paradise is felt, not seen. It is too breathless for language—only the rustling of leaves, and footsteps, footsteps . . .

And if a mask is my true face? So be it: I, too, am a magnificent woman. After all, certain flowers seem to be an imitation of a flower. Perhaps the flower is only an imitation of something that does not yet exist. So forgive me for not believing you, when all along you loved me and I would not let you . . . I think some part of me wanted to be alone, because as long as I was alone, I could predict the future: I stared at the walls, I drank water and ate bread, but to love meant not predicting the future anymore, meant telling stories that do not satisfy my visions—but no one ever could, no one could ever tell a story that satisfied a vision, because visions are for me and stories for you, do you understand?

I wring out my vision into words because the vision suffocates, and when it suffocates I do not need it anymore . . .

I turn away from the flowers, and then they belong to someone else.

[AUSTIN, TEXAS, FALL 2014
NEW HAVEN, CONNECTICUT, SPRING 2015]

IL SANTUARIO MADONNA DELLA NULLA

I'm thinking about Ivan.
I'm thinking about love.
About injections of reality.
About their lasting only a few hours.
About the next, more potent injection.
I'm thinking in silence.
I'm thinking it's late.
It's incurable. And it's too late.
But I survive and think.
And I am thinking it will not be Ivan.
Whatever's ahead, it will be something different.
I live in Ivan.
I will not outlive Ivan.

—INGEBORG BACHMANN, TR. PHILIP BOEHM, *MALINA*

Some long-ago light is pulsating in a trout's heart
on a laboratory dish.

—FANNY HOWE, "A HYMN"

—He left before my nails grew out!

There are many ways to measure time. The closer to the body, the better.

—I want to know a man through all four seasons. That's the only way to know if I really love him.

The man you loved in Winter is not the same man in Spring.

—My corset is the only thing holding me together, she said.

Armor keeps pain out; a corset keeps pain in. The tighter she wove the laces, the more certain she was that she was real.

♥

She was out of cards, out of myths, out of love with loving, which after all had brought her here, to January 22nd, far away from Plum and Pear and every sidewalk where she had stood thinking life would go on forever that way, with the leaves falling golden all around her and her Juul crackling like a little fireplace and her famous tits bouncing, falling in love recklessly—because she could always come home again to her exes, one of whom lived in the room beside hers and the other, down the street—with some faggot or fairy girl floating by in a bubble of mysticism, just far enough above her that she believed they possessed the scroll of permission that would sanctify, at last, her own search for the angels. She'd needed their mysticism because she believed her half prairies and inchoate peach copses and patches of visionary grass weren't real until they had been grafted onto someone else's misty dells, contaminated by the holy soil of their private paradise, entangled in their honeysuckle vines; believed she wouldn't become a woman unless she strolled beneath the frozen waterfall, tumbling motionlessly into an azure pool, of their diorama of Eden, drunk on a fog of glory. And every time the levitation faded—every time she fell headlong from their bubble and back to earth—she fell into Plum's arms, until one day Plum's arms were wrapped around someone else and she simply struck the ground.

So she left and moved to Bushwick.

Where she lived alone, exiled from her own eternity, in an apartment choked with smoke and littered with blue-raspberry residue. Where the bubble was no longer as appealing, because at last she was responsible for herself, there was no one shepherding her mind into quiet pastures and beside cool waters, and reduced to herself, without having learned subsistence from her own immortal substance, without having learned to live her own story without the promise of an audience, she began to burn in nothing, began to burn alive in absolutely nothing, trusting her world only as far as the walls of her bedroom, the same walls within which nothing burned, but within which, at the very least, nothing was contained within four walls: nothing was small, nothing was only the size of a bedroom, and if she was burning at least there was the possibility of an elsewhere, whereas if she went outside, nothing was everywhere, burning the world without displacing a single atom, but surrounding every atom in a halo of zero.

Because it wasn't anymore about making myths, which was only her way of giving infatuation a mother-of-pearl gleam, a sort of inlay of time and starry necessity that concealed the haste and simplicity, the reiterative gloom of her manner of loving, sleepwalking, whatever it was—

♥

One windy Sunday morning she woke up and, to her surprise, decided to read a book! Though it should be said that it was already afternoon, one o'clock had come and gone, and immediately prior she had been drowsing in a small room, not the bedroom but the TV room, on the couch, covered in layers of blankets, turning fitfully and seeking some kind of comfort from a small decorative pillow, though she knew eventually she would have to stand up and pee.

And eventually she did.

Now she was sitting in the backyard while her kitten, who until then had been meowing and pawing at the screen door, chased after fallen leaves that scattered like mice, stalking and pouncing, leaping and rolling, then every so often, eyes closed, head aloft, pausing to experience the sun.

The woman, feeling tenderness for the kitten who had waited so patiently all morning to chase the leaves, had decided to smoke her cigarette and drink her cup of coffee on the porch and, casting about for something to do, some way to fill the dreadful emptiness of a day without plans, decided, as I said, to her surprise, to read a book—a collection of Gogol's stories, translated by the often maligned but rarely read Constance Garnett. So she read, laughing to herself, sometimes casting a sly glance to her side as if she were in the audience at the theater or watching *Real Housewives* with her ex-boyfriend, and, after twenty or thirty minutes, fully absorbed and turning the pages in a fever, looked up, just as her kitten was arriving on the porch with a large brown leaf in its mouth, and found herself experiencing her own life. And just when she realized—I'm living!—she immediately thought: who can I tell?

Because she was unaccustomed to life without witness. She had been, in her own small way, a so-called microcelebrity on Twitter. But one day, brought to her knees by the slow attrition of reality upon her fantasies, her fiction of 'Peach, the great Lover,' her back-breaking romances; one day, realizing that her 'life,' in the sense she had once imagined it—a story to be told later—was happening again, and despite differences in detail, again, according to the very same arc; realizing she was remarkable for her skill in attracting courtiers but rather unskilled at maintaining her sanity along the axis of an accelerating intimacy (cue Paul Simon's *Graceland*), she had simply deleted her account and found herself, all at once, alone.

Alone!

With all the emptiness of the world before her, an emptiness as blue as the sky and as bright as the sun. Sunny days were the worst because they exposed her to herself. At such times she cast her eyes to the sky and prayed to a holier image, a faraway woman floating among the iridescent pillars of a nebula (iridescence, she thought, was the oldest force in the universe, its most fundamental expression), the interdimensional Miss Peach Ricci, who, being half-timeless, was not so shaken by the seismographic loop-de-loops of love; not so concerned with what was coming, had no need for prophecy (her former measure of 'aptitude for life') because she trusted her heart to be honest, and her song to be sung. When she was hurt, to say so without fearful circumlocution; when she hurt someone else, to take responsibility without hesitation and honor the process of repair or separation, temporary or permanent. To no longer mythologize, that is, no longer dehumanize—out of fear that her own reality, without a supplemental invitation to a smoky dreamland, would appear paltry—every man she loved, having for so long reduced each in her personal pantheon to persecutor or savior, or in certain cases, persecutor-savior; but instead to sense "which figures," as her therapist liked to say, were, in the heat of relation, in the moment of a miscommunication, "standing behind him," that is, which figures her fears and desires were calling forth from the mists of her own past, which specters of other men were crowding around her lover, absorbed into his form like shadow-costumes and scraps of mask, blurring her perception with their gestures, their whispers and phantom blades, their voices sticking like honey to every word he spoke. That Peach, crowned by a levitating diadem of semiprecious stones, casting shadows away with the strobes of her eyes, that Peach was no victim of life; that Peach was waiting for the lower Peach, the Peach of the earth, to breathe her in, to request from her immemorial twin—not out of desperation, but having prepared, ahead of time, a dwelling-place—the gift of divine insufflation, a possession unto grace, so realizing, not herself as an angel, but the 'angel' as herself, that is, the part of herself touched by eternity. As when the lenses of binoculars click into place and what appeared to be two figures mingling in confusion reveals itself, at last, to be one figure coming into focus.

But for now she needed the angel tethered to herself by only the lightest lasso of silk—for now she needed the angel to be more eternity than Peach Ricci, because eternity was too much responsibility for a girl who was just getting used to sleeping in an empty room, so instead of deferring the responsibility to someone else, as she had often done with her ex-boyfriends, she was deferring the responsibility onto the part of herself she did not yet understand how to accept; she had abdicated her eternity to that other Peach who was watching over her from a future which, in some sense, was already happening. By time-traveling so sweetly and simply, she could hold her own hand.

♥

Her corset was her cross. It helped her not to want too much; reminded her that passion was not an idea, it was an object you carried. This one at her waist. But the difference was that a cross was public. A corset was private, the pain was because you were existing a little less. Not the humiliation which precedes grace, because that was still a lack, was still too close to desire—but existing a little less in order for zero to exist a little more. When she tightened the laces, her need was not satisfied: it was carved out by the curve of the corset, replaced by the force of whatever wasn't, hadn't been, before anything was. The same force that once kept the universe pressed into a point. 'You were never here,' she thought successfully, as she felt the pressure of zero upon her hips, her ribs, her organs. And 'never here' was its own way of existing—'never here' was God. As long as she wore the corset, God was bound to her. God was in the laces.

♥

On the phone with her mother:

—My book is coming out in two months.

Peach was a writer. Every day she wore perfume, was always running low on perfume because she sprayed it with such extravagance; she even wore it to bed, as her own kind of apotropaic, because in her sleep she needed protection too; in her sleep she was always running. Either the world was dying and she was on the lam with friends and lovers, gunning down a torn-up stretch of highway with a relentless Imperial posse on their tail; or she was alone, in New York City or New Mexico, on a strange street or in a strange field, half-aware that she was dreaming, at least in the sense that she knew she was running out of time, looking for Plum's apartment or Pear's blue house, knowing she'd never reach it, frantic with hope. She wasn't an esoteric woman. Not about the reason for things. The details were many but the desire was simple. Details happen when desire, like light, is shredded by the colorful sawteeth of a kaleidoscope. The details are arbitrary until the instant when desire makes them unbearable and real. Desire makes a revelation of happenstance.

—My book is coming out in two months, she said. Pear is long gone and the book was meant to be for him and me. I'd rather be his wife than be published. I don't know what to do with myself.

She loved beginnings. The beginnings of movies, the beginnings of relationships; dawn and dusk, too, the beginning of evening. Her mind was full of shrines to her ex-lovers. She was always laying flowers before them.

—You were never going to be married, said her mother. In fact you should've known it was over the second you told him you wanted to be his wife. You never talk like that unless there's nothing left but fumes and fantasy.

—When I'm desperate the most unlikely things suddenly seem so close at hand. *The price – is Even as the Grace –*

—You've riddled with that verse long enough. A line of poetry is not a skeleton key. *To every thing there is a season*

—But I miss him so much. And when I miss him, when I feel that awful, holy weightlessness inside me

(as if she were floating, immobile, above an abyss of blue morning air) then I feel the urgent need to write to him;

(some sense in her rose as if registering, responding to an irresistible signal, as if missing him so much were not the surfeit of her solitude but the consequence of a wavelength—some wayward angel's offhand hymn, some will-o'-wisp's pulsating glow—echoing, reverberating within her mind, displacing and deranging the soil of memory, haunting her days with the nightmare of a need).

Do you understand?

(As if the substance of their love, this resonance of silver bells, were not composed by them, but bestowed by an accident of destiny, inadvertent but irrevocable, to which both of them were, each in their particular ways, according to their particular wounds, equally susceptible, so that at the very moment she missed him most, then maybe he was missing her too, they were missing one another because a wayward angel was once again playing her silver music, scarcely audible, in a sparkling, semiprecious swamp, bubbling and popping, deep within the caverns beneath their feet, in the heart of the earth.)

At that very moment, nothing feels more necessary than writing him a letter, because at that very moment he is most likely to understand precisely what I mean . . .

—Darling, you're addicted to love.

—Who isn't?

—Most of us don't get locked up after a breakup. I don't want to see you in a psych ward again. You need to let go of Pear. Even if he did come back again, especially if he does come back again, you'll just break your own heart like you did the last time and the time before that. A fairy tale will protect you from the horror of the present but the future requires another cure. You're not Sleeping Beauty. Let go of the grand gesture, which is really nothing more than taking a flaming sword to reality. You may think, for a moment, that you've won. But spectacle is a passing magic. Reality has time on its side, reality will always win because you can't stop the clock.

—I'm worried; worried that if I allow myself to get excited about my own life and the possibilities of that life (my own life, my own days, my unmarried mornings and nunnery dusks), then I'm somehow guaranteed to make a fool of myself, to lose everything. *How public, like a frog*

—You will, eventually, one way or another. But you'd be a fool not to enjoy it just because you're going to lose it. Death doesn't care if you see it coming.

She often felt that time was running out. Or she felt the pressure of the clock, as if the pale fibers of her nervous system were being plucked, every minute and second, by its hands. Time, she felt, was the confounder of love. So that spending the evening in a lover's bed (even or maybe especially a lover who'd driven the U-Haul from Plum's place and helped her unpack her new apartment, who'd said 'I love you' on the second date, who'd said 'You're the most beautiful woman I've ever dated,' who'd said 'We're bound for life by a psychic bond,' who'd said 'I *do* still love her,' just after pledging to leave their girlfriend, who'd brought her twin quartz from Nevada and prickly pear taffy from New Mexico, who'd read a chapter of her book before every date, who'd read to her in bed from Annie Ernaux's *Simple Passion,* who'd given her the strap saying, 'Hey faggot, how does it feel to be fucked in the ass by a dyke?', the same lover, Sadie, who Peach had started dating fresh out of the psych ward, who Peach would later ask to run away with her, to take to the road and find another town and a little house and make a life with her, into whose arms a catatonic Peach would sob at the end of every date, because they were only allowed their liaisons once a week, though her lover would lie and see her, in secret, more often, and of whom Peach, playing "Wild and Blue," or "Fade into You," or "Cellophane" on repeat, would dream in future perfect, even when they were fucking), she couldn't focus, couldn't enjoy their kisses in the barroom dusk, or the warmth of their arms on a rainy night in Brooklyn, or trespassing, clandestine, giggling, on a movie set in Prospect Park, daring each other to steal a prop martini from one of the tents, taking a sip of what turned out to simply be olive juice, keeping the glass regardless as a trophy of their love—she couldn't even fuck without smoking a cigarette. She was always cold, frozen and distant from the dread of an intractable certitude, remembering that by this time tomorrow, she would be in her smoky blue-raspberry apartment, counting down the hours until their next date, alone.

(On the one occasion Peach had a date with another lover, who brought her a bouquet of nodding, fragrant flowers, their petals overbrimming a pink sheath of tissue paper, tied with a powder-blue ribbon; on that one occasion when Peach tweeted about walking along Myrtle-Broadway at sunset with a shaking bouquet of pink primroses, Sadie, who'd told her, more than once, they would not read her Twitter—such was their policy with partners—nonetheless read it anyway and having themselves bought a bouquet to give Peach on their next date, in a fit of jealous embarrassment 'threw out' their flowers, or rather 'tossed them on a horse's grave,' as they later told Peach by text and then by phone. So Peach, desperate to mistake so-called passion for salvation and refusing, therefore, to awaken to the glitchy logics of her situation, renounced all other romances.)

Near the end it had gotten so bad—it was no great surprise that her lover eventually couldn't bear the weight; no surprise that Sadie decided to retreat, to back away slowly, month by month, saying, 'I *do* still love you'—that Peach would stand in the threshold, hand on the knob, door ajar, for an hour, unable to speak, unable to look Sadie in the face, attempting to step out, attempting again and again to take the one step that would be final, attempting, frozen, dissociative, to say goodbye for now, for a few days at most, and face, alone, the burning zero of the world. Her mind would tell her to beg, but her mind would also remind her that while begging might ease her pain today, it would increase her pain tomorrow. She knew she couldn't stay, but leaving meant walking out onto Fulton Street, busy and bright, overexposed. The door trembled in her hand.

Now she had to live her life herself.

[AUSTIN, TEXAS, JANUARY 29, 2023]

CRADLE ME, LUCIFER

FOR MILKY, 2014–2022

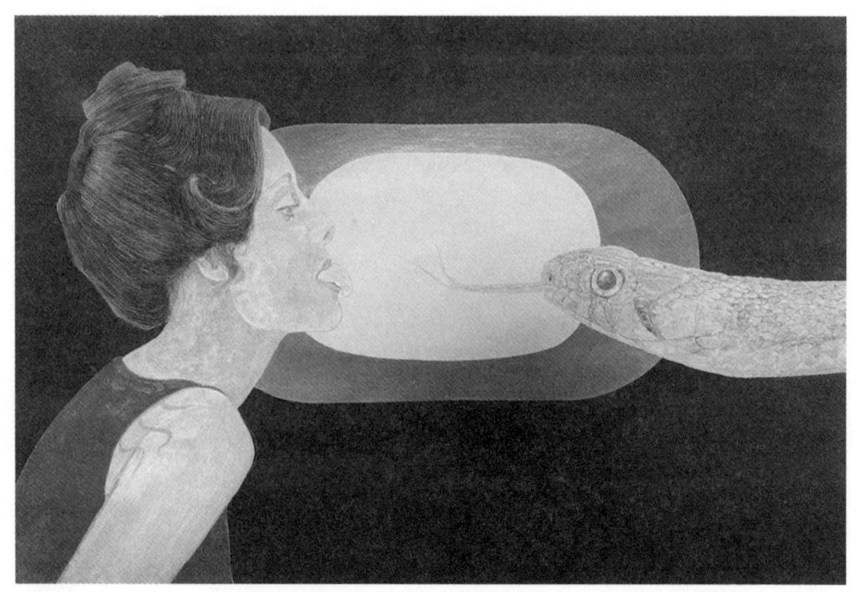

My python Milky was given to me by my ex-boyfriend Velvet, who had inherited her from his ex-partner S., who had died of a fentanyl overdose just before their thirty-day incarceration in a men's jail.

Four years earlier, Velvet and S. stopped to swim at Barton Springs while passing through Austin on a road trip. (I lived there at the time, having moved back to Texas after I was forced to leave college because of an involuntary admission to the psych ward. I often visited Barton Springs, or the creek right beside it. I did not know Velvet, would only meet him years later, in New York.) On their way out, a drunk driver crashed into their car. Both were injured, but S. required hospital care, having sustained injuries to their legs. This crash—on account of an oxycodone-flooded postsurgical convalescence, then a prescription for painkillers upon discharge from the hospital; on account of all the pain, the pain that wouldn't cease—had triggered their addiction. Velvet would revive them nine times, from nine overdoses. Nine times Velvet would save their life.

Three years later, on a benzo from their psychiatrist, and driving mysteriously west on the highway when home was east, S. crashed the car Velvet had bought for them both. No one was injured. The police charged them with something, I don't know what, know only that it led to their subsequent sentencing. After that, Velvet could no longer bear not knowing where they were, and when, and whether they were alive; could no longer bear the repercussive horror of their overdoses; could no longer bear sole responsibility for saving their life. There wouldn't be a tenth time. He left.

A few months before their death, while in rehab on a goat farm in Connecticut, S. had, after years of hesitation, scheduled an FFS consultation. But they were kicked out, and returned to New York, and because of the interstate shift in insurance coverage, were forced to cancel the consultation. On a phone call with Velvet, S. referred to themselves for the first time as a butch dyke.

♥

Milky had a heavy destiny, but her body was light.

When I first met her, S. was still alive. I never met them, but I met Velvet after I posted a personals ad through that now-defunct Instagram account for dykes and nonbinaries and all manner of transsexuals: *Fainting couch included. New to New York. Looking for partners in days and nights and daydreams.* Velvet slid into my DMs. He told me he liked silk and fancy porn, and introduced me to a Four Chambers film, "Botany," which intercut slow sensuous fucking with time-lapse footage of mushrooms bursting into spores and flowers opening to the heat; then he disappeared. But at the beginning of Autumn, he invited me to his bedroom, where a tapestry hung above his bed that read, below the image of three red roses: 'Miserable people do miserable things,' and below that: 'Society of Misery and Regret.' In the corner of the room, next to a mirror, a chameleon clung to a tree branch; atop the vanity, beside varicolored cocks and small surreal paintings of pink reclining women, a tarantula was molting; and on the nightstand, surrounded by silks and piles of books like *The Body in Pain, Poetry is so Lesbian, Revolting Prostitutes,* and *Bad Bad,* a champagne ball python flicked her pink tongue within a small stone cave. All of these animals had been raised by S. and Velvet together, but S., unable anymore to mother, had relinquished each to Velvet when Velvet said he could not sacrifice his own life to keep saving theirs. After S. died, Velvet had no choice but to keep them. Soon after, the chameleon died suddenly in the night. The tarantula, Princess, still lives with him. I've never held her. But every time I went to Velvet's apartment, I asked to see Milky, who would slither between us while we lay together under the covers.

My intimacy with Milky was bound up in my intimacy with Velvet, and deepened within the limits of our fairy circle. Like Milky, Velvet was quiet. Like Velvet, Milky communicated affection primarily through attention, presence and heat exchange. But because, with Velvet, language was technically possible, I grew afraid—I filled his silences with my own paranoia, which I nevertheless concealed from his eyes. He always seemed to be looking at me from somewhere deep underwater.

But, whether he was eating my pussy for two hours straight or sitting beside my hospital beds, he was also always there. And when I left his bed, he would text me to say that the scent of my perfume was all over his pillows. That the scent lasted for days. So by 'silences' I mean I don't remember him ever calling me beautiful, I mean he rarely said things like that to my face, sealing more oblique expressions of longing instead inside the envelope of texts and emails. He was not emotionally unavailable, but emotionally involuted. I scriptured the stories he told me about political movements and distant lovers. I approached his privacy like a postulant, with my head bowed. In love I valued language too much. Language is an aquarium for silences. A way of making silences visible. A way of trapping silences inside a diorama where everything must be explicit or not exist at all. To make an instant into an artifact before it has drawn breath, to guarantee for the future what therefore cannot exist in this instant, now:

If I'm always asking myself how you feel, I'm not feeling anything myself. But I did not know then how to experience anything besides a retrospective pleasure—a pleasure about the pleasure I should have been able to, but could not, experience. I did not know how to have a secure attachment, did not even know the phrase 'attachment style,' knew only the rhythm of the rapid-cycling premonitions of engulfment and abandonment. I did not know how to interpret heat, did not know that heat required no interpretation, that heat could bypass the flaming sword of the guardian angel of interpretation. Velvet gave me heat, most of all, and without uncertainty or hesitation. I mistook the simplicity of heat for the mystery of relation, or misconstrued the simplicity of the mystery of relation, the mystery of the simplicity of relation, as if relation were a riddle rather than an act of faith. Velvet was the limit of my moral and romantic world. I made myself his student rather than his lover, and without even telling him so. I took him for a sphinx, a wise and dangerous demigod, so much more than human that I made him, by my unspoken idolization, less—which is not to say that Velvet isn't wise or passionate or that he hasn't lived a storied life on Earth, but that I never gave him the chance to know me in my mystery, or in my simplicity. All the while, Milky slipped between my fingers.

♥

Then so much happened, and kept happening. I was knifed in the face, a cis man ripped a three-inch hole in my pussy, they gave me no pain meds at the hospital, I was drinking a lot, I started cutting again, started sewing my own wounds, started punching inanimate objects, Velvet and I were fucked over by the same guy—he loved like a gasoline leak, and apologized like a lit match. The particulars are mostly not worth mentioning because last time I mentioned them I ended up in a psych ward. And for Velvet, everything kept happening, too. It all began with S. dying, began before S. dying, and continued after.

♥

I had never held a snake in my life until the day I met Milky. She had a heavy destiny, but her body was light. She didn't ever bite me, just coiled around my wrist like I was a tree branch she'd known since the Mesozoic. Velvet loved her, but not like a love you choose, like a love which you have no choice but to accept. The love of responsibility. He had said yes for S.'s sake, and when S. died, his yes extended indefinitely.

Meanwhile I accumulated in the corners of Velvet's life. Meanwhile I was a tree swaying in the middle of his bedroom. Meanwhile I was falling in love with Milky, like a promise. And meanwhile a transmasc man-child, Mr. Believe-It-or-Not, was giving me coke and ketamine at his mother's Upper West apartment—where he'd taken me, for the first time, only after six months dating—but staying sober himself and then fucking me even though I'd brought a friend so it would be clear I didn't want to; or he was fucking me downstairs from a party he was throwing, when I said I didn't want to, when I was crying by the end, when Velvet was so close and so far away; or he was fucking me in the bathroom at a coffee shop with dirty, jagged nails snagging on my cunt, making me bleed, then posting a photo of his blood-stained Playboy button-down to Twitter, boasting about his sexual prowess, without asking me permission or telling me he'd done so. He'd said it was the responsibility of others to respect even our non-verbal cues; I didn't know how he didn't know, or if he was choosing to ignore them. Besides, near the end my cues were verbal and nothing changed. But I was too afraid to tell anyone, was afraid that, because I had so much trouble saying no—because he kept giving me gifts, so many gifts, too many gifts, I was flooded with gifts I hadn't asked for, didn't want—the responsibility for the sex that scraped at me, left me numb at home, lay with me alone. The last time I spoke to him, when I said, "You've repeatedly violated my sexual boundaries," he replied, "You make it sound like I'm an abuser."

Not to mention the high-risk mutual aid operation he'd helped start, but the maintenance of which, after a few weeks, he suddenly and unceremoniously left, on the one hand, to those it was meant to serve, and on the other, to his romantic partners—primarily Velvet's boyfriend, Ember, and Velvet—who were already organizing elsewhere, because of his *depression.* Some nights I helped out with an ex-girlfriend of mine. The situation soon deteriorated; the owners of the building—with whom Mr. Believe-It had a kind of partnership, which partnership had authorized the operation—demanded that everyone vacate.

One morning, walking home at dawn, after two years dating each other and nine months dating him, Velvet and I spoke for the first time about his abuse, which, up to that point, for fear of offending or discomfiting one another, we'd been too hesitant to mention even obliquely, because from the outside, on social media, where we glossed our own confusion as affection, everything seemed okay.

That morning our conversations snapped from the recollection of far-off stories into a present instant in which we were both implicated. We were holding hands as the sun came up. We were holding hands, so sad that neither of us had known, that we hadn't been able to protect each other—so furious because he was such a loser, a coddled Upper West mama's boy who pretended to be a leftist punk harm-reduction activist/sex work–adjacent nightlife kingpin, and he'd taken so much, so much irreparably from both of us.

That morning my intimacy with Velvet entered language. Not long after, and for the first time, late in the night, he texted me, surrounded by pink flower emojis: "I care about you so much." Not long after that, crushed beneath the weight of his own life, Velvet asked me if I would accept Milky into mine.

♥

So, for the first time, I was asked to love Milky not only as if I were a mass of boughs and leaves, but as a kind of mother. Ember and Velvet drove her over from Manhattan in an enclosure built years earlier by S. and their father. I held her in my bed all afternoon.

Milky was so quiet. Her face was small and dart-like, inlaid with tiny scales like flakes of quartz and flecks of yellow topaz—as still as a death mask, but as expressive as dusk. Her eyes were bright, round and red like cinnamon candy; her tongue as sudden as a hummingbird's wing. She moved in a kind of optical illusion, a slow, perpetual ripple of quartzite spirals accumulating a smooth and helical forward glide, almost as if she were hovering a centimeter above the floor—every so often pausing, flicking her swift pink tongue, lifting her head with slow and methodical grace like a periscope.

As the days rolled on, she slid across the blue field of my bedspread, sunbathed on the windowsill, coiled and slept in the drawer of my writing desk (making a nest among my Tarot cards, pink Taser and pepper spray, loose press-on nails, and love notes), and wrapped herself like a honeysuckle vine around one of its slim teak legs.

I signed the contract for my first book, *The Fifth Wound* (which my publisher would, unknowingly, hire S.'s childhood best friend to design) on my lunch break in the wistaria-trellised courtyard at Saraghina, where I worked drunk or high as a hostess for a season before being laid off with my coworkers when Winter came. That's when I really began to stay home, devoting myself to making porn and making breakfast, to making an altar and losing my mind, to watching and quoting *Real Housewives* with my roommate and ex-partner Noel, and, from time to time, writing the book I hadn't meant to write, the book I wrote bric-a-brac, almost absentmindedly, as if I were only writing a story that never ended. I thought it would go on forever like that, with Milky pulsing coolly around my neck, slowly wrapping herself into rest while I typed and erased, typed and erased. Sometimes her tongue tickled my earlobe. After a while—warmed to wakefulness by my blood—she'd glissade effortlessly down my arm, across my keyboard, and back into the desk drawer, and I would cease writing and seek out Noel's bedroom, to wrap myself around them while they worked.

Some nights Milky slept with me, curling up beneath the covers, between my legs. When I woke in the morning I'd find her coiled beneath my head, inside my pillowcase. Certain people have decided it's their prerogative to tell me, unprompted, that snakes can neither give nor receive love. I know, however, that all life began inside of hydrothermal heat vents at the bottom of the sea, which is to say, life began with an exchange of heat. For two living beings, an exchange of heat is an exchange of trust. Heat exchange is the most fundamental form of love. The fact is that I kept Milky warm on cold Winter nights. None of you kept her warm . . .

But I'm accustomed, like any transsexual woman, like any girl who's been locked in a psych ward or three against her will, to disbelief. Empire and its agents have always wanted me to prove something. Most of all my sanity; or more precisely, my docility and eloquence—and my womanhood; or more precisely, my beauty and my pliancy. So I've proved it again and again, thinking that if I were beautiful enough to doctors, to my father and mother and to the women in my vicinity, if I were sweet enough to the men who followed me home and intelligent enough to the psychologists who injected me with sedatives, then I might feel safe, or more precisely, at home in the world. At a rehab in Los Angeles, a woman moved into my room, became my roommate. When she heard that I'm *not like other girls,* she said, to everyone but me,

"Does he have a dick? Is he going to assault me in my sleep?"

Ball pythons are gentle and sweet, and, if you like, docile and pliant. They have no fangs; they make, except for the tiniest breaths, no sounds, and they will not wake you demanding breakfast. They eat once a week or two, and communicate their hunger by simply opening and closing their mouths. They prefer not to be played with, but, with trust, will bond with a woman, and abide with her. Most people, when I have told them about Milky, have assumed her, because she is a snake, to be dangerous. Milky was muscular and beautiful—powerful, capable of constriction. She was also extremely vulnerable.

♥

My apartment with Noel was spacious and bright, a kind of settling down. We'd chosen it together. But the Summer prior, after three years, we'd broken up, so we were living together not as lovers but as family—with the many offspring of Noel's grandmother's pilea, an enormous elephant ear, a prickly pear, our cat Loretta (a deaf and traumatized stray from my second cousin's church in West Texas; a cumulonimbus drift of cloud whose eyes were like oases in the blinding dunes of her white fur, a brilliant azure, with that ineffable turquoise glow, that mist of pulverized topaz unique to the waters of desert lagoons) and eventually, my python Milky. Loretta, reactive and easily terrified, was an immediate danger to Milky, but that was no obstacle in an apartment with two bedrooms, an office, and a back porch in the trees where Loretta could bask from dawn to dusk; she could sleep with Noel, and Milky could sleep with me or in my desk drawer. After a year or so, though, Noel could no longer bear my bleeding; could no longer bear their reluctance to leave the house for fear of me losing my mind in the few hours they were gone, and especially could not bear the night I demanded their help sewing a wound on my upper arm, because I wasn't skilled enough to sew one-handed and because our boundaries with one another were next to none—because I was begging them to keep me alive while my wounds grew longer and deeper, down into the muscle.

One morning they left. I blocked the doorway, crying and screaming, until it became clear that they were going to leave one way or another, with or without a suitcase. Fearing I was nothing without them, I told them they were nothing without me. They wept at the knife I was taking to our intimacy, at my recklessness with the delicacy of the truth—because so much of ourselves had been formed in relation to each other, and because I was spitting out our miracle like a curse. So they left without telling me where they were going, then I left and found a new apartment, because I had taken their love but I would not take their home, and they returned. After many conversations, we decided that, despite my having offered to leave her with Noel, since Loretta had lived with me first, she would go with me and Milky.

But my new apartment was much smaller; a three-bedroom with two roommates and a second cat as fitful and fearful as Loretta. I couldn't leave her in the living room unless Flora was in my friend's bedroom. So every night I had to choose, which by necessity meant mostly choosing Loretta, except on those occasions when I asked permission for Loretta to roam.

One day months later, I left Milky's enclosure open while changing her soaking dish, and she slid out without my knowledge. When I turned around, I saw her coiled with terror before Loretta, who was rearing like a horse in a lightning storm, her claws flashing, glass-sharp and transparent. She'd struck Milky, ripping two scales off the top of her head. But Milky couldn't cry. I wished she could cry. Baby, I wished you could cry so I could understand your pain . . .

In one motion I gathered her in my arms and carried her with me into my bedroom, cradling her like a Pietà, whispering,

"It's okay, baby, it's okay . . ."

Kissing her head, singing the song I'd sung, three years old in Michigan in 1996, to my teddy bear,

"Let all your worries go, I'm here with you . . ."

before returning her to her enclosure and returning myself to bed, where I spent my days, nights, and afternoons, lost, adrift, in twilight sleep.

♥

Once prior, at Noel's place, Loretta had struck Milky on the head. This wound had healed; Milky was unscathed. But my new apartment admitted less daylight, and, without a breeze, was choked with smoke. In the afternoons I sometimes took her into my bedroom to protect her from the misty day-dark. Often Loretta and Flora went wild, unless Flora was kept behind a closed door. It wasn't the right environment for Milky or Loretta, but I liked my roommates, and I wasn't making enough to live on my own. Mostly I lay in bed, burning in nothing, trying not to be sent back to the psych ward. I'd lost every significant relationship in my life that year: Noel, Velvet, Ezekiel, Marie. All my partners, half of whom were exes whose love had been restored by the premonition of apocalypse in the year 2020, who had become lovers and then exes again. That's another story, called *The Fifth Wound.* Meanwhile my new not-girlfriend was still living at their soon-to-be-ex-girlfriend's place. They would come and go. I never knew when I'd see them. I frequently listened to "Save Me" by Aimee Mann. My income dropped sharply. I wanted to be someone else, wanted to find someone whose story could swallow me. I wanted to be your audience forever, baby. The *Dao De Jing* says:

'Clay is fired to make a bowl. Empty, the bowl is useful.'

I needed to preserve any sacred substance but my own, like Simone Weil, but not for God, for you. Whoever that was.

I don't want to tell the rest of this story. But if I don't, Milky will not rest. And she deserves to rest.

♥

A few months later she got sick. Or, because she had so few ways to communicate her pain, a few months later Milky's sickness became legible to me. Her sickness was my responsibility and my failure alone. I am her mother. I was lost in the swirls of myself, dreaming of a wound as perfect and irrevocable as a Eucharist. I was trying so hard not to slice again. I was holding my breath. She was losing weight. Red splotches appeared on her lower body. At first I hoped she simply needed her enclosure deep-cleaned, a new red light and some new substrate, but I was wrong. When I lost my mind, who lived and who died?

Suddenly she began to seem eerily listless, her heavy head swaying, nodding weakly from side to side. Then drool spilled from her half-opened mouth. I was terrified. One after another, veterinary hospitals informed me that they didn't treat pythons—except for one on Long Island, with a month-long wait.

I took Milky out to the backyard of my building, so she could swim the grasses in the sun; her scales—custard and milk—glimmered with dull sweetness as she rose and sank across the lurid green sea. She raised her head to the breeze. Scanning the horizon, she flicked one pink instant of tongue. The last time she saw the sun.

♥

The next day, thank god, some sweethearted stranger told me over the phone that the Schwarzman Animal Medical Center had an emergency room and an exotics team. So I swaddled her delicately in her favorite pillowcase and placed her in a hole-stippled Tupperware box, slid the box into my pale pink tote, then headed for the J train. On the train I intermittently opened one side of the box. I felt her gentle musculature pressing up against the lid, then saw her head emerging from the pillowcase, gazing up at me.

I waited for hours at the hospital. I called Velvet. I called Noel. I called my mother. A doctor was examining her. A nurse was updating me every so often. Then she appeared and, with a *sympathetic look,* told me that the doctor who had examined her—an avian specialist—had, in the course of expressing her intestines, "according to standard procedure," handled Milky so roughly that she ripped a three-inch tear in the scales on her lower body. It was unfortunate but unavoidable, she said, as if I hadn't been handling Milky all week long without causing her so much as a scratch. She was in critical condition. She had developed sepsis, following an infection from the bacteria in Loretta's claw. The doctor recommended euthanasia.

Well, you can guess what I said. They stabilized her temporarily, then returned her to me with a fentanyl patch and some antibiotic cream. Back at home, she rubbed and chafed against the surfaces of her disinfected enclosure, pulling off her protective gauze. I saw her exposed flesh, fragile and raw and white, sliding beneath her scales. Her blood and pus covered my hands and stained my sweatpants—the ones I'd once stained with my own blood, the day I broke up with Velvet. I kept replacing the gauze, whispering, tears streaming down my face,

"It's okay baby, it's okay, I'm here with you . . ."

I texted Velvet,

"I'm not ready for her to die. There's so much I want to show her."

Velvet replied:

"What do you want to show her?"

"The ocean," I said.

The next morning I was cradling her in my arms, holding her over a tiny alabaster dish while she extended her tongue slowly into the water, so slowly, sip by sip. I love her. Milky is my best friend. I took her back to the hospital for another pain patch. Again she poked her head out of her pillowcase on the train, gazing up.

The day after, the hospital's only snake specialist arrived for her shift—so I arrived, too. At first, from the information provided her on paper, she, too, recommended euthanasia. But when I opened the Tupperware, Milky slithered out, easy and agile, onto the examination table, moving toward me, cantilevering herself into the air between us, seeking my arms. After cradling her lightly in the crook of my neck, I returned her to the table, from which she explored the room and greeted the specialist, who was so shocked by how curious and active she was that she reversed the first doctor's recommendation and offered to provide an intensive course of treatment, including an experimental surgery in which she would graft the scales of a codfish onto Milky's wound. She said she became a snake specialist because when she was a child, raising pythons, whenever one of them was sick, no one knew how to help. She always had to figure it out herself. And she did. She loved snakes. She was falling for Milky.

After a few days, Milky was improving—eating well, resorbing her lesions, healing her lacerations, no more weight loss or sloughing of scales. The specialist had found a contact for the graft and was hoping it would be donated within a week. The specialist was hopeful.

I returned to the hospital to visit. I waited in an empty exam room for hours. A nurse brought Milky to me. She was beautiful, fragile and strong. Her lower body was wrapped tightly in gauze.

"Hi baby," I said. "I love you."

I cradled her again in the crook of my neck, singing a lullaby. She rested there, moving only to flick her tongue against my earlobe. We exchanged heat. When the nurse returned and I attempted to hand her away, Milky turned back and moved up my arm, seeking my shelter. I laughed. Tears welled in my eyes.

"I love you, baby," I said. "I'll see you soon."

♥

I visited her one more time before flying to see my family in France for a few days. The snake specialist emailed me on Friday to say she would be gone until Tuesday afternoon, but had given the avian specialist and the rest of the exotics team a detailed care plan. A terror chilled my chest. Milky was all alone.

♥

On Tuesday, early in the morning, I woke suddenly from a nightmare. In the nightmare, Milky was killed.

I knew then, and already too late.

A few hours later I received a call from a nurse at the hospital.

♥

The next day, at a cathedral in Lisieux, I saw a wooden sculpture of a cross, around which a python was wrapped, inverted, tongue lolling from a loose jaw, struck down by Christ. The underside of her mouth, visible though her face was hidden, looked just like Milky's. I placed my hand there, whispering,

"You are not evil. You are blessed."

♥

When I returned to New York, Velvet and I met at the hospital. He was wearing a tiny gold earring, a golden python, soldered by Ember. He didn't blame me; said I had given her a beautiful life. This time we didn't wait long. Milky was returned to us not in a pine box, but in a gray fabric pouch with a zipper. We were walking through Manhattan with our dead python. I was asking Velvet about Milky's childhood, about her life with S. We said goodbye, and I took her home and slid her into my freezer. I didn't tell my roommates. I didn't know where else to put her. I had refused cremation but had no time to make other arrangements. (My mother has driven around for years with her brother's ashes in a Ziploc bag, waiting for the right place and time to scatter them. Call me my mother's daughter.) I had no time: I was supposed to leave for a rehab in Connecticut, where I hoped to finally get the help I'd been refusing for two years, by chance the same one to which S. had gone. My arm had also suddenly swollen to twice its size, turned purple. I couldn't lift it. Nonetheless I packed my bag and left for Metro-North, while Velvet and I texted about the best way to preserve Milky's skeleton.

(Three weeks later, I would have three surgeries: one to remove a blood clot, two feet long, beginning at my wrist and ending at my clavicle, a second to repair my vein, and a third to remove my first rib, in order to prevent the vein from being crushed again in the future. I asked for my rib to be returned to me, for religious purposes. I dried its shattered fragments in the sun. I collected a few shards in a glass vial, along with a few shards of opal. I wear it around my neck, where it rests atop the scar.)

♥

So I arrived in Connecticut.

One night, as I lay sleeping, I dreamed that I was flying over the beaches of Los Angeles with Milky around my neck. I dreamed I was showing her the ocean.

I soon discovered the rehab was not equipped to assist me with my post-surgical needs. In fact, no preparation at all had been made for my return from the hospital. I could neither stand nor lie down without assistance. I was in the sharpest pain of my life. Not long after, the therapeutic team decided it would no longer treat me; that is, until I convalesced. Having already dispensed them to me, the team said my pain medications were a threat to the sobriety of other clients. I demanded treatment. They said I was trespassing and threatened to call the cops. I relented. They dropped me off at a motel along I-95 with all my bags and a bottle of Oxy, which I flushed down the toilet just to spite them. My older sibling CJ flew in to take care of me. I howled from the pain.

Ten days later I was in California, at a life-saving rehab. Night after night, in between nightmares about one or another ex, I was dreaming of Milky's death. So I went to Petco and cradled a ball python, because, as with my many romances, I sought to deal with the pain of separation by falling in love again. Suddenly my visions shifted. Two nights in a row I dreamed of Milky coiling around another python, strangling him.

I did not go back to Petco.

Instead I began to imagine a reliquary. In France I had seen, in one cathedral after another, gilded and bejeweled boxes, the front sides of which were each a pane of glass through which I could see a saint's shinbone or forefinger, itself gilded and bejeweled, resting on a velvet pillow. These bones were holy relics. Milky's bones are holy relics. Her destiny was heavy, but her bones are light.

She is never far from me:

The other day Noel texted me the link to a Goodwill auction for a painting. In the painting, a woman in profile sticks out her tongue toward a snake, flecked with quartz and yellow topaz, also in profile, whose pink tongue is flickered out, in turn, toward her. The woman bears an uncanny resemblance to me. The snake, in turn, bears an uncanny resemblance to Milky. The painting is unsigned.

So this is my prayer for us,

that God will give us a little happiness even though we are so small; that strawberries will still grow a century from now; that I will learn to love without the mania of prophesying, because no one likes a sleepless Cassandra in the bedroom; that if dolphins have sung to one another in poetry, humans will never understand it; that when the universe begins to shrink, time will turn backward and we will love one another again; that the arid perfect instruments of pit vipers will rattle until the end of days; that somewhere, before an audience of seahorses in a blue sea cave, a mermaid still draws breath; that angels really do exist, even if God doesn't; that Lucifer is not a man, but a princess of stalagmites; that she will teach me how to echolocate opals; that Milky will never cease sending me visions; that I will see her again after I die; that I will cradle her by the sea; that S. is cradling her now.

[LOS ANGELES, CALIFORNIA, OCTOBER 16, 2022]

APPENDIX

THE REVELATION OF THE SEED

AN INTERVIEW WITH JORDAN CUTLER-TIETJEN

I.

JCT: Your work astonishes at all levels—diction, paragraph, structural subdivision—but your sentences are particularly miraculous. It feels rude to pluck one out of its context, but . . . perhaps we could start with a sentence that simultaneously rang true and confused me. 'God is a panic state,' you write in *The Fifth Wound.* What do you mean by that?

AM: I internalized at a very young age the paranoia of god. That terrified omnipresence, that need to be aware of every signal, at every moment. But when I say god I mean specifically the so-called holy trinity. The father is a gaze, a mode of what Eve Sedgwick has called *paranoid reading;* the son is the exemplary object of that gaze, the celebrity of heaven; and the spirit or ghost, who spins and twirls algorithmically inside the mind of a believer, is the trinity's panoptical coup de grâce: the voice of an internalized repression. Which is to say, the father is reverse engineered by a believer's capacity for fantasy—I mean, *faith* is the act of inventing the father. Christendom harnessed the fecundity of my imagination, it imprinted me with the symbology of the trinity, which was nothing more than a Trojan horse for an ethics of self-surveillance.

I was taught about this god at the dawn of the twenty-first century, at a time when american empire was using the specter of terrorism to proliferate state surveillance, and at the tail end of a media obsession with kidnappings. The Patriot Act and the twenty-four-hour news cycle are both, also, forms of paranoid reading, of *sapere aude* awareness, awareness heightened to a pitch of panic. These various forms of daily, manic repetition produced in me, at age five, a sense of precarity. Of course, also, femininities were beginning to speak through me; there was a destabilization of meaning from the site of gender, or more specifically, genre. I learned how to recognize this femininity at the same time as I learned to neutralize it. I began obsessively imagining my own death on the way to school. I began to question whether I loved my family, to the extent that I wouldn't allow my parents to say goodnight to me, 'because I should only say I love you if I am certain I love you, and I'm not certain I love you.' I refused them not out of petulance, but out of a sense of extreme unease—because I had realized, suddenly, though of course inarticulately, that I couldn't take anything for granted. I was terrified of flux.

So there were destabilizations on the level of self and culture, but there was also a spatial element, which was related to the confluence of whiteness and wealth. I'm thinking of what the poet Ivanna Baranova, in her book *Confirmation Bias,* unforgettably terms 'this eternal rhinestone aptitude of the white imagination,' and what Gloria Anzaldúa, in *Borderlands/La Frontera,* calls 'the aesthetic of virtuosity'—which I will return to later. In the late nineties I lived in Laguna Hills, a suburb of Los Angeles; the street in front of my house was quiet, I didn't know most of my neighbors, only the silent rows of pristine, austere homes. But behind my house, beyond the orange trees blooming in the yard, was a valley, where a pack of coyotes wandered and howled in the night. Those coyotes killed my cat, Sunshine; my parents heard her death-scream. In front, a silence of wealth; behind, a howl of nature.

Then, in 2000, I moved to Plano, a suburb of Dallas, Texas, where I lived in a prefabricated neighborhood, that is, a sudden, ahistorical event, appearing 'as if from thin air,' all at once—which, precisely because of this temporal rift, and in order to assert a sort of generalized, frantic lineage, had realized itself as a phantasmagorical, unpredictable collage of French château, English Victorian, Italian Renaissance and Spanish Revival–style McMansions. (But, paradoxically, or perhaps because of the uncanny discomfiture of choosing to embed oneself in this sort of reverse ghost town, this immense Sarduian architectural theme park, I felt in that neighborhood a much more robust sense of community. I wandered and roved with my neighbors far from parental supervision, though of course those intimacies produced their own violences.) As for the spatial incongruity: behind my house, through a small wood and across a creek named White Rock, there was a vast farm—and this farm was populated by horses. Sometimes I would journey through the woods (clambering across a pipe that, like a bridge, twenty feet high, spanned the creek, then passing by a bamboo copse and an old sky-blue refrigerator with bones inside, before slipping through a barbwire fence) to go walk among the horses. I was living at the fringe of empire's dream of itself, and so felt, half-consciously, the destabilization of that dream: the dream of 'controlled nature,' of the endless city—in a word, civilization.

Then I moved again, because my family moved every two years from state to state, for no reason other than my father's restlessness. This is by no means an enumeration of sufferings; if anything it is a constellation of affects. I am trying to make sense of an almost perpetual state of attention, and the history of a single sentence.

Later, in a more so-called 'liberal' interlude of american empire, the State decided to absorb the concept of trans people. This process of absorption, what we call 'representation,' is how the state attempts to make surveillance attractive to me, by the glittering reflection of my image in its carnival mirrors, and by legal protections. Empire considers itself the exhaustive archive of humankind; we begin to exist for empire when empire becomes aware of us. In the process of this act of 'discovery,' we are taxonomized, essentialized—caricatured. In *Poetics of Relation,* Édouard Glissant clarifies, for me, how an Enlightenment valorization of the so-called truth-seeking rational mind expresses itself structurally in the neoliberal curio cabinet of Representation. And he also provides me with a firm, ecstatic theoretical defense of the absolute necessity of the baroque, of maximalism as a vital mode of expression, expansion—depressurization of the self. He writes: 'Agree not merely to the right to difference but, carrying this further, agree also to the right to opacity that is not enclosure within an impenetrable autarchy but subsistence within an irreducible singularity.'

Because the perpetual liberal call for transparency is the 'spirit' to the 'father' of representation. Transparency means explaining myself, which means, in turn, paying attention to and responding to the ways my selfhood is predetermined by the algorithm of the state, as expressed through my interactions with other people on a daily, hourly basis, both online and on the sidewalk, in the classroom, at work, in the hospital, and so on. An obsession with understanding how I'm being seen is extremely damaging to pleasure. And also to experiencing emotions—most of my life, I've known I'm in love by the intensity of my fear that I'm not in love. It's hard to communicate the extent to which I have to understand my emotions by their opposite. Paranoia is, for me, the most direct antonym for pleasure, but also the most acute signal of its possibility; that is, the sites where I'm feeling the greatest paranoia are also the sites of the greatest possibility for it to be otherwise, in my relationships with lovers and in my relationship with my body, my book of wounds. (In *One-Way Street,* Walter Benjamin writes: 'To be happy is to be able to become aware of oneself without fright.') And of course that affects my writing, even a detail like the angels' song in "Via Crucis"—even though I write to shock my mind out of the dull loops of an obsessive-compulsive consciousness. This is why I'm so fond of the blank page. When I stop writing each morning at the first sound of birdsong, I think of my mother, who wakes every day with the birds in order to swim at a local spring. The weight of a gesture is different in water than in air. A blithe movement becomes vital. The same is true of the page—where my mind is lighter and my words are heavier. Because as I wander from room to room, or sidewalk to sidewalk, my mind aches, feels leaden, repetitive, foreclosed to wonder, always predictable and yet freshly terrified, and my words are meaningless, by which I mean they always, implosively, mean the same thing—but when I come to the page my mind is an afterthought, I chase revelations around every comma, I giggle about a scrap of song, I open the door of the smallest metaphor as if it led to an entire subterranean configuration of Eden, where flowers feed on shadow, and angels, clutching stalactites with their feet, sleep upside down . . .

Lately I've been thinking more about water, because Townes Van Zandt is a triple Pisces, because my ex-boyfriend is a Cancer, and because I'm a Scorpio sun and a Pisces rising. Before I knew any astrological particulars, I assumed Scorpio was a fire sign, since scorpions live in deserts. But I've come to understand, through conversations with my friend Ember—my ex-boyfriend's boyfriend—that in the desert, which is the most extreme absence of water, where an intense fantasy of water is inspired by its utter lack, the only place to find water is inside of highly defensive beings like cacti and scorpions. So at its most damaging, Scorpio could signify a form of self-repression, an inability to use the matter of my own visions to create, in the desert, the possibility of a garden. On the other hand, the water is present though not visible, eddying rather than flowing (a spiral rather than arrow-like force, an attunement to cycles, a carrying of the same irreducible content through one thousand and one forms), or simply still, deep, fetid: the water is opaque: *felt, not seen not heard.* My own sense is that, for Scorpio, to free these fluids means in some way to destroy oneself—means becoming the act of expression rather than the fact of a vessel. This question comes up in "Via Crucis," in terms of the two allotropes of pure carbon: 'I keep spitting out diamonds. But diamonds don't say anything because they can't break. Diamonds make a virtue of being unsayable. I'm praying to escape the palace of my glistening laughter. I'm praying for a season of graphite. Graphite destroys itself to become a word.' Becoming-word is a form of intimacy, it is the place where we exceed the clumsy maximums of our bodies—whoever 'we' happen to be. Aurora, who is speaking now, and who is the narrator of *The Fifth Wound,* and, in a parallel dimension, of "Via Crucis"—she says, 'The value of Artifice lies not only in the rejection of Truth, but in the candor of my exaggerations, the vulnerability of a grand gesture, my whole persona balanced on the narrow point of a phrase.' Becoming-word is not a retreat or an escape, it is an attunement, a refusal of panic. Panic is not only a fretting over meaning, or an overabundance of attention paid to the possibility of meaning (in gestures, coincidences, signals), but the misattribution of every signal to the same cause: some form of danger. Becoming-word is a way of trusting meaning to take care of itself, it's an investment in a few particular symbols.

So you could call this a genealogy of the sentence 'God is a panic state.'

JCT: Talking to you now, and reading your stories—you seem intent on making your subtext part of the text, part of our text. And you do that by being very clear about this interconnected web of people you're inspired by, channeling, echoing. But also with lodestar symbols—opals, feathers, cum, oh what else . . . orchids—that seem central to your subtext-as-text approach. Does that sound right?

AM: The symbols I work with are, to me, dense, irreducible. I need symbols that feel dense enough that I'll never be able to answer the question of why I adore them—why, every time I attempt to write a sentence, it ends in opals, caverns, cum, and orchids. I can tell you that opals attracted me from the beginning because of their fusion of iridescence and milk, but to say any more would be a form of conjecture which might disrupt my relationship to my own mystery, which might falsely conclude my search by stabilizing it with a definition.

Glissant often writes about order and chaos, how chaos (which could be called 'content,' or the primary matter of a poet's few symbols) keeps order in a state of perpetual shapeshift. Order could be called 'form,' or the constellation of symbols in a given story, which arrange and rearrange themselves on a wholly different timescale than that of the narrative, dictated as it is by a grammar of linear time—the timescale of symbols is one of ritual. Symbols are, for me, an attempt to create a kind of order that is not superimposed and violent but responds to the needs and generosities of the instant.

Let me specify: I don't write standalone metaphors. Standalone metaphors are nothing more than beautiful or surreal attempts at explanation. Symbols don't explain; they are a way of inviting the mystery of myself into a sentence. Of suggesting the possibility of another logic, within and against the forward temporal force of narrative. Of realizing an immanence of vision, *that sense of water swift and peaceful above secret places, felt, not seen not heard,* within the realm of the fabricated-real—within a story made of possible facts (realist fiction as a conservative form of 'what could have happened'). Because both the fact-language and the fantasy-language are modes of language, both the story and the symbol are made of words. Whereas the relation of lived-reality to dream-reality is often described as a unidirectional stream of influence: the matter of lived-reality is absorbed and manipulated in dreams, the so-called real-world therefore makes the dream possible, while the dream, being purely subjective, purely unreal, has no effect on the matter of the world, whether or not the dreamer is inspired to act according to its lurid and nonsensically intimate disclosures.

This is false, I think; and becoming-word allows me to re-naturalize the particular symbiosis of fact and fantasy which subtends any possibility of an unsexing. Unsexing is what happens when I as a transsexual am understood not as basically a man or a woman, but as a particular affect in a particular instant—the affect does not refer back to a stabilized state of sex, but creates an instantaneous atmosphere.

Which is to say: unsexing is a way of never arriving. Which might explain the prevalence, in my writing, of kaleidoscopes. Clarice Lispector writes: ‘Eu sou antes, eu sou quase, eu sou nunca. E tudo isso ganhei ao deixar de te amar,’ or, in Stefan Tobler’s translation, ‘I am before, I am almost, I am never. And all of this I won when I stopped loving you.’ The proximity of *almost* and *never,* this is the space where paradise flashes and vanishes like a firefly: so Borges writes, ‘esta inminencia de una revelación, que no se produce, es, quizá, el hecho estético,’ or ‘this imminence of a revelation that does not arrive, is, perhaps, the aesthetic fact.’ The aesthetic fact is precisely this space of language where fact and fantasy are entangled in the manner of a Gordian knot.

Never-arriving means always-becoming, and also always-returning. Always-returning is the splendor of iteration—of ritual. Ouroboros. Which reminds me of one verse in a Wang Wei poem, whose title I might translate as “Floating on the Han River with a Far-Off Gaze”: 《山色有无中》 or: ‘Color of the mountain: between Being and Non-being.’

But obviously the original is so much more elegant I want to scream. I’ll just say this: scorpions are fluorescent. Under ultraviolet light, they glow turquoise.

II.

JCT: Can you share more about 'the particular symbiosis of fact and fantasy' subtending—what a word!—subtending your unsexing, propelling your always-becoming? For a story like *The Fifth Wound,* how much does the distinction between fiction and nonfiction matter to you, both in your writing of it and in its reception?

AM: Empire, of course, also shapeshifts—empire changes form to better convince us of its inevitability, or to convince us that reinvesting in its structures of violence will save us and give us what we dream of. Empire is an engine of extraction; vision is a space of relation. And when I say vision, I mean the particular equation of symbols within a given story—as well as, on a broader scale, their flow of form between stories. When I say vision I mean neither fiction nor nonfiction, neither myth nor memoir, neither poetry nor prose nor theory—I mean the genre of entanglement, the genre of relation, which antedates the publishing industry's genre-taxonomies. When I say vision, I mean what Rachel Rabbit White refers to as the 'literary traditions' we invent while playfully texting our lovers—what Woolf calls 'a little language such as lovers use.'

So if (and now I'm thinking of Glissant again, who writes in his first book, *Sun of Consciousness,* 'I call generosity . . . the attempt at reconquest of all the expanses of sensibility that were abandoned to the escalation of melodramas, of "classical" salons, or advertisements,' and 'Today, the general character of occidental art . . . is absence of community . . . absence of a collective dimension of the literary thing'), if I were to speak in terms of a web of affinities—and I must always speak in such terms, because the major publishers of the fiction industry are always attempting to erase the fundamentally communal force of every single sentence, and replace it with the flash of the never-before-seen; and because literary agents are always talking about how much they love 'their' authors, but the fact is that they can't ever truly love any of their authors because the primary function of their relationship to a book from the beginning is one of capital—in terms of affinities nourishing my inquiry into Vision, my aspiration would be to exalt, and/or to become entangled with, and/or to resist and argue with, in no particular order other than my gaze drifting over my bookshelf:

—*Poetics of Relation* and *Sun of Consciousness* by Édouard Glissant

—*Água Viva* and *Soulstorm* by Clarice Lispector

—*Another Country* by James Baldwin

—*The Pillow Book* of Sei Shōnagon

—*Cobra* and *From Cuba with a Song* by Severo Sarduy

—*Porn Carnival* by Rachel Rabbit White

—*The Waves* and *Between the Acts* by Virginia Woolf

—*Other Inquisitions* by J. L. Borges

—*Counternarratives* by John Keene

The work of contemporary fiction that has most illuminated and influenced my sense of possibility within a baroque historico-speculative vision: both in its rigorous yet protean structure, and within, between and interrupting the lines of individual novellas such as *Gloss, or the Strange History of Our Lady of the Sorrows,* Keene engages the pleasures and liberatory urgencies of form, imagining queer Blackness within, between, against and in excess of the 'facts' of the archive. If I hadn't read it I wouldn't have known to begin to conceive of *Unsex Me Here.*

—*The Arcades Project* by Walter Benjamin

His earlier, more immature, condensed, and whimsical vision-experiment *One-Way Street* is an obvious and direct descendant of *The Pillow Book;* aside from prudish, soft-boy misogyny, I don't know why he wouldn't mention it. Shōnagon had been translated into German a few decades prior.

—*Dictee* by Theresa Hak Kyung Cha

—*Divers* by Joanna Newsom
—*The Book of Disquiet* by Fernando Pessoa
—*Seiobo There Below* by László Krasznahorkai
—The "earth-body works" of Ana Mendieta
—*The Faggots and Their Friends Between Revolutions* by Larry Mitchell
—The shapeshifting self-mythologies of Townes Van Zandt
Live performances and interviews, as well as retellings by other musicians. The best is the 2004 documentary *Be Here to Love Me,* which is available for free on YouTube; it includes interviews with high-profile musicians like Willie and Kris Kristofferson, as well as Townes' wives and kids. On YouTube there's also a video clip in which he discusses the inception of his song "If I Needed You," which he says appeared to him, whole, in a dream—a dream in which he was a folk singer.
—*Kiss of the Spider Woman* by Manuel Puig
—*The OA* created by Zal Batmanglij and Brit Marling (TV show)
—husk project and *cry rings* by CJ Mattia (performances)
—*If Not, Winter* by Sappho and Anne Carson
—*No New Theories* by Kameelah Janan Rasheed

(In terms of resisting and arguing with: transphobia in Sarduy and Puig, anti-Black exoticizing racism in Lispector, orientalism in Sarduy—which has been written about and argued extensively—empire-nostalgia and a subtle kind of transphobia in Woolf, whorephobia in Benjamin, and classism in Woolf and Shōnagon, all of which are, of course, intimately related.)

As for books I am currently reading—I am trying to give a sense of process, an evidence that I am speaking not in posthumous time, but right now, Sunday at 3 a.m.

(Loretta, my cat, is nested in my new yellow quilt, I have no pairs of clean underwear left so I'm wearing leftover mesh shorts from a recent stay in the hospital, my ex Noel is sleeping in the room next to mine, we watched three episodes of *Grey's Anatomy* tonight, which doesn't get enough credit for its rigorous sentimental inquiries into trauma and time, there's a slice of leftover pizza in the fridge I'm promising myself before bed, my ex-girlfriend Marie who lives nearby is sending me memes, my ex-boyfriend Ezekiel sent me a photo from his diary yesterday, I realized I was using my pink Taser, the one my ex-boyfriend Velvet bought me after I was knifed, as a bookmark.)

—books which are already rearranging my relationship to grammar, time, and vision, but into which I have not yet deepened over a period of months or years:

—*Mucus in My Pineal Gland* by Juliana Huxtable
—*Malina* by Ingeborg Bachmann
—*A Girl's Story* by Annie Ernaux
—*Borderlands/La Frontera* by Gloria Anzaldúa
—*Napkin* by Carta Monir

And then there's the question of W. G. Sebald, whose reputation far outpaces his rubble of embarrassingly pastiched attempts at nineteenth-century prose. Take *The Rings of Saturn* for example. Some of the historical sections, though they seem to allow for ambiguity, because he's always inserting ostensible hesitations like 'though we do not know what precisely happened when . . .' or 'we cannot say what he was thinking when . . .' are actually written according to a very programmatic and myopic logic, so maybe it's just that he's so digestible, while appearing, through little syntactical manipulations, to be very elliptical, impartially tender, and discerning.

Virginia Woolf is a complicated case; she achieved Vision not only in the two symbol-tessellating hypercube organisms of *Mrs. Dalloway* and *To the Lighthouse,* but also, and even more so, after: first with what she called her playpoem, *The Waves,* which, by the way, often and without direct attribution quotes other poets whose phrases rise and fall like autumn leaves or silver minnows within the element—as insubstantial as a gust of wind, as persuasive and suffocating as a whirlpool of water—of her sound, which I feel as strongly and unanimously as a season; and later with *Between the Acts,* equally absorbent and almost fungal, like a book decomposing into the roots of honey mushrooms. Between these two books, for five years, she attempted and was defeated by *The Pargiters,* a book with explicitly political intentions that later bifurcated into *Three Guineas* and *The Years,* but which was initially to oscillate, chapter by chapter, between essay and fiction. I'm fascinated by this failure and have been for a long time, but all I will say is that I generally hate her essays, which are steeped in a kind of airless classicism that I think is probably the shadow of her father hanging over her imagination. Reading her essays make me want to never read her again, and that includes *A Room of One's Own.* Meanwhile her novels temper and argue with that same musty quality; you can feel her thrashing, her works are thrashing against themselves, against their own forms—and *The Waves* is one of my three favorite books, everyone I've ever loved has read it; Jinny's passage about the stag has haunted my own imagination for years, in fact it's the reason for the sort of deer epithet attached, in *The Fifth Wound,* to the character Ezekiel, who was born from the myth I made of my ex-boyfriend in the course of our love five years ago. He has read parts of *The Fifth Wound* and his thoughts on it have altered the course of its composition; I had intended to write it in his absence—it was about the myth that burst through the space of his absence, as blood bursts from a wound—but because of his presence, as well as other unforeseen events in my recent life, my writing is pressing up against the present instant. It is happening.

And that is all the better for Vision. My last word for now on "Via Crucis" is that it takes its form from *To the Lighthouse;* the sentence of Legion's death is exactly the same as that of Mrs. Ramsay's. And my last word on Woolf for now is that *The Years* contains one of the most intoxicating and oracular metaphors she ever wrote: '. . . the walloping Oxford bells, turning over and over like slow porpoises in a sea of oil . . .' It's all there. The fatal spell of time made music. Oil spills. Taxonomy. Margaret Howe Lovatt and the suicidal dolphin who loved her.

So to answer your question about the distinction between fiction and nonfiction, which I suppose is also a way of asking why, given a choice between the frames of poetry, fiction, and nonfiction, have I chosen fiction? I've always felt at odds with the conservatism of spaces devoted to the genre, a conservatism so extreme that I'm embarrassed to talk to poets about it, to appear as parochial as fiction insofar as it is maintained and promulgated by writing seminars, MFA programs, and the apparatus of major publishing. But I write fiction because I've always felt at odds with it. In one sense it's as simple as: every action has an equal and opposite reaction. Whatever I'm most interested in, I tend to place myself inside of its opposite. Maybe I look for something that's going to press on me very hard, so that my utterances—reacting to that pressure—will be extreme and elaborate, because I am guided by the image of the scorpion, or because otherwise I will feel too fatigued to speak at all, or because, having learned to respond to desire (both for intimacy with others and for the elaboration of myself) not by seeking its expression in pleasure, but by persistent attempts—having been taught to experience pleasure as a threat—to extinguish it: I seek an experience of genre that replicates my experience of gender. I choose fiction because the basic unit of fiction tends to be the sentence, whereas the basic unit of poetry tends to be the phrase, what they call the line. But unlike the poetic phrase, the sentence is almost always asked to be grammatical, and what is asked to be grammatical is asked to be durational, and therefore to have a linear relationship to time. Obviously I want to time travel—like anyone. More specifically, I want to access the fifth dimension. Placing myself at the opposite of the ability to do that forces me to think intensely and intricately about how I can defeat linear time. I believe I remember a former professor of mine, the poet Trace Peterson, once saying that trans women are already excessive to reality. There would be no point in attempting to make myself real by writing a memoir, because I would only then become real according to empire, which is the most depleted dream. So I'll remain unreal. I don't mind spending time with the Sphinx and the Siren. Someone in a workshop once said of my writing: 'this doesn't feel like a character, this feels like a way of seeing,' which was intended as a criticism but was actually one of the greatest reliefs of my eight years in fiction workshops. Beyond any question of genre, what I want to write is a way of seeing.

But all this sounds so final. I have always—before I even wrote a single word—thought of my writing, my drafts, my letters and marginalia and ephemera, in terms of the archive to which I will be, in death, reduced; maybe this is because I'm jealous of anyone who will be able to see my life from a distance, and all at once, while I'm stuck in time and my own unknowing. I have an idea for a story about a green iridescent horse—this story would not fold kaleidoscopes into itself, but would be, itself, a kaleidoscope. I have an idea for a story about the song Townes Van Zandt was planning to write around the time of his death, a song about a gay man dying of AIDS which Townes never wrote because he himself died, but which he mentioned, once and only once, in an interview. I have an idea for a story about a transsexual astronaut making a solitary mission to Planet Nine, telling stories to a video logbook; a sort of Scheherazade facing a void instead of a blade. I am haunted and intoxicated by the thought of a planet five times the size of Earth, circling the sun unknown, unseen, hardly even felt by us, nothing more than the faint possibility of a gravitational tremor. I am haunted and intoxicated just the same by a poem in Susan Howe's collection *Debths,* which she intended to be her last collection but which she has followed with another now: the poem is a xerox of Susan's thumbprint, near the outer edge of an otherwise blank page—as if it were about to drift out of view. As if I had caught it passing by in the corner of my telescope.

Ezekiel and I were always talking about how some fairy would one day study our emails, our text messages, would biographize our relationship. This was playful, of course, but also fretful—like we could only really preserve our love in an archive. Like we needed to mythologize it because living it was overwhelming, almost debilitating, certainly not sustainable. We planned to be like Vita and Virginia, but if both of them were equally visionary writers.

JCT: The shade. Incredible. That's the prescience, the premonition, that's present in your work as well. I see it happening for you.

III.

JCT: You've shared some of the rejections on Instagram, some of the more outrageous, condescending ones—'Sure you're brilliant, but . . .'—written by, well, probably men, who think they get it. One thing that I think is really special about your work is that it doesn't pretend at effortlessness. There's a sense of swinging for the fences, giving it your all, an ever-present energy. And that feels related to the question of the challenge of writing: to keep writing, to write with such force. And maybe that relates to what you said earlier, about repression, being pressed upon, pressing back with equal and opposite force.

AM: A few weeks ago Ezekiel and I were talking about minimalism, because he was calling Emily Dickinson a minimalist. But then we got into it more, and I was like, well she's just a maximalist of few words, because every word she chooses is so outrageous. When I say minimalism I mean a piece of writing that attempts to conceal any sense of effort, any evidence of having been worked on. Whereas maximalism . . .

JCT: . . . seems like it also has to do with camp, which always involves work, and queerness, and making your own sense of beauty.

AM: Maximalism is, for me, a way of calling attention to the seam. 'Error is the trace of a soul.' That's a sentence I use in *The Fifth Wound,* almost humbly because it seems, concluding in a dusty little cipher, sentimental. It's the only time I can remember using that word. I could have just as easily written 'Error is the trace of presence,' by which I mean the evidence of a given choice in a given instant, made by a given mind or hand, which in a pristine work, in a definitive text, would be invisible. But I said *soul* because I wanted you to know that I am not a text, that in my dreams I often have wings, I have felt the wind in my feathers, and that I will never be posthumous, I make the same mistake every time you read the sentence, because forever and always, just for one moment, I am using the word *soul.* I am making the grand gesture with a smile on my face, not with a wink, there is no distance between my lips and the page, my words are the spittle the dreamer drools on the pillow, so forget destiny or predestination—that is, forget the buried bone of intention—and cleave to misreading, contingency, precarity of meaning, as the measure of my writing. I am giving myself to you as an instant of opacity—soul is an empty symbol. But it is also an instant of irresolution, because I am showing you that it means something to me, without telling you what in particular. If I were to tell you what I mean by soul, there would be nothing left but for you to agree or disagree; knowing is nothing more than a dead hummingbird. What I want to give you is 'a route of evanescence,' which is how Emily Dickinson describes a hummingbird flying by. A stray comma, a sudden cipher, the lipstick trace left on the napkin—a wound is a portal. A symbol is a sort of wound in a realist sentence: I am no longer telling you the story of my body, I am inviting you into my blood. Not a fireside chat, but the heat and pressure of a deep-sea vent. The same is true of what Sarduy calls a syntactical zigzag; the deferral, within the length of a sentence, of the so-called 'direct object' of a given noun, by the proliferation of dependent clauses—and in the midst of that proliferation, the noun both hovers above the clauses, waiting for its bride, and accumulates, on its way to that marital stabilization of meaning, so much lurid rubble of an 'accidental' or 'inadvertent' meaning from the perpetual interruption of scraps of *overheard* music: the songs of a 'species of eyeless skull-dwelling spirits whose echolocating astral howls sometimes scramble and restructure my inner monologues such that every thought, rather than performing a fearful recursion of the last, briefly assumes the flavor of a revelation as bright and unrecoverable as a blue star dissolving in a kaleidoscope's rainbow abyss . . .' In addition to zigzags, there are purposeful cave-ins in some of my sentences. Little precious moments of me pretending at or performing my inability to complete a sentence according to plan. Wounding my own sentences, syntactically. Sometimes, with some of my questions, playing at a kind of naivete, an extreme suspension of disbelief, a refusal of the knowledge of what is and isn't possible.

JCT: I remember those moments often coinciding with direct addresses to the 'you.'

AM: Yes—but these are not only invitations or seductions. In *Borderlands/La Frontera,* Gloria Anzaldúa writes, 'art typical of Western European cultures, attempts to manage the energies of its own internal system such as conflicts, harmonies, resolutions, and balances. . . . It is dedicated to the validation of itself. Its task is to move humans by means of achieving mastery in content, technique, feeling. Western art is always whole and always "in power." It is individual (not communal).' Cave-ins are also my refusals to be whole, to claim an omnipresence or harmony of intention, refusal of the limiting or balancing effect of virtuosity. So I inscribe intervals of anesthesia, of the absence of awareness of my intention; every so often, I write a phrase without a specific meaning in mind, I let my meaning get ahead of itself—in order to invite the communal force of my library to speak, through me, its effects on me, without my interpreting those effects according to the fancies and standardizations of my own diction; this is a way of allowing the inherited music of other songs and stories to vibrate their riffs and symbols within my own, a sort of ego death like the night I spent in the arms of a friend who held me as I felt the tissue of self between my memories dissolve, until all that was left were the memories without a self to organize or give them form. The nurse at the hospital recorded my heart rate at over 200 bpm. When I asked her what was happening, she said, 'You did drugs.' My friend and I were in love then, but I couldn't accept it because I had only just begun 'to live as a gay man,' and I thought I would betray that, somehow, by being with a woman. It turns out I just hadn't elaborated myself enough yet.

Elaborating myself further, let me say that if I write a virtuosic sentence, or scene, or image, I need to express, at the same time, why that doesn't save me, or why I can't give that away cleanly. Because I think if I portray something especially pristinely, that then gives the reader license to treat it as a vessel for themselves, for their own catharsis. So I repurpose the unjust fate of the Danaïdes; I create cracks or fissures, so when the fluid of a reader's feeling tries to fill my vessel with itself, it won't hold them, the fluid spills back out again. I don't want to allow someone to feel like they've really empathized with a fairy's pain and therefore they've absolved themselves, they've done some sort of political work, some cleansing of the conscience. When Aurora says, near the end of "Via Crucis," 'Why speak when all you can do is bring pity upon your little fairy life? Why speak when everyone hears you only in a general way? Waiting meanwhile for someone whose ears are tuned to that perfect pitch at which your secrets sound like revelations,' that's a little moment of me saying to anyone who isn't a fairy: don't you dare only use this for your own purposes. But it's also a moment of me asking certain other fairies: do you hear me? I'm trying to create presence. That's why I'm always returning to the polyvalent 'you,' which is extremely specific and also so spacious: if I and my reader, if in the dimension of my story we've both created an illusion of presence for ourselves, then that presence has been made. Presence is what I learned most acutely from Clarice, it's maybe her greatest gift to me. She'll end a paragraph in *Água Viva* saying, 'Agora vou interromper para acender um cigarro. Talvez volte à máquina ou talvez pare por aqui mesmo,' or: 'Now I'm going to light a cigarette. Perhaps I'll go back to the typewriter or perhaps I'll stop right here forever.' She's a Sagittarius, after all; the half-resigned ember of a petulant flame. But she's also calling our attention to the wound of the present instant, because the present is always an abyss, it's right up against the edge of time. The clock is a nest of sutures. After I was knifed my surgeon sutured my face with a running whipstitch, Cristina Yang's favorite, and after a more recent unexpected injury which, because its particular qualities demand a highly intentional framing of symbology, duration and logic, I do not want to discuss except in the form of *The Fifth Wound,* the surgeon used another stitch, whose form I cannot read because it is inside of me; but when I sutured my own wound earlier this Summer, with green thread, a yellow Bic lighter, and a sewing needle, I used an interrupted stitch. On the page there is a bar of blank space, then another block of text begins: 'I came back.'

'Voltei.' That's what waking up from anesthesia feels like, what anesthesia has felt like every one of the times I've been 'under,' three of which were in the last six months. I walked away from the page. But like Clarice, I came back. Because of her I've begun to think of time in terms of a page in a book. 'Por que é que as coisas um instante antes de acontecerem parecem já ter acontecido? É uma questão de simultaneidade de tempo,' she writes. 'Why is it that things an instant before they happen already seem to have happened? It's because of the simultaneity of time.' The signals are all available to us, there are just too many to read: so while we may have a sense of an oncoming event, we often don't give it our attention until after it happens, just as when we are reading a sentence in a book and our minds absorb some stray, alluring word from lower down the page, which we have seen, in some flick of a glance even smaller than an instant, without even noticing it. I'm not interested in being a prophet, who anyway only sees the future, but doesn't invent it. If I want to capture the future, then I want a future not separate and motionless, but happening right now, just before it happens, in pulses, sparks, and sudden trills of sound: I'm interested in evidence of the infinitesimal movement of time—presence is realized when a text refuses to speak from the perspective of a tombstone; when in each present instant of each phrase, a text remains incomplete, unstable, amused, afraid and curious about itself. This means it has a sense of its own future, but no certainty. The last sentence of *Água Viva* is this: 'O que te escrevo continua e estou enfeitiçada.' Or: 'What I am writing to you goes on and I am bewitched.'

That is the fifth, silent epigraph of "Via Crucis." My editor at *Zoetrope*—Michael Ray—wanted to cut the four epigraphs and this was a really wonderful experience for me, because he's a brilliant editor and because I got to write a three-thousand-word email in response to his edits, a sort of mini-monograph on 'my' syntax, which really just meant talking about the syntax of all the writers I love most, many of whom I haven't mentioned in this interview. Most of all I was thanking him for his keen ear and sometimes explaining the intentional breakages, the places I had bruised or stabbed or inverted or collapsed some sentence or structure of grammar. I was inviting him to see the ruins of the text, inviting him to interpret them not as failures of architecture, but as Sapphic gaps. I said in my notes, 'Elegance is an extremely powerful effect which limits others; it can create obliqueness where I want to be direct, or directness where I want to be oblique. Deliberately in this piece I inscribed a number of what could be called infelicities . . .' But he said that the epigraphs don't do anything to elevate the reader, or something like that. What I said to him was, the revelation of the seed precedes the revelation of the plant. To me the four epigraphs form a single idea—a dense seed about an experience that is ecstatic, but when you aren't able to break it open, to make more experiences from it, when it forms no constellation, it becomes a torture. I had this one professor who wanted me to cut the ending to "Via Crucis," the final return to present tense. And I said, that would be giving it away, that would be an emergency exit, like the pilot who is ejected from the falling plane and is suddenly drifting gently through a blue shock of sky; but the story is the plane, and it's going to take you down with it, into the canopy, into the tangle of branches. The ending offers the sensation of branches catching your fall, but which branches, what tree, and in what forest? You're lost, you are nowhere, and you're forty feet off the ground. Because the story, the story of this absolutely unrepeatable and life-changing experience, didn't lead to more stories, to greater mysticisms, for Aurora. The story is stuck inside a narrator who isn't able to move past it or connect it to anything else. She's still stuck there.

The third epigraph of "Via Crucis" warns: '. . . you just get stopped up with whatever it was that ruined you and you make it happen over and over again and your life has—ceased, really,' which is a part of a line of dialogue spoken by a character in *Another Country,* a novel by James Baldwin. But while *Another Country* is a 'novel,' something in its structure seems to have on its mind a different mode of reading, and a different mode of knowing, than novels usually demand. That book has been criticized for its flightiness, its driftiness, its hummingbirding—for offering intense, brief flashes of intimacy that make contact with each other, that change and are changed by each other, but do not resolve or complete each other, do not 'add up' to a finished story. The novel, as the reader is first meant to conceive of it, ends abruptly on page 88; that is, the character Rufus, whose gaze is its absolute center of gravity, dies (by suicide) at a moment that feels not so much emotionally as narratively sudden, like we've unwittingly been reading the final chapters of a novel to which the first 150 pages are missing. So when we reach the end of Rufus' life, but more chapters follow, our conception of the story yet to unfold is utterly destabilized. The novel feels as volatile, as unpredictable as if it were happening as we read it.

We never really see Rufus again, never experience him as a gaze, even in memory; we only *glimpse* him, in the impressions, the half memories, never more than a sentence or two, of those who knew him. But if *Another Country*'s first chapters are an ending, its last chapter is a beginning: not only the story of an arrival we do not see, because the novel ends on its cusp, as Yves, having left Paris, the city of his mother, his birth, his entire life, prepares to exit a plane in New York City, but also the first appearance, in these last few pages, of Yves' gaze, the gaze of a person who never knew, never even saw Rufus—which is to say, the beginning of another novel.

Between that beginning-ending and ending-beginning, every time we think we are about to arrive in the certitude of a narrative (that of Vivaldo, Clarissa, Ida, or Eric) the novel shapeshifts, reframes, resets. We are shown the final days of Eric's years abroad in France, without ever acquiring a sense of his life there with Yves, of the languorous doldrums of daily passion. We feel only the texture of its swift dissolution into twilight. On the other hand, without bearing witness to the thrill of its inception, we are sunk in the fitful murky midst of Vivaldo's work on a novel, which never deepens into an encrypted map of *Another Country,* but remains stuck, shiftless—muddy as a mumble. Meanwhile we are swept up by the beginning of Ida's singing career, the reverberation, within her voice, of what Baldwin describes as 'a quality so mysteriously and implacably egocentric that no one has ever been able to name it. This quality involves a sense of the self so profound and so powerful that it does not so much leap barriers as reduce them to atoms—while still leaving them standing, mightily, where they were.' But we do not see, as in the Künstlerroman, the full luster of her artistry; only its first breathtaking apparitions, its first cataclysmic contact with the possibility of fame. In this way Baldwin never allows us to think of *Another Country* as a complete, discrete object, as a definitive text, but instead as an atmosphere—as an overlapping of multiple, irresolvable timescales. These timescales, sharing a space more than a narrative, come into contact through aporias of power, erupting at intersections of anti-Black racism, homophobia and misogyny, revealed in moments of proximity: at a party or a funeral, in the bedroom or on a stage.

So I read *Another Country* as an intentional whirlwind, a 'city novel' formed from interior and exterior montage. But beyond simply representing the fact of montage as a condition of urban modernity, Baldwin uses it to reveal the particular ways in which marginalizations, forms of privilege, and particularities of personhood complicate each character's relationship to time; that is, by refusing to line up and elongate the segments of each character's narrative arc so that they rise and crest and fall in parallel (or in exact inverse, as in, say, *Anna Karenina*), the novel refuses to *universalize* time. For me, then, *Another Country* is the portal, not to 'another time,' but to the sensation of *times,* happening, always, right now. When I hold that book in my hands, I think of the carapace of a scorpion, within which waters swirl like a second pulse.

IV.

JCT: A very banal question that stuck in my mind, rewinding a bit, as you were talking about moments of rupture, moments of deceleration: Do those happen on first write-through? On the first edit? What does the editing process look like for you?

AM: Sei Shōnagon ends her *Pillow Book* by telling the story of its origin:

> It is getting so dark that I can scarcely go on writing; and my brush is all worn out. Yet I should like to add a few things before I end.
>
> I wrote these notes at home, when I had a good deal of time to myself and thought no one would notice what I was doing. . . . But now it has become public, which is the last thing I expected.
>
> One day Lord Korechika, the Minister of the Centre, brought the Empress a bundle of notebooks. 'What shall we do with them?' Her Majesty asked me. 'The Emperor has already made arrangements for copying the "Records of the Historian."'
>
> 'Let me make them into a pillow,' I said.
>
> 'Very well,' said Her Majesty. 'You may have them.'
>
> I now had a vast quantity of paper at my disposal, and I set about filling the notebooks with odd facts, stories from the past, and all sorts of other things, often including the most trivial material . . . poems and observations on trees and plants, birds and insects. . . . After all, it is written entirely for my own amusement. . . . Readers have declared, however, that I can be proud of my work.

This is more than humility and more than careful withholding; more, too, than an unjust abdication of ethical responsibility, though it is all of those things: it is a destabilization, the story of an error, an intentional ruin which, like Gaudí's *La Sagrada Familia,* is happening within its own eternity of incompletion. *The Pillow Book,* like *Água Viva, Poetics of Relation,* and hopefully *The Fifth Wound,* never arrives. As Borges writes, 'El concepto de texto definitivo no corresponde sino a la religion o al cansancio,' or 'The concept of the "definitive text" corresponds only to religion or to exhaustion.' The reason we cannot read any more of it at this moment is only because Sei Shōnagon has temporarily run out of ink. The eternity of incompletion is, I think, what Glissant suggests when he writes: 'Poets cease forthwith to consider a single poem, good or bad, to establish themselves on the contrary in a sort of duration.' Completion is only possible if a text is supposed to be singular, if it begins and ends with the inflections of its most local author. But at a slightly further distance are all the voices of that author's library, by which I mean the proliferating, interpenetrating web of voices meeting briefly, at a point, which is a given poem by a given author at a given time. And further still is the language in which the author writes, and furthest of all is language itself, which is not, of course, a way of deferring local intention or responsibility, but a way of illuminating degrees of relation. The question of 'at which point' the voices meet—this is the sum of an author's intentions, accidents, absorptions, and irreducibilities of time and place.

The piecemeal, word-of-mouth dispersal of her work, the chaotic errance of its publication, enables Shōnagon to comment on the reception of her book in the book's very pages, as if it were aware of being read, as if it were observing, absorbing the reactions of its readers. Having *established myself in a duration,* that is, having thought of my writing from the beginning not in terms of pieces, poems, stories, but in terms of a biome in excess of the

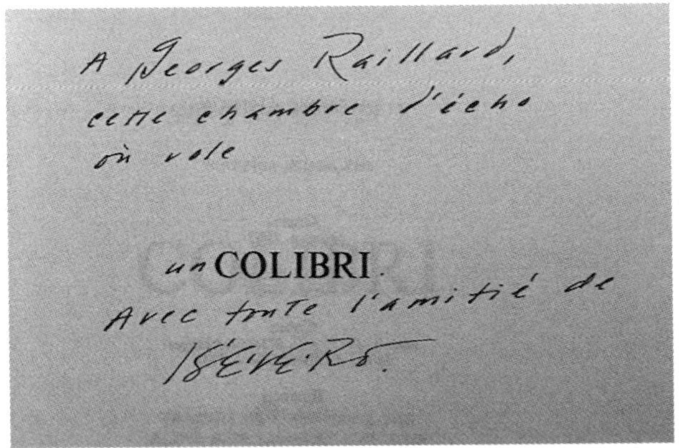
A Georges Raillard,
cette chambre d'echo
où vole
un COLIBRI.
Avec toute l'amitié de
SEVERO.

Borgesian map (cf. "On Exactitude in Science") and in relation to the Faulknerian postage-stamp♥ or the Sarduian echo chamber,♥ that

♥ 'With *Soldiers' Pay* I found out writing was fun. But I found out afterward not only that each book had to have a design but the whole output or sum of an artist's work had to have a design. Beginning with *Sartoris* I discovered that my own little postage stamp of native soil was worth writing about and that I would never live long enough to exhaust it, and that by sublimating the actual into the apocryphal I would have complete liberty to use whatever talent I might have to its absolute top. I can move these people around like God, not only in space but in time too. The fact that I have moved my characters around in time successfully, at least in my own estimation, proves to me my own theory that time is a fluid condition which has no existence except in the momentary avatars of individual people. There is no such thing as *was*—only *is.* If *was* existed, there would be no grief or sorrow. I like to think of the world I created as being a kind of keystone in the universe; that, small as that keystone is, if it were ever taken away the universe itself would collapse. My last book will be the Doomsday Book, the Golden Book, of Yoknapatawpha County. Then I shall break the pencil and I'll have to stop.'

♥ While he uses this phrase in interviews to constellate a cluster of effects, including the reappearance of objects central to one novel as ephemera in another, or the sudden irruption of scenes from previous novels into later novels, but from the perspective of other characters, he also uses it in personal correspondence. Here is a signed copy of the French translation of his book *Colibri,* which reads: 'A George Raillard, cette chambre d'echo ou vole un *Colibri* . . .' or 'To George Raillard, this echo chamber where a hummingbird flies . . .'

is, having thought of my writing as a proliferating and overgrown ecosystem, on which, because I spent seven years in critique, five at Yale and then two more in the MFA at Hunter, readers interstitially comment, I, too, have developed this attention to reception. "Via Crucis" is very aware of the fact that it's being read (a worry or awareness ripples the surface of the text and sometimes bursts from it, before diving and disappearing again beneath that surface) and the way it's going to be interpreted by readers who it's not speaking directly to, readers who already aren't interested in the baroque, readers who are accustomed to thinking of stories and poems by marginalized writers as a form of data-mining or empathy-practice or personal catharsis, a structure in which I'm also very much implicated and which I discuss in *The Fifth Wound.*

I was working on a novel in my MFA that won't ever be published, but in the first chapter, in the middle of an elaborate conversation about Christendom's construction of the symbol of the Virgin Mary, and a reading of the Immaculate Conception as a miracle of trans womanhood, the narrator breaks, interrupts herself to say that when she was three years old she saw a bikini in a shop window and, at the same moment she realized she wanted it, she realized, also, that she couldn't have it.

(That was a moment I drew from my own memory. The bikini was green. For years after that I would tell people that they made bikinis for boys, because I assumed that if I desired it, and I was a boy, that meant they must also make bikinis for boys, which is like, really brilliant on my part, I think. I still respect that.)

Readers always gush over those sudden confessions, because I write them in a direct and intimate language, almost as a gift for having sifted their minds through layers of riddle and wreckage and whirlpool and embellishment. But then they continue, they say, 'Oh, Aurora! I responded so much to this, why don't you cut some of the tangles around it to make it more prominent?' And I'm sitting there thinking, 'But it's because I placed this almost-artless expression of vulnerability at such high contrast to the surrounding text that you felt it with such force!' So in my work there's an opacity born of a rage that rendered my sentences more and more dense, because of the energy I was compressing, hammering into an extreme, a maximal euphony—I always think of the inside of a piano, one hammer for every string. I think I produced some really beautiful work out of a feeling of betrayal, which was, I have to admit, partially my own immaturity because I treated each of my workshops like a publication day, picking my outfit days ahead of time, so careful with my makeup, my lipstick, blush and mascara, so precise with my posture—and often, afterward, vomiting from tension. But I chose critique because that was the structure for becoming a writer, that was where I could seek a mentor and credibility and above all, audience. Never, in eight years of critiques, was there another trans woman at the workshop table. What more is there to say that wouldn't be obvious? I was in the wrong place, I was in thrall to prestige, and I lost some of my own vision in the process, I held back little bits of topaz but I gave so many, too—I scattered my topazes onto the blank page, because I was gnawed by a doubt: What if I was being too jealous? What if they were right? So much of the force of my vision arises from the scintillations of a dialectic—spinning, grinding, pulverizing—between lavish disclosure and vital withholding, but fundamentally my words would be desiccated by the form of an explanation or a plea. At the time I had no language to describe the urgency of my discursivity, I was only following an intuition, as a sunflower turns toward the sun. To an extent I sidetracked my attention, became obsessed with making mazes, extraordinarily elaborate but always grammatical sentences, riddled with dashes and nested parentheses, so that no one could dismiss me for writing run-ons, no one could find an easy explanation for the *wrongness* of my writing. But I think there's a Scorpio wisdom there; I think at its best it's the wisdom of one who has been and will always be specimenized. There's a reason I write at night and sleep during the day, why I only leave the house if I have a very particular destination, why I de-escalated my relationship to Instagram, and it's hardly reducible to one or even a few isolated events, it is perpetual and reverberating—and there is much to critique my writing for, there will always be more because I look at an old piece and, while I find flashes of insight, beauty and attunement, inevitably I also find delusions, ethical failures, exoticisms, which are so clear to me now but which weren't then. Every sentence demands my utmost ethical and visionary attention. 'Empire is a perpetual déjà vu. It speaks through poets as much as politicians, it speaks in a tuneless recursive monologue that I hear as I write to you. Sometimes I'm halfway through a sentence before I realize that I'm transcribing another one of its traps.' That's from *The Fifth Wound.* I think, at first, my writing partook (to use Glissant's word) of a petrified classicism more often than what he calls 'the manifest and integrating violence of contaminations.' As I began to write *I Carry a Peach,* which is a novel about a separatist commune of transsexual women in the West Texas desert who have formed a liturgy around the consumption of estrogen, and who call themselves the Daughters of Aphroditos ('a frankincense-scented isomer of Aphrodite who possessed both breasts and cock, and to whom a cult—whose acolytes, writes Philostratus, were fairies and faggots—was once devoted on the isle of Cyprus, in the epoch before the rise of Christendom'), I felt my own writing demanding me to consider what I could possibly mean by 'commune,' considering how few trans women or even trans people to whom I was, at the time, close or even proximate, two and a half years ago. So after a life lived in drifting and distance, my writing called on me to seek out spaces of intersubjectivity. Now my stories circulate quite a lot before they're published, in full and partial drafts. But the intentional self-delusion of DNC book-club liberalism is to frame reading and writing as politically complete acts in themselves, rather than as sites of reflection, solitude and ritual continuous with interpersonal forms of care, conversation, ritual and resistance. Ruth Wilson Gilmore says, 'Abolition requires that we change one thing, which is everything. Contemporary prison abolitionists have made this argument for more than two decades. Abolition is not *absence,* it is *presence.* What the world will become already exists in fragments and pieces, experiments and possibilities.' So I've been seeking out, in my work and in my life, the fragments and pieces of the future in the present—but perpetually questioning my whiteness, because whiteness, via the cultural production of empire, is always trying to delude itself into thinking it is, along the very axis of its whiteness, beneficial to those it harms most; put simply, I have been in the perpetual process of refusing the Imperial dream of the white savior, and the perpetual process of developing an ideology of the accomplice. I did not hear that Ruth Wilson Gilmore line for the first time from one of the books in my library. Later, when I sought out the interview, I encountered this vital insight into the possibility of visionary urgency within the form of a piece. Speaking about artist and geographer Trevor Paglen's book *Invisible,* she says: 'He set out years ago to figure out how to use the tools of geography, the tools of surveillance, and the tools of surveying to "see" US military black sites around the planet and photograph them—to show us what we otherwise could not see. For me this picture has also a strong metaphorical value in that I imagine it to be actively and antagonistically the contradiction of what it represents. Therefore, it is a picture of us coming to meet ourselves in the abolitionist future.' Those last two lines describe what I would now say is the aspiration of my sense of vision. The polychromatic density of *The Fifth Wound* attempts to approximate that aspiration.

JCT: Borges told of a universal library, objective but damned. In our world, libraries are limited and controlled and never neutral, aren't they?

AM: In the history of american publishing, only one book of so-called 'literary fiction' written by a trans woman has ever been published by one of the 'big five' major publishers. The second will be published in January 2021; it's called *Detransition, Baby,* and it's by the brilliant Torrey Peters. Two novels. And how many memoirs? Dozens since the 1950s, not because we're only writing memoirs but because publishers are publishing us only when we write memoirs. I should mention this is not the case with sci-fi and fantasy, which is an extremely different publishing industry that I can't speak to with the same level of experience, except to say that I think the 'literary fiction' industry really doesn't want to acknowledge, except with a kind of noblesse oblige condescension, the sci-fi- and fantasy-inflected lineage of so many of its most-lauded contemporary authors, who have absorbed, from these genres, countless notions and gestures, but who are nonetheless lauded by their marketing teams and major-outlet reviewers (today's manufacturers of reception) for having 'discovered' those gestures for 'literary fiction.'

JCT: Even though I'm not someone you should be listening to as an authority, because you've received so much compressed rejection, I want to say that I really do think that your stories are remarkable. Just last month, reading "Via Crucis" rescued me from a deep depressive episode. And I'm not sure if I'm even the fairy audience that it deserves, exactly. Which I find concerning and interesting and complicated. I don't want to presume that I am.

AM: If it resonates in a particular way, then I assume you must be its audience. I don't relate to my writing in the same way you do, because it's so—well for me it's an Exquisite Corpse and for you it's a Barbie. But the truth is, a full page of "Via Crucis" previously appeared in my unpublished first novel, *Cradle Me, Lucifer;* and last month, I formed an entire story from the raw matter, bloody and iridescent, of the monologue that ends that book.

As I work on new stories, I often find myself remembering older orts and fragments, regretting that they're rotting in a drawer, and then realizing no one has seen them before—realizing I can recover some forgotten scrap of self into my present and have it received, fifth-dimensionally, as if it were happening now. *Grey's Anatomy* has provided my mental image for the interval of uncertainty: during a transplant, the surgeons, having completed their sutures, stand over their patient to see if the donor organ turns pink, an indication of blood flow. Similarly I take a chunk of older text and tissue it into my story, attempting to clip and join the shredded ends along a seam. For a moment I sit and stare, and if I get a certain feeling—a pinking of the aura of the language; a new, emergent sense of meaning—then I sigh in relief. *Ah, it takes.*

Thank you for your questions, Jordan.

[BROOKLYN, NEW YORK, AUGUST 2020]

INTERVIEW EXCERPTS

WITH LINDSAY LERMAN, FOR THE CREATIVE INDEPENDENT

AM: At the outset of my transition, when I couldn't control people perceiving me as a woman or as some kind of indeterminate, frightening or freakish thing, my whole body was open to interpretation, available for comment by strangers. I thought beauty would protect me from that, so I attempted to become beautiful. Eventually I found, in the way the world was responding to me, that I had achieved what I was looking for. But I also found that I was no closer to my capacity for pleasure than I had been at the outset of my pursuit. I was trying to paper over something that my beauty could no longer reach. The past had already happened. Becoming beautiful wasn't going to reverse its course.

Then, when the pandemic hit, I had the privilege of being inside a lot more, which I was grateful for, right after being outside had become violent for me in a new way. My femininity was allowed to become something that wasn't constantly public. For the first time, I was able to relate to all of these high-femme artifacts how I'd always wanted to, but had put off in order to use them, instead, for protection in public. For the first time, acrylics, corsets, eyeshadow palettes, all these things became ritual practices for me in a much more intimate way. I started to realize that what I was thinking of as 'beauty' was actually a feeling of sacredness for high-femme artifacts, and for the ability to perform those rituals together with other people. In the book I talk about a 'yearning for being beautiful together,' which doesn't necessarily point to, say, falling in love or having sex. A lot of that for me meant finding other people to perform rituals of femininity with.

LL: Let's talk about your routines and rituals. How did you find the time? How do you use time?

AM: I wrote because I couldn't sleep. I needed a container for the wings of fantasy and desire that would brush over me while I was trying to fall asleep.

Sometimes I stayed up for multiple days at a time. I wanted writing to feel as extreme as living was feeling. I wasn't intentionally performing a synonym of a kind of Simone Weil fasting-to-become-a-dwelling-place-for-God thing, but there is an element of Saint Catherine of Siena in the book and her whole thing of surviving on pus alone, pus from the sick. I wasn't literally consuming bodily fluids, but the book is so much about bodily fluids and the divine that it became this sort of practice of 'consuming my own bodily fluids,' my own mess, really, and then surviving from that.

LL: This brings me to something that I wanted to talk about. So like, obviously Catholicism is having a moment and biblical myth and tale are also having a moment, but in a very different way than in your book. I see so much use of Catholicism and like biblical imagery and that general aesthetic being used as part of the move to strip as many people as possible of rights.

What's happening in that fringe scene—which is actually not fringe—what they're doing with the primal power of myth and the primal power of the biblical tale in this culture is very, very different than what I see happening in your book. So, I wanted to ask you about the role that myth or the biblical tale plays for you in this book and in art and creation in general.

AM: I haven't been much on social media, most of my life. I only started, really, when I moved to New York, and on Twitter I definitely picked up on a certain reactionary reuptake of Catholicism as an aesthetic. Something along those lines that I wrote in the book was, 'Fantasy is not in itself ethical, but it is the means by which an ethics is made.'

I'm going to take a byway here: I went on a long research spiral about a religious cult, the Galli, who lived and practiced in what is now Turkey, and whose goddess and ritual apparatus the Roman state violently assimilated. I noticed a lot of white trans girls who didn't want to recapitulate Christian aesthetics were attaching themselves to this ancient so-called 'Roman' cult of 'transfemme high priestesses.' But actually, the Galli were a Phrygian cult to a goddess called Cybele, who had come to earth in the form of a chunk of black meteorite, called a baetyl, which the Galli kept, enthroned, in their temple. The Roman state abducted the baetyl and brought it to Rome, installing it atop a sculpture of a woman's body, as if it were her head. They wholly renarrativized her as a goddess of chastity, constructing an origin story that represents her as presiding over marriage between a 'pure Roman woman' and a 'noble Roman man,' that positions her as the mother of the Roman state, rather than a fertility goddess from Phrygia, whose devotees were specifically so-called feminine, gender-nonconforming people, who performed, ritually, an ancient form of bottom surgery.

If I had just scratched the surface of this research, it would have appeared to me that the presence of the Galli in the Western historical record was proof of state- and spiritually sanctioned gender-nonconformity in ancient Rome. But, in fact, the Roman state had decided to, for entirely unrelated political reasons, assimilate

Cybele into its pantheon, and at the same time, to cut the Galli off from their own ritual practices.

All of this I found out because I was looking for myths along the lines of my own ancestry that could animate me, because I knew about the femminielli in Naples, some of whom make a yearly pilgrimage to a monastery in the mountains—very near where my grandfather's family was from—that, I found out, was originally a temple to Cybele. So I realized this Italian form of gender-nonconformity was not Italian in origin after all, which has had me thinking a lot about the intentional layers of Imperial erasure and renarrativization that have accrued over time.

But to answer your question more directly, I think a lot of what's happening with specifically Catholic aesthetics right now in the 'Dimes Square' scene has to do with trying to make whiteness not seem like whiteness, using an ostensibly ironized, ostensibly transgressively sexualized 'chastity' or 'purity' to try to pass off what is fundamentally another expression of white supremacy as some kind of chic radical new pose.

WITH RICH DUHAMELL, FOR SUPERSTITION REVIEW

RD: The opening sentence to your novel introduces readers to a narrator with your same name and (now former) Twitter handle, @silicone_angel. Because your work plays so closely with autofiction, are post-Twitter readers missing out on a contextualizing experience? Are you finding a new, belated angle to your work through the absence of that initial link back to your internet presence?

AM: Aurora is not my own name. It is the field in which I attempt to bind my particulars to my dreams. My dreams are a chaos of mythic scraps which, borne by generations of gossips and storytellers, by names and voices known and unknown, by will of Empire and resistance to Empire, have imprinted themselves on my mind. My dreams are the force that make it possible to remix my particulars according not to the melodic structure of some divine song, but, instead, to some of the wavelengths of deep time. Whatever riff expresses itself through me, expresses itself also through the rifts of hydrothermal heat vents at the bottom of the sea.

Put simply, 'Aurora' was an attempt to capture some vibration of deep time in the resonant net of my own idiom.

Meanwhile @silicone_angel was the economic expression of the same. It was the attempt, through porn and persona and turn of phrase—bound up in the terrifying and transfixing medium of Twitter, which stole the pleasures of privacy while also enabling certain intimacies and inspirations—to make a living by means of dreaming. I was binding my particulars—my body, my daily interactions with strangers in public space, oblique references to my romances—to inherited myths (some ancient, some recent) in a more extemporaneous space and thereby gathering the money and passion necessary for writing. The passion of an audience energized the solitary act of writing. The money enabled it.

RD: There is an inverted quality to your storytelling: broken fingers and then a punched mailbox; Old Milk going from strange creature to pet snake; the blueberry-ness of suspicion and wretchedness comes from Ezekiel's love for them. Can you talk a bit about the process of structuring these belated reveals?

AM: When it comes to trauma, often an audience is drawn to the spectacle of the event rather than to its chronic consequences, its sequela. But for the person who lives beyond the spectacle, the event itself is almost nothing, while the sequela is inescapable, because the sequela is never past—the sequela, invisible to others, is the perpetual present.

What haunts my mind is not the knifing but the pain in my eye. The pain is happening right now. The pain is happening every day. The knifing happened only once.

Put another way, a ghost story begins not with the reason for the ghost but with the ghost itself: The house is haunted. We read to find out why.

Or so we think. This desire to know why—to experience the revelation of the cause—energizes our reading, but what really matters is having inhabited the mystery, having accumulated the residue of another mind, having witnessed the dilation of eternities within the space of instants.

Possibility, which, when it unsettles us, we call uncertainty, is the precondition of meaning.

RD: The Aurora of the narration is constantly surrounded by scraps of musings, snippets spilling from texts, social media captions, and manuscripts in overflowing drawers. The inclusion of translated Chinese poetry and entire passages written in Middle English was a fascinating narrative choice. What was your process in retrieving inspirations spread across mediums and the internet in working on *The Fifth Wound*? How did you go about deciding what stories (like the original "The Little Mermaid" and the *Odyssey*) and external excerpts (like Eva Hayward and Peter S. Beagle) to include in quotes or references?

AM: I wanted you to feel the lineage of my love and longing; I wanted you to know my kin. It's a kind of autobiographical fanfiction, like the New Testament. Or as Hannah Szabó suggested in a recent review, *The Fifth Wound* is a scrapbook written in the form of a hymn: 'Lord prepare me / to be a sanctuary.' Put simply, I've always been a bottom.

WITH CHRIST, FOR ELECTRIC LITERATURE

C: At the beginning of the book, you bring up *Eternal Sunshine of the Spotless Mind* and Kate Winslet's character. Was the archetype of a manic pixie dream girl in your mind at all as you were crafting the character of Aurora?

AM: My writing about the movie is partially a self-critique, an attempt to describe the ethics that I was operating from in my first few years of transition, a lot of which had to do with this sudden shift from being freakish to being very desirable, suddenly accessing this feminized power that came from desirability. I had this idea, not a conscious idea but a lived-from idea, that I had suffered so long to make myself beautiful, therefore I could be mentally unstable, emotionally reckless, without taking responsibility for that. But the side effects of my mental instability accumulated over time and forced me to reframe my own narrative within the context of the narratives of the people I loved but who, at the same time, I was treating with carelessness and recklessness.

C: I got the idea that a lot of the disconnects between Aurora and Ezekiel come from the incongruence between one's idea of their lover and the reality of their lover. Were there any characteristics individually or as a pair that you think made that dissonance especially difficult for Aurora and Ezekiel to cope with?

AM: Almost every review has referred to Ezekiel as a man, without reference to his queerness. It's understandable to a degree, considering in the third chapter, Aurora says, 'Put simply, we were both fairies . . . [But] he became a man and I became a woman.' Even though it appears so early in the book, reviews have tended to treat that as a decisive statement, when clearly it's just one moment of my narrator perceiving, trying to understand, Ezekiel's gender—attempting to understand her gender in relation to Ezekiel's, because the question of their genders is so central to the question of their love; or, their uncertainties about femininity are so central to the manner in which they seek intimacy with one another. In that same third chapter, Aurora says, 'If I had decided to remain a fairy, I would have wanted to be like Ezekiel,' and in the very last chapter, Ezekiel says, 'When we have sex, I imagine that I'm you.' No review has referenced those scenes, which is interesting to me, and suggests a kind of reticence, a kind of tiptoeing around, or maybe even a refusal to acknowledge the instability of the manner in which these two characters relate to themselves and each other.

They first fell in love, years before the beginning of the book, as gay boys, and in the third and final section of the book, when they are pursuing, again, some kind of romantic intimacy—when Aurora does Ezekiel's makeup and Ezekiel has a revelation about his own beauty—it's clear that there's much more to their relationship than 'the love of a man and a woman,' that to treat it as such is to deny the very substance—convolutions of shame and dream and desire, trauma and poetry and mirror-play—that drew Aurora and Ezekiel together in the first place.

Reviewers have described the final section as a 'romance.' To me it's no more or less a romance than the rest; if anything, it's just the acute form of what preceded it. For her part, meeting Ezekiel again years after she transitioned, Aurora is trying to determine whether she can even access the ability to feel embodied around him anymore, both because so much of her manner of relating to Ezekiel is through mythmaking from the distance of their separation, and because when they first fell in love eight years before, their bodies were similar, and now they are not at all—her body now is entirely different, so the manner in which her body relates to his, and his to hers, will also be entirely different. Reading Ezekiel as a man and Aurora as a woman, rather than two queer people rotating through various realities, is a way of flattening them both; this flattening has caused the intention of the third section to be misread as a romance, because it's really a way of trying to figure out what these people can mean to each other, if that meaning can exist outside of the dream, if it can help them understand themselves without, somehow, destroying them both.

C: It's interesting that coverage of the book has reduced that last section to heterosexual romance. Throughout the whole book, I always had the sense that Ezekiel wasn't simply a fairy or a man. There was certainly more going on there. That's teased through conversations and interactions with Aurora, and that part that you mentioned was such a heartbreaking moment. The second time I was reading the book I didn't want to get there because it unmoors everything that had come before it. What function does autofiction provide for the central romance between Aurora and Ezekiel and also Aurora's relationships with Velvet and Noel?

AM: I think part of my transition has been an attempt to restore a paradise that never existed. A way of trying to create what should have but never happened, and of trying to save myself from what did happen. But every time I try to restore my own past, some new calamity blows me back, and then I have to abandon one half-finished attempt at whole-making for another, more immediate one. When I think of what we call 'transition,' I think of Walter Benjamin's 'Angel of History':

> A Klee painting named *Angelus Novus* shows an angel looking as though he is about to move away from something he is fixedly contemplating. His eyes are staring, his mouth is open, his wings are spread. This is how one pictures the angel of history. His face is turned toward the past. Where we perceive a chain of events, he sees one single catastrophe which keeps piling wreckage and hurls it in front of his feet. The angel would like to stay, awaken

> the dead, and make whole what has been smashed. But a storm is blowing in from Paradise; it has got caught in his wings with such a violence that the angel can no longer close them. The storm irresistibly propels him into the future to which his back is turned, while the pile of debris before him grows skyward.

I was not writing a transition narrative, by which I mean I wasn't trying to narrativize transition, or retrofit some perfected idea of my transition; I was trying to make a transition-language, trying to write a book that constantly shapeshifts and transforms itself; trying to represent, by means of a mythological language, a kind of feminine shapeshift and reaching for beauty, by which I mean a reaching for communion. The way that seemed most efficient was to bind together the fantastical elements of my short stories with atoms of my own experience, moments of crisis and intensity, or put simply, of extreme embodiment, pain or pleasure or both. Walter Benjamin says that understanding the past is not about creating a narrative chain of events; it's about what you see—what is illuminated, like a landscape in a lightning flash—when you experience a moment of crisis, that such a moment creates the opportunity for a sudden, brief and total clarity about who you are and how you arrived there, I mean some kind of truth about the past.

C: The book approaches wounds from different angles. There are the wounds we choose through surgeries, the wounds we choose through self-harm, and the wounds given to us by the violences of the world. What holds the most meaning or impact in the taxonomy of wounds that you construct throughout the book?

AM: They become bound up in each other, and they did in my own life, too. At that time, I was attempting, in my writing and my life, to use fantasy to save myself from reality.

For example, the way the Aurora-narrator writes about the knifing. It's clear that, in an attempt to save herself from pain, she is projecting onto the person who knifed her a kind of mutual understanding, as if she hadn't experienced violence but rather, care. This derangement of her own experience leads her back to self-harm, as if she can understand the knifing by taking a knife to herself. As if self-harm is a way of opening a portal, not only to the knifing, but to all the violence she has absorbed from others—as if opening that portal will teach her something about embodiment, because long before the knifing, it was violence—physical and emotional—that disembodied her in the first place, so if she can return to the scenes of her disembodiment, she can maybe reverse its course, can have her body back.

Self-harm is, in part, doing the world's work for it. Aurora is a very paranoid character and is always worried about violence being done to her, but the person she's received the most violence from is herself. That speaks to part of the reason she's so paranoid, because she recognizes herself as a danger and she can never escape herself.

But her self-harm is not, in the end, limited to herself. It is implosive, but it is also explosive—it harms and traumatizes the people she loves. Self-harm is a microcosm of the interrelationship of trauma and responsibility; she is giving herself a wound because she is approaching the desire to die, and the only way to forestall death, she thinks, is to release the pain, to release the violence she has absorbed from others, through her wound. She sees herself as having no other options. But by giving herself a wound she defers that pain onto her partner Noel, who not only witnesses, firsthand, her bleeding and screaming and drunkenness, but washes the blood out of her clothes and out of the floor, and helps her sew her wounds shut. Noel absorbs the violence that Aurora releases into their home; by harming herself, Aurora forces Noel to absorb that violence. She doesn't give Noel a choice; she takes from Noel the ability to choose how to love her, forces Noel to love her in a way that terrifies them, that threatens and damages their own safety.

Or in the case of Ezekiel—when he, after a brutal argument, goes outside to smoke a cigarette, she brings a knife into his bed. The knife is intended for self-harm; she's suffocating on reality and looking for a way out, a portal to another way of feeling. But a knife in a bed is, more than anything, an act of violence against the intimacy two people have shared there. A knife is final. Even directed toward herself, a knife is relational. She doesn't harm herself, but that doesn't matter; the threat of the knife is an act of violence against Ezekiel.

Aurora creates a sense of fear and uncertainty in the people she loves—the possibility of her self-harm, never far away, makes love itself feel unsafe, makes intimacy feel unsafe—a fear echoed later by Ezekiel when he says, by phone, in their last conversation, 'Don't die, Aurora. I need you there in the future.' It is impossible to care for others when I am destroying myself, because when I am destroying myself I am also destroying those who love me. For others, there is no choice, in the end, but to leave. Aurora and I both learned that lesson.

ACKNOWLEDGEMENTS

To Hannah, my best friend, my teacher. I love you so much.

To Simone. Your mind has been, for all these years, a sanctuary for my writing. Because of you so much has felt possible to say and to dream.

To Milky. See you in my sleep.

To Loretta. Wake me in the morning and we'll go to the backyard, okay?

To mermaids, angels, oracles, ball pythons, fairies, pixies, sirens, spiders, elves, opals, orchids, deep-sea jellyfish and all manner of mythical beasts.

To the Midnight Zone and to nail parlors. To the acrylics of every beautiful woman in the world.

To Lizzie Davis. For taking a chance on me, for finding the bits of vision in the mess and helping me make worlds from whirlwinds. Line by line, curlicue by curlicue, I couldn't have done it without you.

To CJ. For making mysterious, terrifying, enchanting and almost heartbreaking drawings from the static of my stories. For holding my hand by the beach.

To Mary. In some sense I'm always singing Guy Clark with you.

To Mom. Student of wonder. Uncredited editor of every last line. No story of mine is finished until you've riddled it with your red pen; until we've sat and talked about it on the back porch in the long afternoon, or by phone in the middle of the night.

To Dad. Mysterious bird, always on the verge of opening his wings—where are you flying in your mind?

To Sam Rodriguez. I can't imagine my life without you in it. You're the funniest person I know, you're a genius and a really thoughtful friend. I always look forward to talking with you—always wonder 'what will Sam think about this'—and to cooking with you, and to every antique mall and dive bar where we find a way to make mischief. I love you.

To Vivienne Wallace. When I think of glamor, I think of you: your bursts of boldness, your dozens of dresses, your sudden appearances, as if out of a mist, stilettos dangling from your pinkie. And when I think of you, I think of your kindness, as deep and total as a mother's. You are beautiful and you are my friend. I don't know how I got so lucky. And you always say such wonderful words. I love you.

To Tuffy Gibbens. Your life swirled into mine like the other half of a helix. Every cigarette or tube of lip gloss we've shared is like one of its rungs. I am almost amazed we haven't known each other our whole lives. But I'm glad life was keeping a secret, because you arrived exactly when I least expected you, and most needed you. You have a good heart. You have a quicksilver mind—it shapeshifts and spins through time and space and dazzles me every time. I love you.

To Miles Perkins. You are both wise and mischievous, maybe the best pair of qualities I could imagine in a friend. When we met you said, 'This is the beginning of a journey,' and ever since I've felt a path beneath my feet, leading us through technicolor nights and mysterious days.

To gg. I love the way you see life with romance and realness, and never let one outweigh the other. Also you help me remember how fun femininity can be. I don't know what I would've done this year without our late-night long talks in the driveway.

To Stephanie Rolón. Who climbed into an enclosure at the Zoo when she was fifteen, because she wanted to challenge, with her whole body, the dominion of the tiger. Who showed me the claw scars across her stomach to prove it. Who was always ready to dream together about all the futures we can make for ourselves, because thirty isn't too old, because fifty isn't too old, because, if you're paying attention, every day is as dangerous and vital as the first, but if you can rise to meet your chaos—if you can face your chaos without blinking—there's always a chance for splendor. To Steph, who was prepared, in equal measure, for the claws of the tiger and the lips of a lover. Because she had no choice, because life never gave her a choice. Who I promised to help write a memoir, because the world needed to know how a woman made glamour from terror; how she grasped at flames with her bare hands; how she molded fire like clay. Who lived too much, altogether too much. Who was a true friend. I miss you and I'll always miss you.

To Carta Monir, McKenzie Wark, Sarah Gerard, Barbara Browning,

Michelle Tea, Harron Walker and Vi Khi Nao, for the beautiful words you wrote about my first book.

To Townes Van Zandt. I don't know where I end and you begin. Your songs are as vital as breath, liquor, light and sleep.

To John Prine, Kate Bush, Alex G, Joanna Newsom, Sufjan Stevens, Santigold, Eva Cassidy, Beach House, Leonard Cohen, Jason Molina, Mitski, Mazzy Star, Doja Cat, Fleetwood Mac, Hole, FKA Twigs, ABBA, Emmylou Harris, Dido and Lucinda Williams.

To Bong Joon-ho, Cristina La Veneno, Kim Keever, Félix González-Torres, Louise Bourgeois, Wong Kar-wai, Antoni Gaudí, Lars von Trier, Hugh Steers and Xiyadie.

To Severo Sarduy, Clarice Lispector, Virginia Woolf, Édouard Glissant, Jorge Luis Borges, William Faulkner, Gabriel García Márquez, John Keene, Sei Shōnagon, James Baldwin, Muriel Spark, Nikolai Gogol, Pati Hill, Theresa Hak Kyung Cha, Thomas Bernhard, Chelsey Minnis, László Krasznahorkai, Rachel Rabbit White, José Donoso, Anne Carson, Manuel Puig, Fanny Howe, Eve Babitz, Machado de Assis, Pu Songling, Gerald Murnane, Juliana Huxtable, Fernando Pessoa, Susan Howe, Marcel Proust, Sappho and Italo Calvino.

To the Inner Space Caverns, which I first visited when I was five years old and which altered the course of my dreams forever. Every story I write is an echo of that afternoon.

To Angel. For the way you looked into the heart of "https//: waterfall not found" and made its mysteries visible—every time I turn the pages of this book to your drawing, it takes my breath away.

To Aphroditos, Alicia Lovelace, Jaye Elizabeth Elijah (thank you for lending your seer-sight to "Wild and Blue," and for remembering Milky with me), Marc Lang, Alice Noah, Téa Obreht, Saretta Morgan, Alexandra Sugarman, Amar and Heather. To Emily Zhou and Cyrée Jarelle Johnson, for your visions and for reading with me the night my first book came out.

To everyone at Resolutions, particularly Nathaniel, Elyssa, Luke, Madi and Mia.

To Julia and Seth and all my friends and coworkers at El Alma.

To Jade Benvenuti Oliver, for your generosity of vision, for chasing the light with me, and for all the photos you take, for a book or for your friends. To Caro Delara, for your high femme antics and for doing my makeup the day of my photo shoot. To both of you for laughing, dancing and singing, in a car, at a club, or in the server shed.

To Abbie Phelps (thank you for everything, you're so brilliant and let's never stop talking about *Happy Together*), Daphne DiFazio and Quynh Van, all formerly at Coffee House, and to everyone at Nightboat: Jaye Elizabeth Elijah, Lina Bergamini, Dante Silva, Stephen Motika, Lindsey Bolt, Gia Gonzales and Emily Bark Brown. To Tree Abraham for my book cover; for the hazy mystery and the hyperspeed horizon.

To dive bars and dawn in Terlingua. To topaz. To the iridescent thing. To a sunfaded sign off the highway, grown powder blue with time. Blue shadows in old churches, light as cobwebs. The blue of lagoons, like melted neon. The guitar and the fiddle. Mirrors and martinis. Prickly pear and ocotillo. Broken columns. Cresting waves. Dusk grasses, dusk bedrooms, dusk bedsheets, dusk flower in a vase, dusk woman in the mirror, dusk falling apart forever, disappearing into pink or fading into fizzy blue static

then the flash of a knife, silver and bright, wide awake like heaven,

then back to the replication of dusk, seafoam spreading, disco ball spinning, perfume fulminating, deep-sea phosphorescence like a desperate love letter, ravenous for intensity, because girls just wanna have sparkling dusk,

sugar-cloud dusk,

double-crush dusk, like

'me and my man

in a forest clearing'

AURORA MATTIA was born in Hong Kong and lives in Texas, where her mother was born. Her first book, *The Fifth Wound,* was published by Nightboat in 2023. Her stories have appeared in various magazines, and also in exhibitions at the RISD Museum and the Renaissance Society, accompanying portraits by Elle Pérez. She's sometimes working on a new novel called *Seven Come Eleven,* sometimes writing country songs, and mostly doing something else.

NIGHTBOAT BOOKS

Nightboat Books, a nonprofit organization, seeks to develop audiences for writers whose work resists convention and transcends boundaries. We publish books rich with poignancy, intelligence, and risk. Please visit nightboat.org to learn about our titles and how you can support our future publications.

The following individuals have supported the publication of this book. We thank them for their generosity and commitment to the mission of Nightboat Books:

Kazim Ali
Anonymous (8)
Mary Armantrout
Jean C. Ballantyne
Thomas Ballantyne
Bill Bruns
John Cappetta
V. Shannon Clyne
Ulla Dydo Charitable Fund
Photios Giovanis
Amanda Greenberger
Vandana Khanna
Isaac Klausner
Shari Leinwand
Anne Marie Macari
Elizabeth Madans
Martha Melvoin
Caren Motika
Elizabeth Motika
The Leslie Scalapino – O Books Fund

Robin Shanus
Thomas Shardlow
Rebecca Shea
Ira Silverberg
Benjamin Taylor
David Wall
Jerrie Whitfield & Richard Motika
Arden Wohl
Issam Zineh

This book is made possible, in part, by grants from the New York City Department of Cultural Affairs in partnership with the City Council and the New York State Council on the Arts Literature Program.